PRAISE FOR RITUAL CRIME UNIT

In this series

Under the Skin
Disturbed Earth
Spirit Animals

SPIRIT ANIMALS

An Abaddon Books™ Publication
www.abaddonbooks.com
abaddon@rebellion.co.uk

First published in 2016 by Abaddon Books™, Rebellion Publishing
Limited, Riverside House, Osney Mead, Oxford, OX2 0ES, UK.

10 9 8 7 6 5 4 3 2 1

Editor-in-Chief: Jonathan Oliver
Commissioning Editor: David Moore
Cover Art: Sam Gretton
Design: Sam Gretton and Oz Osborne
Marketing and PR: Rob Power
Head of Books and Comics Publishing: Ben Smith
Creative Director and CEO: Jason Kingsley
Chief Technical Officer: Chris Kingsley

UK ISBN: 978 1 78108 477 9
US ISBN: 978 1 78108 478 6

RITUAL CRIME UNIT

SPIRIT ANIMALS

E.E. RICHARDSON

ABADDON
BOOKS

CHAPTER ONE

"You know, I bet bloody RCU London don't get called out to this many farms." Pierce grimaced to herself as she squelched across the mud towards the derelict barn. Wellies might have been an idea, but they were probably beneath her dignity as DCI in charge.

Not that there was anyone around to see as she struggled across the fields after her much younger and fitter constable. The building they were headed for was clearly long-abandoned, windows now just empty holes in the crumbling stone walls, the mossy roof slates dangling like loose teeth on the verge of dropping out. The neighbours' reports of people lighting fires ought to have been a matter for the local bobbies, but mention of caged animals being taken in had bumped it up the chain to the Ritual Crime Unit. Could be an illegal skin shop, making unlicensed shapeshifting pelts.

Or it could just be squatters with pets. Technically, as a DCI, Pierce ought to be exempt from these kind of shot-in-the-dark preliminaries, but the RCU's northern branch had all of five officers to police an area covering half the country. In theory, they mostly consulted and let local forces do the grunt work; in practice, any case with a whiff of magic was a hot potato that no one wanted to keep in case it made a mess of the crime statistics. Even in these days of global information networks, magic remained a rare and poorly studied art, and the law was always scrambling to keep up.

Besides, Pierce had her own reasons to take a personal interest in any case that might involve shapeshifters. She stretched out her left shoulder, still feeling a twinge where the silver skinning knife had stabbed her, months before. The man who'd delivered the blow, a skinbinder she'd known as Sebastian, had supposedly died in police custody, but Pierce had her doubts. He'd had powerful friends.

Probably too powerful to have set him up in a place like this. She sighed, suspecting this wasn't the smartest use she could have chosen to make of a frigid February morning. Staggering uphill over steep muddy fields was a job for the likes of her young constable, Gemma Freeman, a tall, athletic black woman with her hair pulled back in a bun who still looked like a schoolgirl to Pierce's eyes.

Still had the perky attitude as well. "At least we're out in the fresh air, guv," she said, turning back to flash Pierce a bright smile.

"That's debatable." There was a reek coming off the old barn, worse than your typical farmyard manure. Animals, definitely—and not very well-kept or healthy ones, either, by the smell of them. Pierce gestured for Gemma to take up a position beside the doorway, and knocked on what was left of the precariously leaning door.

"Police! This is the Ritual Crime Unit!" she said, raising her voice. "Identify yourselves and come out of the barn."

No sound except the wind rattling the roof. Any people inside might just be keeping quiet, but she'd expect animals to make a bit more noise if they were here. She nodded to Gemma, and the constable gave the leaning door a shove; it fell inward with a splintering crash, only loosely attached by the bottom hinge. The brittle wood crunched under Pierce's feet as she stepped over it, squinting in the half-light within.

The stench was even worse inside, rolling off the rows of wire cages stacked up against the far wall; the smell of the animal shit that caked the bars mingling with the all-too-familiar stink of decomposition. None of the huddled lumps of fur and feather slumped inside the cages appeared to be moving.

Gemma made a small sound of dismay as she followed Pierce inside. "All dead?" she asked, taking in the situation at a glance.

"It would appear so." Not from natural causes, either—not so soon after the reports from the neighbours. The animals must have been put down *en masse*, apparently too much of an inconvenience to cart away from the scene when the going got hot. Pierce walked along the line of cages, more to take inventory than to look for signs of life. The dead animals were a bizarrely eclectic mix: a badger, a barn owl, what might have been a lynx, even a snake. Some semi-exotic, some mundane, but none of them particularly large.

"Well, whatever they were doing in here, they weren't making shapeshifting pelts," she said. An enchanted pelt would allow its wearer to take on an animal form, but only one of roughly comparable size. The country's few authorised skin shops typically worked with the bodies of big dogs, deer and horses; the less legal kind, exotic predators smuggled in from abroad.

"Recognise this, guv?" Gemma asked, nodding towards the far end of the barn. There was what appeared to be a ritual altar set up, an eight-sided stone slab raised above a fire pit ringed with carved stones. A cross-shaped iron frame stood above the arrangement, a heavy butcher's hook hanging down from the centre. Two concentric rings were drawn around the whole lot in the dirt, the straw that strewed the rest of the barn fastidiously swept away from the circle.

"That's a new one on me," Pierce said, pulling on a pair of evidence gloves as she approached it cautiously. "But I know the setup for a blood ritual when I see one."

The caged animals were clearly intended as sacrifices, probably fed and watered just enough to keep them barely alive until they were needed for the ritual. But the mismatched assortment puzzled her; sacrificing animals of such different sizes and natures would bring widely variable results. Had the ritual-workers been experimenting, trying to find the perfect animals for their purposes? That was even more dangerous than if they were following exact instructions from a ritual text.

Because this setup looked all too carefully assembled to be just clueless amateurs buggering about. Pierce bent down as she approached, trying to get a look at the rune-carved stones around the fire pit.

And felt something shift under her foot beneath the straw. A subtle shivery tingle passed over her skin, like the barely perceptible drag of a spider's web. She froze.

"Constable Freeman?" she said stiffly.

"Guv?" Gemma said warily.

"Would you mind clearing away the straw around whatever I'm standing on, *carefully*, and telling me if I've just set off a trigger rune?"

After thirty years on the job, Pierce recognised that shivery sensation all too well. She'd just crossed a magical barrier.

She held her position, half-crouched, as Gemma hunkered down beside her. Her muscles were already threatening to cramp. She didn't dare even look down to watch Gemma's progress as she brushed the straw and dirt away from around Pierce's shoe. If she'd just primed some kind of magical trigger, any wrong move could potentially set it off.

After an eternity in which Pierce's muscles screamed protests and a minor itch at the back of her head swelled into a maddening urge to scratch all over, Gemma finally sat back on her heels and frowned. "Right. Okay, then," she said, though it sounded anything but. She drew her phone to take a photograph of whatever she'd uncovered, and brought it up so Pierce could see the screen without having to move.

It didn't look good.

The object her foot was resting on appeared to be a small

stone slab, dug in to lie more or less level with the dirt floor of the barn and then covered over with straw. The surface was painted with symbols that her shoe now partly obscured. Underneath the slab ran a steel wire, no doubt connecting a ring of more such trigger stones around the altar.

"Well, bollocks," Pierce said, with feeling. She took a deep breath, fighting a sudden wave of vertigo that made her feel as if she was somehow in danger of falling off a slab of stone less than an inch thick. "Right, then, constable," she said, doing her best to keep her voice even. "What does your PRMC training tell you about that?"

Pierce had been doing the job since long before the force had offered anything as arcane as a certification in ritual magic; she was dubious of its usefulness when it came to assessing whether job applicants could actually hack RCU work in the field, but it did at least come with a more up-to-date grounding in magical theory than the patchwork knowledge Pierce had picked up over the years.

Gemma chewed her lip as she considered what could be made out of the design. "Right," she said eventually. "So far as I can tell, it's a variation on a standard tripwire trigger. I don't know what kind of enchantment it's tied to—can't really see that bit—but it'll go off if you disturb the position of the stones."

"Figured that much," Pierce said tightly. "How much can I move without setting it off?" Her back was already threatening to spasm.

"I don't *think* it will go off just as long as you keep your foot on the stone," Gemma said.

"Oh, well, that's all right, then." But she did ease her other knee down to the floor, to relieve some of the trembling tension. "I will need to pee at some stage, constable," she pointed out. Probably quite soon, given she was currently resting on a magical landmine.

"I think you could probably safely substitute your touch for someone else's without setting anything off," Gemma said, musing aloud.

"That means somebody else volunteering to step in here and take my place," Pierce said. And she'd better not be thinking of doing it herself. "No deal."

"What about using one of the animals?" Gemma suggested, turning to look at the row of cages. "I doubt the enchantment's sophisticated enough to tell the difference between a living being and a dead one—these magical triggers are complicated enough to create without adding a load of unnecessary extra conditions."

That sounded like some pretty ropy theorising to her—but when it came to magic, ropy theorising was frequently all they had. Pierce gave a curt nod. "Fine. Bring me the corpse of Basil Brush, then." At least she wouldn't have to worry about putting another living creature in the firing range, police constables included.

She waited, sweat trickling down her back, as Gemma moved off toward the row of cages. Despite assurances, Pierce didn't want to tempt fate by twisting round too much to look, so she had to track her progress by listening to the creaks and rattles of the cages.

Gemma eventually returned bearing the blanket-bundled form of the dead lynx, but Pierce stopped her with a raised hand before she could get too close. "Right, that's far enough," she said. "Put it down on the ground beside me."

"Guv, it's probably better if I'm the one who—"

"That's an order, constable," she said.

Gemma looked briefly mutinous, but she clearly wasn't certain enough of her ground with Pierce to argue it. She stooped to lay the lynx on the ground, the big cat's tufted head flopping back lifelessly with jaws slightly agape. The air of death and excrement in the barn was so pervasive that being up close made no difference to the smell. "Right. Now sod off," Pierce ordered. "No sense you being in the area of effect if this doesn't work." She flapped her free hand as Gemma reluctantly retreated a few paces. "Further than that, constable. Out of the barn, down the field, and keep moving. Someone's going to need to write the superintendent a report if this thing brings the barn down."

She waited until Gemma had obediently left before turning her attention to the task at hand. Replace her foot with the lynx's paw. Right. Easier said than done: that thing looked heavy, and she couldn't really twist around to pick it up with both hands without shifting her foot on the stone more than she liked. She was going to have to drag it towards her, and hope like hell she didn't disturb the hidden wire buried under the dirt while she was doing it. Pierce grimaced as she reached out to tug on the corner of the muck-encrusted blanket with her left hand, remembering only then that it was her weak shoulder.

And the lynx was a dead weight. It refused to move at all in response to her first careful pull, and she yanked harder with a frustrated huff. The blanket dragged clumped straw and dirt along in its wake, and she cringed at the thought of the steel wire running just under the surface.

At least now the big cat was close enough she could grab it instead of the blanket—and, small mercy, she'd managed to put on some evidence gloves before all this began. She hauled the unfortunate animal towards her by one of its mangy front limbs. Long legs and big furry paws: unquestionably a wild creature, not a domestic cat. Where had the ritual-workers sourced it from? Could be a lead.

If she made it out of this barn alive to pursue it. Right now her only concern was whether one of those big paws would be heavy enough to keep the stone weighed down. She draped it over the end of her shoe and slowly inched her foot back out from underneath. So far, no boom. But as soon as she let go of the slack paw it started to slip away, and she made a frantic grab for it, heart racing.

It wasn't going to stay in place on its own. Steeling herself, Pierce pinned the paw with her right hand and shifted her grip to the matted scruff of the lynx's neck. With another great heave, she managed to lift the thing bodily off the ground and lay the heavy head down on top of the paw to keep it weighed down on the stone. When she very carefully peeled her fingers away, the head lolled sideways, dark lips parting, but it stayed where she'd put it.

Pierce closed her eyes and took a long, shuddering breath, wishing she believed in the power of prayer, or could at least think of a more inspiring final thought than *please don't fuck this up*. Nothing came to mind. But delaying was only going to make it harder. She eased her foot out from under the weight of the lynx's head and off the stone.

No reaction.

Pierce resisted the urge to let out a great gusty sigh of relief; she wasn't home yet. Still moving very, very slowly, she set her knee down on the straw-covered ground and shuffled backwards away from the stone. There was a tense moment as she pulled her trouser leg out from under the beast's body, but though it shifted slightly, it stayed where she'd arranged it.

She pushed herself up from her kneeling position, feeling a twinge from her unhappy back but managing to make it upright without staggering. Still wary of disturbing the precarious arrangement, she took a soft step backwards. Another. Keeping her eyes fixed on the dead lynx, she edged all the way back through the barn to the open doorway.

Where she found Gemma lurking anxiously just outside.

"Constable Freeman, I can't help noticing you have not sodded off to the requested distance," she said.

"Sorry, guv," she said, not sounding terribly repentant. "The substitution worked, then?"

Pierce picked her way out past the remains of the fallen door. "Well, I haven't—" A chunk of rotten wood shifted under her feet, and she cursed and grabbed at the doorframe.

From further in the barn, there was the almost inaudible sound of something shifting. Pierce lunged forward, shoving Gemma away from the doorway just as a wall of flame exploded out from the altar.

CHAPTER TWO

BY THE TIME the fire brigade had arrived, there wasn't much of the crime scene left to be preserved. Though the stone walls were still standing, the roof had collapsed at the altar end, and the straw had carried the flames to the animal cages, adding the stench of burning flesh and fur to the haze of smoke. A thorough dousing from the fire hoses helped to ensure that any evidence that hadn't burned would still be ruined.

They were still awaiting permission to re-enter the building when Pierce's phone rang. Seeing her sergeant's name on the screen, she wandered away from the scene to answer it. "Deepan. What's up?"

"Might need you for a consult on this case, guv," he said. "Are you free to come out to the scene?"

"As a bird, unfortunately—my evidence just went up in flames." She grimaced at the still-smouldering barn. "Is this the ritual murder?" she asked. "I thought you were out there with Dawson."

DI Dawson, her ostensible new second-in-command, was becoming a bit of a thorn in her side; he'd been brought in to run the RCU while she was out on medical leave with a shoulder injury, and she suspected both he and her superiors had expected her to politely shuffle off into early retirement instead of coming back to take the reins. Somebody up there was apparently still hoping that she'd take the hint, since they'd yet to divest her of Dawson despite the fact her team was too small to need a second senior officer. He tended to behave as if he was still in charge, and certainly wasn't inclined to call her in for a second opinion on one of his cases

"I am, but I think this one might be linked to one of our cold cases," Deepan said. "Before my time, though, so you'd know better than me."

"Which case?" Pierce said, trying to mentally pull up the details of the call that had come in early that morning. Not much to go on, as she recalled: a killing down in Nottinghamshire that was suspected of being ritual murder. That was one crime that definitely justified the RCU showing up on-site instead of just remote consultancy, but in her experience it was over-reported—most of the time the supposed occult elements were just attempts to disguise a more mundane killing, or nervy investigators jumping the gun over oddities at the scene. She'd been happy to let Dawson take this one to keep him out of her hair.

Deepan hesitated before answering. "I really think you should come and see the crime scene for yourself, guv," he said. "If I'm right, this is a big one, so I'd rather you see it clean than have me put ideas in your head."

Ominous. "All right then, I'll come down," Pierce said, transferring her phone to a shoulder clamp as she reached for her notebook. "Just tell me where I'm going."

THE BODY HAD been found in a graveyard, which might have rung a bell, but honestly, it rang all too many: there were few locations would-be occult killers liked better, aside from convenient sets of standing stones. A broad perimeter had been taped off around the site, and Pierce was stopped at the gate by a young PC who looked a bit overwhelmed. Rural beats could be busier than most supposed with only a few coppers to cover miles of ground, but ritual murder was still a little out of the ordinary.

"DCI Pierce, Ritual Crime," she said, showing her warrant card and RCU badge. Her sergeant, Deepan Mistry, was already jogging over to meet her as she ducked under the tape.

"Oh, good, you're here," he said with a relieved smile, pushing back his hair. He was a chubby-cheeked lad who still looked younger than his thirty years to her, though he was starting to pick up some lines from the strains of the job. Or maybe that was parenting two small girls. "Crime scene's down this way, if you want to take a quick gander. The locals are getting a little bit twitchy about leaving the scene as-is for this long, but I wanted you to see things *in situ*."

She donned a set of disposable crime scene coveralls, and Deepan led her on through the rows of graves to a wooded area a little further back from the road, probably intended to allow mourners a quiet space for private reflection. Though it wasn't quite private enough for performing human sacrifice. "I take it we don't think the victim was killed here?"

Deepan shook his head. "No, guv. But the corpse was laid out with a bit of ceremony—that's part of what pinged me as familiar. See what you think."

He gestured her on through the trees to where a denser cluster of police and forensics personnel surrounded the body. She recognised the bulky, shaven-headed shape of DI Graham Dawson among them, but left him to his task of lecturing the forensics team so that she could scope the scene out before he butted in with his opinion.

The victim was a young man, laid out among the trees in classic coffin pose with his arms folded over his chest. Early twenties, maybe, with a relatively muscular build—not the first choice of a killer looking for easy prey. Nothing else too distinctive about his appearance at first glance: white, square-jawed with shortish brown hair, unshaven past the point of stubble but short of a true beard. Hard to tell if that was a sign of being held in captivity or a fashion choice.

His eyes had been closed, though dozens of razor-fine cuts over his face and neck and exposed arms gave lie to the impression of peaceful repose. Those cuts had been made while he was still alive to bleed. Yet aside from the inevitable discolouration and the effects of lying outdoors for some hours, the corpse was remarkably clean, clearly bathed to remove excess blood and the worst indignities of death. His clothes were pristine enough that they either had to have been removed before any trouble started and replaced after his death, or they'd been supplied by the killer.

Which made the choice of outfit interesting. Not the ceremonial robes you might expect of ritual symbolism, nor the formal or fetishistic choices of a killer intent on displaying their victim at his best, but strangely casual: tracksuit bottoms, a sleeveless black T-shirt with a small logo on the breast, colourful trainers. She crouched to peer at the soles: no visible sign of wear, and the other clothes looked new too.

Deepan was right. This was ringing some bells. Healthy young victim, fit and in the prime of his life, dressed up in sports gear... and of course that criss-cross web of cuts, evidence of ritual blood-letting. Pierce moved to crouch by his head, looking for the sign that would confirm it.

There, just under the edge of his crew neck on the left side: two deep round puncture wounds spaced about an inch and a half apart, like a snakebite.

Pierce sat back on her heels with an explosive huff of breath. Shit almighty, what had she done to deserve *this*?

Deepan appeared discreetly by her shoulder. "Thinking what I'm thinking, guv?" he asked in a low voice.

"Depressingly, I probably am." She accepted his hand up, rising from the ground with an unhappy groan. "Right, grab Dawson, but let's keep this chinwag away from any other ears for now." Mention the Valentine Vampire in front of anyone old enough to remember the previous killings and they'd be seeing it in the papers the next day.

She retreated to a quiet corner of the graveyard, and Deepan followed a moment later with DI Dawson in tow, or rather striding out ahead of him.

"Right," he said brusquely as he reached her, jerking a thumb back at Deepan. "Your boy said he recognised this, but he wouldn't say anything without a second opinion. What's the news?"

Pierce pressed her lips together. She wasn't exactly thrilled at the prospect of letting a glory-hound like Dawson know this one was a potential career-maker, but she could hardly keep him out of the loop either. "He's right," she said. "MO has all the hallmarks of the Valentine Vampire murders."

Dawson narrowed his eyes, obviously trying to place the name—not one that Pierce had ever been thrilled with, but it was what that had stuck in the public's imagination, and there was no shifting these things once the press got hold of them. "Serial killings in the 'nineties?" he said.

Pierce had already been doing the mental calculations, and she didn't much like the answers she'd come up with. "The first set of three murders was in February '87," she said. She didn't always remember the details of older cases, but she had good reason to remember the dates in this one. "There were three more seven years later, and another three seven years after that. We were ready in 2008, but there were no killings reported." In situations like that you could only hope your serial was either already dead or banged up for life for an unrelated crime.

Deepan had already done the maths. "And now we've reached the next interval."

They had—and as the only member of the department who'd been around for the original killings, Pierce should have been on the alert for a resurgence, but after the skipped interval and what with the chaos of everything else that had been going on lately, it hadn't even crossed her mind.

"So the killer's resurfaced," Dawson said.

"Possibly," Pierce allowed. "Possibly not. We could easily be dealing with a copycat. There was a book published just before the last set of killings was supposed to have been due—Christopher Tomb. Remember him?"

Deepan let out a startled chuckle. "Oh, wow. Yes, I do. He was on all the talk shows, with the dyed black hair and the earrings and that red velvet jacket."

"That's the one," Pierce said with a grimace of a smile. "Anyway, he wrote that godawful sensationalist book—*On the Blood Trail of the Valentine Vampire*, I think it was called—and publicised the details of the murders far and wide. He always claimed he had an anonymous source who used to be a member of the killer's cult, but most likely he knew someone who'd been at the scenes."

"Or he could be our killer," Dawson said.

"Too young," Pierce said, shaking her head. "He'd have been fourteen when the first murders took place."

"Old enough," he said flatly.

"To kill? Yes. To subdue and slowly ritually murder three healthy young men and transport the corpses? Not without help. Besides, we checked him out thoroughly at the time. In school for the first round of murders, at university down in Sussex during the second wave... He's not our man."

"But he could be the copycat," Deepan suggested.

"It's a possibility, but let's not get married to it," Pierce said. "After that bloody book was published, anybody in the country could put together a mock-up that passed muster." But despite the long years since the last one, this scene had the ring of authenticity to her. "All the same, we've got to operate on the assumption that this *could* be the original killer, returning after a break in the pattern." It might indicate jail time, or a period spent overseas or hospitalised for some reason or other—all potential leads, if they could only pin down some suspects to start testing them against.

On the other hand, it could indicate another three murders had somehow passed under their radar seven years ago. She would hope not, with the details of the case so well-established in the public consciousness, but with the RCU's overstretched resources, it was depressingly possible.

But that wasn't the main concern right now. Pierce pushed aside thoughts of possible past mistakes to focus on the current scene. "The victim," she said. "Any possibility of ID?"

"Already done," Deepan said. "Membership card for a gym in Newark-on-Trent in his pocket, complete with ID photo. Nottinghamshire Police sent somebody over, and it checks out. Matt Harrison, twenty-three years old, living with flatmates in Newark—according to them, he didn't come home the night before last, but they weren't worried because he texted one of them to say he'd met a girl. The family have already been notified."

"Pretty cocky murderer," Dawson said. The killer had to have been the one to dress the victim; she doubted the card had been left there by accident.

But cockiness fit the profile of the Valentine Vampire. "And fond of symbolism," Pierce said. "The gym card goes with the clothes—emphasizes that the victim was young and strong and healthy. All of the past victims have been athletes, joggers, on competitive sports teams... we believe that the killer's intent with the blood-letting ritual is to absorb the victim's vitality to increase their own strength." Whether the ritual actually worked, or if it was all in aid of a bit of occult hokum... well, who could say with these things?

"One thing we do know for sure," she said. "Whether this is the original killer or not, our murderer is deliberately echoing the Valentine Vampire's past patterns. If that holds true, we can expect two more deaths before February is out." She fixed both of her subordinates with a serious stare. "Let's see that it doesn't happen."

CHAPTER THREE

PIERCE LEFT DAWSON in charge of liaising with the local police, hoping he wouldn't antagonise them too much, and drove back to the police station that served as the RCU's base of operations. Too small to merit their own dedicated building, they worked out of a set of offices and labs on the second floor.

She climbed the stairs and pushed through into the open-plan office that housed her team of detectives—along with a mountain of paperwork, stacked up around the computers that were supposed to have taken its place. Entering the information from the old case files into a fully computerised database was the kind of work in progress that never actually progressed; with one small Yorkshire-based team handling the caseload for the whole of the north, any supposedly free moment they snatched at the computers had to be used to answer consult requests.

Fortunately, Pierce had two constables and a sergeant to filter through those, so that only the more interesting ones got to her desk. The final member of her team was manning the computers as she arrived: Constable Eddie Taylor, a lanky ginger-haired lad in his late twenties with a broad Brummie accent and a nervous disposition that he hadn't yet shaken off despite several months in the job.

"Ed!" she barked as she came in, snapping her fingers. "Whatever you're doing, if no one's in immediate danger of death, you're reassigned. I need you to pull everything we've got in the files on the Valentine Vampire murders. You'll have to go a way back—they started in '87 and ran through to just after the turn of the millennium."

"I know the case, guv," Eddie said with a sombre nod. "I remember the last murders—our mom wouldn't let us walk home from school while the vampire was out there."

That made her grimace, and not just for the depressing reminder that most of her co-workers had still been spotty teenagers back when she'd been a forty-something sergeant battling to get her boss to listen to her.

"Don't let yourself get sucked in by all the media drama, constable," she said. "I've been working this job thirty years, and I've yet to see evidence that there's any sort of supernatural creature out there that wasn't either a human using magic or a spirit temporarily summoned by a ritual. We're looking for a human killer, not some kind of vampire." And maybe if her superiors had listened to her about that fourteen years ago, they might have caught the bastard back then instead of wasting their time on dubious vampire lore.

"We thought the murders had ended in 2001, but either the killer's just resurfaced, or we've got a well-informed copycat on our hands," she said. "Get familiar with those files. We need to know every relevant detail." She sighed. "Better get a copy of Christopher Tomb's book as well," she conceded. "If it's a copycat, they may well be working from that."

"Yes, guv."

Pierce shrugged her jacket off and was treated to a waft of smoke and worse, reminding her of the morning's escapades. "Gemma been back in?" she asked.

"Er, briefly, guv," he said. "She had some evidence for the labs, but she's gone back out on a follow-up to the grave disturbances in Bridlington."

"Right. I'll be next door," Pierce said. "Get on and find those files."

'Next door' was the Magical Analysis department, home of the RCU's array of specialists and researchers. They were an eclectic bunch, inevitably snowed under with far more cases than they could reasonably process: it was hard to get the budget for a field of analysis that was still mostly experimental and tough to demonstrate in court. Magical rituals were always difficult to predict, repeat or record, and even when they did successfully produce results, it was an uphill struggle convincing the legal system to accept them.

Pierce poked her head into the first office on the left: Sympathetic Magic, the domain of Jenny Hayes. At a petite five-foot-one, she was barely visible behind the wall of evidence boxes and file folders on her desk.

"Jenny! Did my bright-eyed and eager young constable bring anything back from the barn scene this morning?" Pierce asked.

"Claire!" Jenny popped up from where she'd been rooting through one of the boxes stacked beside her, pushing her wavy hair back from her glasses as she straightened. "Heard you were doing your best to blow yourself up."

"Well, I do try," she said. "Was anything rescued from the rubble?"

"Not much," Jenny said with a grimace and a shrug, and waved her vaguely on down the hall. "Wasn't really anything substantial enough for me to make much sense of—I think it's all gone down to Simon in Ritual Mat."

"Oh, is he in?" she said. "Truly, we are blessed."

Simon Castle was their expert in identifying ritual materials, the closest thing the Magical Analysis Department boasted to a legitimate forensics job. He was also a busy little bee, frequently spending the few hours the department could afford him prowling the region's occult markets and magic shops to pick up comparison samples. Ideally he should probably have an assistant doing that kind of scut work for him so he had more time to devote to the analysis, but while they were wishing, why not get them *all* assistants, and a departmental pony?

Besides, the finicky little sod would probably refuse to accept anyone else could do the job to his exacting standards anyway. Pierce supposed it took a particular kind of mindset to devote your life's work to studying the mysteries of the occult and then make your speciality comparing the composition of one shop's bag of allegedly magical mixed herbs with another. But at least he got results that made sense to a judge and jury, which was more than could probably be said for the rest of them. She gave Jenny a nod of acknowledgement and headed on to Ritual Materials.

Simon's personal fiefdom was not much bigger than Jenny's tiny office, but despite having just as heavy a workload he still managed the mind-boggling trick of keeping things well-organised. The room was flanked by two matching rows of tall metal cabinets, and on top of them stacked sets of tiny plastic storage drawers, the kind that elsewhere might be used to hold nuts and bolts. Here they were employed to store Simon's many material samples, all individually labelled in neat, sharp capitals. At the back of the room was the equally tidy, well-organised lab area.

Simon himself, an extremely tall and very thin man in his forties who'd had the same short-back-and-sides haircut for the near-decade that she'd known him, was currently perched spider-like on his lab stool, in the midst of dripping some kind of liquid solution onto a test stick. Pierce waited in the doorway for him to finish, knowing from experience that there was no point attempting to chivvy him along.

Eventually he received whatever result he'd been looking for, made a detailed note of it on the form in front of him, then set everything down and swivelled around to face her. "Chief inspector," he said, clasping his hands together and raising his chin expectantly.

"Simon. Any word on the evidence recovered from the barn scene this morning?" she asked.

He pressed his thin lips together disapprovingly. "As I already told your constable, the samples were hardly in any fit condition to do anything with."

"Couldn't be avoided," Pierce said. "The whole place went up around our ears—we were lucky to come out with *anything*."

"It's debatable whether you did," Simon said. He rose and stalked over to one of the cabinets, opening the door to retrieve an evidence list that he'd apparently already filed. He raked it with a dubious eye. "Unknown yellow powder, contaminated with ash and molten plastic. Heavily melted stubs of wax candles. Burned leather pouch containing herbal residue. Small metal container of possible bone chips... that's about the only promising item on here."

"Well, I'm sure you can work your magic even with that much," she said.

He gave her a stern look. "It's hardly magic, chief inspector, just expertise and careful work. And no amount of expertise can make the results any better than the samples."

It could be a real effort making conversation with Simon at times. "Then please do what you can," she said. "What about the altar? Did that survive the fire?"

He looked vaguely irritated to be consulted on something he no doubt considered outside his department. "I understand it was heavily damaged by a falling roof beam," he told her. "The centre slab was shattered and the alignment of the other stones destroyed, making reconstruction difficult. I believe Cliff has the photos." He closed the folder and placed it back in the cabinet. "If there was anything else?" he asked, lifting his eyebrows.

"Not yet," she said. "But make this case a priority. The people behind these animal killings are still out there, and if they're leaving that kind of booby-trap on their equipment, then they're a dangerous bunch. I need anything you can get me on what they were up to and where we can track them down."

He gave no particular gesture of acknowledgement as she left, and Pierce suspected he was going to go right on handling his cases according to whatever priority he saw fit, as per usual. Still, at least he was always efficient.

She headed on down to end of the corridor and the Enchanted Artefacts lab, the largest and best equipped in the department. It was the base of operations of Clifford Healey, their expert on identifying and rating the threat level of occult objects that they'd seized from crime scenes. As this was mostly achieved by a process of hazardous trial and error that often amounted to poking them to see how they reacted, Pierce generally entered the room with a degree of caution.

There were no obvious sounds of chaos, and a quick glance through the wire-reinforced window didn't suggest an imminent crisis, so she pushed in through the heavy fire door. "Cliff! Got a minute?"

Stooped over one of the lab benches facing the door, he smiled at her and held up a finger, vaguely indicating the headphones in his ears. She loitered in the doorway while he finished drawing out a charcoal magic circle on a large piece of art board, then straightened up and excavated his music player from a pocket under his lab coat, tugging the headphones out of his ears.

"Claire! What brings you to my humble abode?" he said with a bright smile. He was a big man, somewhere around his fifties with broad doughy features and hair that had retreated to two greying islands at either side of his head.

"You get those altar photos from our crime scene this morning?" she asked.

Cliff gave an apologetic grimace. "Yes, but I'm afraid there's not much to be made of them," he said. "I have your constable's notes on what she remembers of the arrangement, but the main altar stone was shattered by the roof collapse, and the other rune stones knocked out of alignment. Without more of an idea of the nature of the ritual being conducted, I doubt there's any way to reconstruct it."

She pulled a face, though she hadn't expected much better.

"Well, thanks, anyway." She started to reverse out through the door, but Cliff beckoned her back.

"That said, I do have some possible results for you on…"—he lifted his eyebrows meaningfully—"that personal project we discussed."

Cliff trying to be circumspect was a bit like something out of a pantomime, but nonetheless, Pierce felt herself tense as she stepped back inside and closed the door. "You managed to put a date on that shapeshifting pelt?" she asked.

At the end of December they'd made a bust on a group calling themselves Red Key, who'd been attempting to raise a major demon. Alarmingly organised and well-supplied, they'd had at least one bona fide warlock in their employ, and a number of shapeshifters acting as the muscle. The shifters—always difficult to contain—had mostly been killed in the chaos or escaped, but Pierce had successfully arrested one in panther form.

He wasn't talking… but the shapeshifting pelt they'd seized from him just might. The maker's rune inside had been Sebastian's. And if Cliff could prove the pelt had been created *after* Sebastian supposedly died in a car accident last October…

"I'm afraid there's a limit to how precise I can be," he cautioned, moving over to the racks of metal shelving at the far side of the room and retrieving a manila envelope from between some boxes. "Frankly, dating pelts has traditionally been a matter of centuries, not months or weeks, and the little work that's been done on newer skins has naturally been angled towards establishing whether artefacts were made pre- or post-legislative reforms in the last few decades."

"You don't need to sell me on how hard you've been miracle-working, Cliff," she said. "I'll believe your expert opinion."

He opened up the padded envelope, and carefully tipped out a smaller sealed plastic bag containing a single strand of black hair—or, she assumed, panther fur. He held it up to the light of one of the standing lamps set up near his workspace. "I'm afraid the results of the earlier testing have faded somewhat, but if you will observe the subtle banding by the root of the hair…?"

She squinted at a hint of red or gold tint that might be a trick of the light on the plastic. "Your eyesight's better than mine," she said.

"Not my eyesight, my contact lenses," he corrected with a smile. "I do have enhanced photographs, in any case." He fished a much-magnified photo of the panther hair out of the envelope, the colours artificially brightened to show bands of colour shading from a bright gold near the root through a spectrum of reds into black.

"Now, as I say, this is an imprecise and untested methodology, and I certainly wouldn't want to hang the success of a court case upon it," Cliff cautioned, "but I acquired some samples from legal pelts and subjected them to the same test." He tipped out two more photographs and laid them out side by side with the first. "Now, this one here was a pelt made about eighteen months ago—note how the test for enchantment shows much less distinct results?"

The bands of colour on the hair in this second photo were dramatically duller, a deep rusty red at the root and a narrow, near-invisible smudge of brown.

Cliff tapped the third and final photo. "And this one was taken from a pelt that was enchanted just this past November."

In this one, the bands of colour looked much more similar to the first, but when Pierce rearranged the pictures to compare the two side by side, she could see that the bands on the original picture were still a fraction brighter and more visible. She raised her head to look at Cliff. "So this means that our pelt was enchanted more recently?"

"It's hardly a smoking gun," Cliff cautioned, raising a finger. "There could be any number of factors influencing the results—variations in the ritual, a more talented skinbinder with a higher quality of skinning blade... perhaps even the type of animal that provided the pelt. Your sample is from a black panther, whereas both of my comparison hairs were from large dogs. I'm afraid there simply isn't enough research on this kind of comparative testing to control for all possible factors."

"Disclaimers duly noted," she said, but she could feel the

buzz of vindication nonetheless. Maybe it wasn't outright *proof* that Sebastian had still been alive and making pelts after his October arrest and supposed death, but it was certainly cause for suspicion—especially when the official story stunk to high heaven. "It's a start, at least."

"A good lawyer would rip it to pieces as evidence, and rightfully so," Cliff warned.

Pierce grimaced. "We're a long way from getting this in front of a lawyer," she said. Not when it came to the kind of case where government groups had permission to walk in and seize her evidence, prisoners died in too-convenient accidents, and the skinbinder she was chasing had the capability to turn murder victims into skin-suits for impostors to wear.

"Keep this safe," she told Cliff, handing the photographs back. "The people who busted Sebastian out of his cell aren't the kind to respect due process."

But now she had a loose thread to begin tugging on.

CHAPTER FOUR

THOUGHTS OF CONSPIRACIES would have to keep, with a major murder investigation in the pipeline. Pierce headed back into the office to see what Eddie had dug up on the Valentine Vampire. "All right, constable," she said, grabbing the nearest chair that wasn't buried in files, "refresh my memory."

He looked a little flustered as he rifled back through his notebook, but that was his default response to being put on the spot; he seemed to have his facts together as he cleared his throat and began.

"Erm, the first wave of murders took place between February fifth and twenty-first, 1987. Three victims: all white males, aged between twenty-one and twenty-six. Two were members of sports clubs and one was a marathon runner. The bodies were left posed in or near graveyards across South and West Yorkshire. All victims showed numerous ritualised cuts across the face and upper body, and identical puncture wounds at the base of the neck, which combined with the discovery of the second victim on February fourteenth led the media to come up with the name the Valentine Vampire."

Her disdain for the name must have showed, because he cleared his throat and hastened on. "Er, there were no leads in the initial investigation, but the murders were assumed to have stopped until the body of Neil Sherrington was found in a graveyard near Horncastle on February third, 1994. It wasn't immediately linked to the Valentine Vampire murders of the 'eighties until a second body was found in Grimsby a week later. Again there were three victims, all following the same profile. The third body was left at the same location as the first, shortly after the police were pulled out of the area."

"Cocky sods," Pierce said. And neither of those sites were all that far from today's body near Newark-on-Trent. Maybe the killer was playing the same trick again, circling back to old haunts once the heat was off.

"Yes, guv," Eddie said with a dutiful nod, and checked his notes again. "Erm, the third set of murders began with the discovery of the body of Andrew Cole near Rotherham on February sixth, 2001. Nine days later the killers dumped the body of a second victim in Hemsworth, but this time there was an alleged witness, a man called Alan Waite who claimed to have been out looking for his lost wallet after he'd dropped it on the way home from the pub. He was briefly treated as a suspect, but found to have been out of the country at the time of the 1994 murders. Questioned by..." He leaned over to consult one of the opened files. "DI Raymond Carlisle and Sergeant... er, you, guv," he said with a blink.

Pierce gave a terse nod, vaguely remembering the interview, though the man himself was a faded ghost in her memory. She wanted to say middle-aged, overweight, balding... but how much of that was recollection, and how much just her mind sketching in details borrowed from a thousand others like him she'd interviewed in her career?

"He gave us a description of the vehicle used to dump the bodies," she said. "But he also gave us a load of complete guff about the people driving it." What had started out as a halfway-plausible description of a woman or maybe a long-haired man driving and a bald man in the passenger seat had quickly swollen with 'remembered' details until the woman was beautiful and pale as death and the passenger could have starred in *Nosferatu*. By the time the media got hold of him, Waite was prepared to swear he'd witnessed the Nosferatu lookalike restored to strength by drinking blood from the corpse.

After that it had been impossible to quash the assumption the killer was a real vampire—especially with DI Carlisle all too eager for an excuse for why the police hadn't managed to make any arrests yet.

Eddie clearly had enough sense to skip over the details of Waite's dubious witness statement. "The police received a tipoff about the van?" he said.

Pierce nodded. "Anonymous female caller claimed to have seen it coming and going from a boarded-up house in York, and that the people living there had tried to recruit her into their cult. Based on her information, Carlisle believed that the cult leader would be confined to the house in daylight hours, and organised a dawn raid."

"But they weren't there?" he said.

"Nope," Pierce said grimly. She hadn't been either—and she couldn't help but think that maybe, if Carlisle hadn't considered her surplus to requirements, she might have realised it was all about to go horribly wrong... "Firearms went in and found the place empty except for a coffin in the basement. When they opened the lid, it blew up in their faces. One officer was killed and two injured. The whole thing was probably a setup from the start—we found the third body in a graveyard fifty miles away a couple of hours later. It must have been dumped there the night before the raid."

About as comprehensive a cock-up as you could ask for.

"One of the officer's statements mentions a possible suspect at the scene of the raid," Eddie said, consulting his files.

"Oh?" Pierce frowned a little, racking her memory, but if she'd ever been informed of that detail she'd forgotten it since.

He peered at the page again as if he might have been mistaken. "Yes, um, Firearms Officer Leonard Grey—"

"Leo Grey?" That caused her head to snap up. "He was part of the raid?"

"Er, yes, guv." He turned the folder to show her the statement sheet. "Is that significant?"

Pierce glanced at the signature, and then the written statement above it. A terse summation of events, much as she might expect from the man. "Not directly," she said. "But I know him. He's got good instincts." He'd *had* good instincts, she supposed; he was retired now, another victim of the clusterfuck of a case that had been their pursuit of Sebastian. "Go on," she told Eddie with a nod.

He swallowed. "Um... there's not much here, guv," he admitted. "According to Grey's statement, he was stationed outside the building in case of attempted escapes, and spotted a young woman watching from the park across the street who he considered to be acting suspiciously." He flipped through a couple more pages inside the folder. "I don't see any evidence that it was followed up."

Meaning that it might have turned out to be nothing—or just gone ignored in the chaos of the disastrous raid. No way to ask DI Carlisle about it now: he'd died of a heart attack five or six years back. Depressing, how many of her former colleagues who'd managed to actually make it out of the job alive were now dropping like flies as time caught up.

But Leo was still around, even if he was retired. Pierce checked her watch and stood. "Right," she said. "I'm going to see if I can talk to Leo Grey. Maybe he remembers some details about that raid that didn't make the reports."

And even if he didn't, she still owed him a visit that she'd been putting off for far too long.

LEO WAS MORE than willing to meet with her immediately—in fact, his eagerness at the prospect of being involved in police work made her feel guilty that her pretext for seeing him was such a long shot. Enforced retirement had to chafe for a man only in his forties who'd kept himself in good shape before he'd been injured. Pierce hadn't seen him since the hospital, but with the state that he'd been in back then, she doubted he could be back up to full strength barely four months later.

The address that he directed her to was a modest terraced house in a village on the edge of the Dales. After much circling of the narrow streets in search of somewhere to legally park, she made her way back on foot and pressed the bell.

The door was opened by a small woman in blue jeans and a knitted cardigan: Leo's wife, whose name unfortunately currently escaped her. Ruth? Rose? Something like that. Pierce had only met her briefly at the hospital, though she'd made a good impression, a calm, pragmatic woman who seemed well-suited to her equally phlegmatic husband.

"DCI Pierce," she said, with a warm smile. "Leo said you were on your way. You're looking well."

That was questionable after the day she'd had, but she supposed that when Rose—she was nearly positive it was Rose—had seen her last she'd been newly released from her shoulder surgery and still half-stoned on painkillers.

"Sorry to butt in on you at such short notice," she said. Often a bit of a social wobble adjusting to the half-forgotten fact that other people had families and lives outside of police work. "I shouldn't take up too much of his time."

"Oh, do," maybe-Rose said cheerfully, stepping back to let her in and gesturing her down the narrow hallway. "He'll be delighted to have something to do. He's never been much of a one for being cooped up around the house. Leave him alone for five minutes and he's putting up shelves and talking about re-tiling the bathroom, and never mind that he's still supposed to be resting that leg."

On their last case together Leo had taken a brutal battering from a shapeshifter in a chimaera pelt, an unholy hybrid patchwork of animal skins. He'd come away with an ugly laundry list of injuries: broken ribs, a shattered kneecap, claw wounds through the muscle of his thigh, and probably worst of all to a man accustomed to being steady-fingered on the trigger, a nasty crushing injury to his right arm and hand that had left him with nerve damage.

Pierce was guiltily aware that she hadn't been keeping up with his recovery as well as she should. He was a taciturn man at the best of times, and a few brief phone calls hadn't told her much about his medical condition: the fact that his status had gone from medical leave to early retirement said more than anything he'd shared directly.

Maybe-Rose led her through to the front room, a warmly cosy sort of space with dark wooden furniture, alcoves full of books and CDs, and a brown leather suite. Leo himself was sitting in one of the armchairs, and she couldn't help but think that he looked older and more worn than she remembered. He'd always had an ageless sort of quality, craggy features and sandy blond hair that hid the signs of grey, but where he'd always been lean he now just looked stretched thin, the angles of his face etched more sharply, like a portrait repainted by a less forgiving artist.

It was disconcerting to see him in casual clothes instead of his ever-present uniform and tac vest; his chinos and grey jumper were somehow even more of an upset than the hospital gown Pierce had last seen him in. She couldn't help but notice a cane tucked beside the chair.

The gravelly voice, though, was still the same as ever. "Claire," he said with a curt nod, about as effusive a greeting as she ever got from him.

His wife leaned over to give him a brief kiss on the cheek. "Right, I'm off to Lucy's," she said. "I'll have my mobile with me, so call me if you need anything, otherwise I'll be home about nine." She headed out, and Pierce and Leo sat in slightly awkward silence for a moment as they listened to the sounds of her departure, neither of them much inclined to small talk.

"So," Leo said, sitting forward once she'd gone. "You need my help on a case?" He looked newly alert, like a bloodhound perking up at the hint of a fresh scent, and she felt bad that she had so little to offer him.

"Looks like the Valentine Vampire might be back to his old tricks," she said. "You were at the raid in York in 2001, right?"

Leo nodded; no doubt he had little trouble calling the case to mind after it had gone so badly. "Yeah, but there's not much to tell," he said. "Suspects had already cleaned out before we got there, and left the place wired to blow. Killed Bill Winston from my unit—I wasn't even in the building at the time."

Pierce nodded in return. "In your report you mentioned spotting a woman you thought was watching the house. I know it was fourteen years ago, but if you can remember anything..."

It was a long time, but if Leo was like her, he'd probably spent many a sleepless night in the years that followed dwelling on the details of the botched raid, trying to find the different call he could have made.

He closed his eyes to think, and without that penetrating gaze to distract her, Pierce could see new lines on his face. She darted a glance at his right hand where it rested on the arm of the chair, but the signs of the surgeries had healed and what damage remained wasn't visible on the surface.

Leo rubbed his temples with his left hand. "There was a woman," he said. "Girl, really—I'd have guessed she was a teenager if she hadn't been so poised. That was what drew my attention: you pay close attention to body language when you're going in armed. Hers was... wrong. Too calm. Not scared or excited, just watching us to see how it went. I was about to call in for somebody to detain her when it all went to hell. By the time I got another chance to look round she was gone."

"Got a physical description?" Pierce asked without much hope. It had been too long. Somebody should have taken all these details down immediately after the fact, even if nothing had come of it.

He pursed his lips. "Young," he repeated. "Mid-twenties at most. Very pale, and I think dark hair, but it could have been dyed. Main thing I remember is she was wearing a silver necklace with something like bat wings on it." He touched his chest vaguely. "Thought that might have been significant."

"Maybe," Pierce agreed. It was something—or at least, it would have been something fourteen years ago. After all this time, with the leads long grown cold, it was a woefully thin description to hang any kind of witness hunt on, and they both knew it.

She sighed, out of any questions that he could usefully help with, but feeling it was too soon to leave. She fished for any other avenue of conversation that wasn't just a blunt enquiry about his injuries.

Leo rescued her, sitting forward in his chair as it became clear her line of questioning had petered out. "So, I hear the skinbinder we went through all this shit to arrest died in a car crash during a prison transfer," he said. "That stink as much to you as it does to me?"

"Like a dead fish down the back of the radiator," she said with a nod. "You're right—I'd bet any money somebody extracted him. Either his own people, or those government wankers who kept trying to take over the case." The Counter Terror Action Team, a group she'd never heard of before or since. "They were obviously pretty eager to get control of the one skinbinder with the know-how to make pelts from human skin." Pierce hesitated, wondering if she could trust him with her wilder conspiracy theories. "And that's not all that stinks. My old superintendent—Howard Palmer. You heard that he retired?"

Leo cocked his head. "You think they forced him out?"

"Worse than that." She pressed her lips together, assembling an argument that still felt almost too paranoid even to her. "He came to see me in the hospital after I'd had my op—or at least, somebody claiming to be Palmer did. Looked and sounded like him, but the way he was acting was all wrong. Nervous, police uniform in a mess... I'd have been willing to call it stress if he hadn't been missing his silver watch."

With the details of their last shared case probably still even fresher in Leo's mind than in hers, it took him barely a moment to twig to the implications. "You think he was replaced by a shapeshifter."

Pierce let out a huff and shook her head slightly, aware how mad it sounded. "Maybe I'm nuts," she admitted. "But he's completely disappeared. Supposedly moved to France, and didn't leave contact details behind him." And there was no way to know if the new superintendent who'd taken his place was an innocent patsy or part of the conspiracy.

She was relieved when Leo nodded thoughtfully rather than dismissing it out of hand. "It's possible," he said. "The people involved in this clearly have a long reach." He straightened in his seat. "Any leads?"

"Maybe," she hedged. "I had a run-in with a group calling themselves Red Key back in December: organised, well-funded, and they had a whole bunch of shapeshifters working for them. Only managed to arrest one of them, but he was wearing a pelt with Sebastian's maker's mark. I had our Enchanted Artefacts man analyse the pelt's age—the results wouldn't stand up in court, but he swears it was made *after* Sebastian supposedly died."

Leo drew in a long breath and nodded slowly. "So that's the start of the trail," he said. "If Sebastian's alive, we need to find him." His gaze sharpened as he focused on her. "You said you apprehended the shapeshifter. Still alive?" he asked.

She nodded. He was last time she'd checked—and she checked pretty frequently. "Had a suicide rune on the roof of his mouth, but we knew to look for it this time." Unlike the decidedly unpleasant outcome the last time they'd arrested one of Sebastian's crew. "Didn't manage to get a word out of him in questioning, though."

"Well, he'll have had time to stew by now," Leo said. "You confront him about the age of the pelt?"

She shook her head. "Not yet. Cliff only came back to me with the results today."

"Then we've got time to press before anyone finds out you've got something," Leo said, standing up. "We should head over there right now."

Pierce could have pointed out there was little reason to bring Leo along for that, but she didn't have the heart.

"All right," she said. "Let's go."

CHAPTER FIVE

PIERCE HAD CAUSE to doubt the wisdom of bringing Leo along with her as she watched the painstakingly slow, stiff way he bent to lace his shoes, and again as she accompanied him to her car; he hadn't brought the cane, and his limp seemed to worsen even over the short walk to where she'd parked. She wondered if the reason he'd opted to leave his wife a note was less to avoid questions about where they were going, and more to avoid ones about whether he was up to it.

But it would have felt like unnecessary cruelty to question his accompanying her now, and besides, maybe she was just feeling guilty, seeing only how far he'd fallen and not how much he'd already recovered. He'd always been a steady, sensible sort of man, and who was she to question his opinion of what he could handle?

All the same, as she drove, she was conscious of him shifting restlessly in the passenger seat beside her, constantly stretching his bad leg as if to ease a cramp. She'd seen him hold almost perfectly still for hours before when the job demanded it.

But he didn't have that job any more, and how could she argue with him seeing this through alongside her when it was thanks to her dragging him into this mess that he'd lost it?

"You know this place they're keeping him?" Leo asked her, after fifteen minutes of driving.

Pierce nodded. "Secure facility off of the M62." In theory a shapeshifter should be no more dangerous than any normal human being once they'd been stripped of their pelt. In practice, magic wasn't so easily and neatly contained, and there were stories of shifters who'd spent too long in their pelts retaining some animal traits even without it. When it came to keeping them contained after arrest, it was best not to take chances.

The Yorkshire Enhanced Offender Institution had high metal fences tipped with razor wire, and a guard on the gates who took the time to actually study Pierce's warrant card when she showed it. She'd called ahead and made arrangements, pleading time-sensitive questions as an excuse for the short notice, but there was still some bureaucratic wrangling to be done and forms to be filled in before they were finally cleared to see the prisoner.

"I doubt you're going to get much out of this one," the prison officer escorting them cautioned. "Gone feral. I've seen it before—scratching at the walls and howling, biting, losing the ability to use tools... Oh, the psych people try to work with them, of course, but there's only so much you can do. Put one of those skin suits on and it starts messing with your brain. People weren't meant to be other shapes."

"Mm," Pierce said neutrally, and forbore from pointing out that it was her own field of expertise. In truth, she supposed, it was scarcely anyone's area of expertise. Most of the literature on long-term aftereffects from shapeshifting came in the form of highly dubious historical accounts of men that had become 'near beast in mind and manner,' and some pre-war experiments where the poor sods had been studied under such inhumane conditions it was hard to know whether to blame the magic or the testing.

"Has Tate spoken since he was brought here?" she asked. The shifter hadn't said word one to her or anyone else who'd tried to question him when he was first arrested. Even the identification was no more than provisional: dental records taken when they'd dealt with the suicide rune concealed inside his mouth had come up with the name of Martin Tate, but they'd been completely unable to find any other up-to-date details on the man, and Tate himself hadn't responded any better to that name than to anything else they called him.

Maybe six weeks in custody would have given him time to start reconsidering his options—though judging by the prison officer's sceptical grimace, she was thinking not.

"Non-verbal since he came in," he said. "Doesn't appear to respond to commands, though you never know how much these guys are faking. But he's in line with some of the worse cases of animal behaviour we've seen." He sucked in a dubious breath and shook his head. "I don't know what you're expecting to get out of this, but the prisoner will have to stay secured. No phones or internet-capable devices inside the interview room; nothing sharp or that can otherwise be used as a weapon. You'll be monitored on CCTV from outside the room—if you move beyond the demarcation line on the floor or the prisoner gets violent, the interview will be terminated immediately."

It was a familiar spiel to her, but Leo listened with a level of serious attention that seemed to placate the prison officer's obvious dubiousness. "I'll be monitoring from outside, as will the main security office," he said as they reached the suite of secure interview rooms. "You'll be recorded the whole time you're in the room. Interview room two, on your left."

They entered the interview room, a sparse affair with the table and chairs securely bolted to the floor and nothing else on hand for the prisoner to grab. Not that he could have anyway: his arms were fixed to the metal frame of his chair with silver cuffs, leaving him unable to lift them more than a few inches or properly stand up. The chair was set well back from the interviewers' table, inside a magic circle etched into the concrete floor. Pierce glanced up, and saw a mirror of the design marked on the ceiling. Heavy duty magical containment; it shouldn't be necessary for a shifter stripped of his pelt, though it might well be for other prisoners who couldn't be so easily separated from their magical enhancements.

There were two chairs on the other side of the interview table; Leo took one, but Pierce stayed standing, leaning back against the rear wall to observe Tate in the flesh for a short while.

His hair had grown back a little from the close crop he'd had when he was arrested, and he'd developed a scruffy beard, suggesting he wasn't shaving himself and no one else was prepared to do it for him; there was something in his near-smirk that suggested he wouldn't be above snapping his teeth at anyone who got that close. He was a well-muscled man perhaps in his mid-thirties, and even cuffed there was an air of coiled menace to his posture that put her in mind of a cat ready to pounce. His loose-fitting prison T-shirt didn't quite cover the intricate tattoo that spread from the back of his neck down across his shoulders: an hourglass made up of interlocking strands that resembled a stylised letter S.

The skinbinder Sebastian's mark, a perfect match to the rune inside the pelt that would allow him to use its magic.

Pierce watched him jitter in the chair, restless in spite of the restraints. When she'd first interviewed him, shortly after his arrest, he'd been much more collected; perhaps the prison officer was right, and he was starting to go feral after too long deprived of the chance to shift into his animal form.

But she wouldn't bet it wasn't a performance. His head was always shifting, tilting in a not quite natural manner, as if trying to make use of eyes and ears that weren't the same shape as the ones he actually had—but when his eyes passed over her, there was too much intelligence there for a man completely gone over to animal instinct. He recognised her, that much she was certain. There was something here that she could work with.

A strained silence filled the room as they sized each other up. When she'd seen enough, Pierce moved forward unhurriedly to take the seat beside Leo, folding her arms on the tabletop—a posture that meant leaning forward slightly, showing no fear of the potential threat across the table.

"So, Mr Tate," she said. "How's incarceration treating you?" No response, but he was watching her. "I imagine you must be getting a little bit restless by now. Muscles giving you trouble? I hear it's hard, getting used to being stuck in one shape when you've spent your time shifting at will."

She didn't make more than a cursory pretence of waiting for a response. Always better to proceed calmly and casually as if everything was going to plan and the interview was a mere formality; let the interviewee know they had knowledge that was worth something to you and they'd do their best to skew the bargain further in their favour.

Assuming they were prepared to bargain at all. Tate hadn't proved an easy nut to crack so far; she could only hope that by now he'd undergone some softening as it sank in that he was likely to be in here for a very long time, and his former allies didn't seem too fussed about hastening his release. Six weeks on the inside stretched an awful lot longer than it did in the outside world.

And even if Tate was a true fanatic for the cause, being deprived of his enchanted pelt would surely be taking its toll. Certain types of magic could be pretty addictive—and addicts, as a rule, didn't stay loyal for long to anyone who couldn't get them their fix.

"I'm afraid if you refuse to speak even in your defence, you're definitely not going to be leaving this place any time soon," she said. "We have you caught red-handed on possession of a class two restricted artefact, shapeshifting without a licence, and attempted murder—and unless you're prepared to provide evidence that proves otherwise, then you're still in the frame for at least one other murder carried out by a panther shifter in the vicinity. You prepared to give us information on any other shifters you know of that could potentially clear your name?"

Pierce raised her eyebrows enquiringly, but unsurprisingly, the possibility of reexamining a charge he was almost certainly guilty of anyway didn't make for much of a carrot. Since she certainly wasn't about to dangle an impossible offer of early release or transfer to a regular prison, there was little she could promise in return for his cooperation.

He was still pretending absolute indifference to the fact she was even speaking—and she was still sure that he understood every word she said. But even if she was trying to persuade the man, her best route in might be appealing to the animal.

"No? Then you're going to be in here for the long haul, I'm afraid," she said. "Might be a good time to start thinking about creature comforts. I'm sure you'd appreciate more exercise time—a chance to go outside, get some air." She sat back to stretch, glancing around pointedly at the bare walls. "What do they feed you in this place? Getting enough meat? Maybe if you work with us, something could be arranged."

The prisoner said nothing, but he bared his teeth in a silent snarl, rattling his cuffs. Beside her Leo subtly shifted, as if reaching to check on the firearm that he no longer carried.

Time to bring him in on things and see if the stick was any more effective than the carrot. Even unarmed and far below strength, Leo was remarkably good at exuding a sense of quiet threat.

"Perhaps you recognise Mr Grey here," Pierce said, tilting her head towards Leo. "Or maybe you don't, if you weren't quite as high up in your bosses' confidence as you think. He's been involved in our investigation from the start, and he's helped bring some very interesting information to light." All technically true statements, if misleadingly assembled. Now for the big push. She sat forward, folding her arms on the table.

"We know your panther pelt was made by a man who calls himself Sebastian. We know it was made considerably more recently than should have been possible, given that he's supposed to be dead. And we know that makes *you* a liability to the people that you're working for, with that tattoo still on your shoulders. You think there aren't techniques to prove who gave you that tattoo and when? Rituals that will prove that you had contact with Sebastian after his apparent death?"

She was bluffing, but the odds were there *was* something to find, if they dug deep enough. It was an avenue of investigation, but a slow and risky one: cooperation from Tate had much higher odds of netting them the bigger prize.

And maybe she was actually starting to get through; he was looking steadily more twitchy. "Now, maybe you're feeling pretty confident in here, and fair enough—it's a secure facility, after all. Nobody should be able to get in here to come after you. Unless, maybe, you have some reason to believe that the people you were working for have some way to compromise that?" She tried to catch the prisoner's eye, but his head was down, his shoulders taut with tension.

Leo huffed dismissively beside her, the first noise that he'd made since they'd entered the room. "I think it's pretty clear that we're wasting our time here," he said, though it was the opposite of what Tate's body language was suggesting. He recognised the time to apply pressure, just as well as Pierce did. "There are other sources who are far more likely to be cooperative."

She turned halfway towards him, making a show of setting her hands on the tabletop to stand. "Well, in that case," she said, "we may as well just—"

Tate lunged forward as if triggered by some unseen signal, yanking at his cuffs and snapping his teeth in a violent snarl. The sound that tore out of his throat was a hoarse, rasping cry that shouldn't have come from any human being. Pierce jumped back from the spitting, gnashing jaws by instinct, stumbling over the bolted-down chair as she tried to push it back. He shouldn't be able to reach her—but the silver cuffs were clanging and scraping against the chair, and she was all too aware they were made to stop magic, not brute strength.

Leo scrambled up beside her, slapping once again at his side for the Glock full of silver bullets he no longer carried, and she heard him curse as he put too much weight on his injured leg. Tate was growling and thrashing against the restraints, his wrists already blooded from the cuffs as he mindlessly threw himself forward. The glint of alertness that she thought she'd seen in his eyes had given way to wild animal madness.

She was turning to call for assistance, but prison officers in riot gear were already flooding in, armed with Tasers and batons and barking orders: "Outside! Out!" She and Leo were manhandled out of the interview room and the door slammed shut behind them. It wasn't quite soundproof enough to cut off the yelling and sound of spray canisters discharging.

The prison officer who'd first escorted them in hurried over from the CCTV station. "You need to leave this area," he said. "Interview's over." It was clear they'd get nothing out of Tate in this state, but Pierce still mentally cursed as they were hustled away from the scene; the days in isolation or medical care he'd more than likely win for this stunt would give him plenty of time to collect himself and prepare for any further questioning.

"When can we re-interview?" she asked.

"Not my call," her escort said tersely. "You're going to have to leave the building. No visitors on site when there's an incident in progress." Never mind her DCI status or their collective years of experience dealing with magical offenders— it was clear that right now she and Leo were just inconvenient members of the public getting in the way of the staff.

Of course, Leo actually *was* retired now. As they were escorted back out to the gate, Pierce glanced around to see how he was doing. The speed at which they'd been bundled out and away from the interview room didn't appear to have done his bad leg any favours: his limp had grown dramatically worse, and his face was tight with pain as he rubbed the heel of his hand down his thigh. The February cold couldn't be helping either; his movements were stiff as he climbed back into the car, struggling to secure his seatbelt until he gave up and twisted awkwardly to do it left-handed.

Pierce looked away to give him some privacy as she started the engine. "Well, I'm not sure this got us anywhere that was worth the hassle," she admitted, running a hand over her face and stifling a yawn. Between this morning's escapades and all the driving, this had been a very long day already.

And it wasn't going to get any shorter if she sat zoning out here. With a sigh she flicked the headlights on, illuminating the shadowed grounds beyond the fence—and a figure in a long coat walking through them. As the man turned to glance up at the sudden light, Pierce recognised him with a jolt.

Jason Maitland, head of the so-called Counter Terror Action Team: the man who'd interfered every step of the way in her attempts to arrest Sebastian, and one of the prime suspects for having helped fake his death.

What the hell was that bastard doing here?

CHAPTER SIX

PIERCE SCRABBLED FOR her phone to take a photo, but before she could find it in her pockets Maitland was gone, heading into the building by a staff door. She didn't know if he'd recognised her past the glare of the headlights. "Shit," she huffed, sitting back.

"What?" Leo asked, squinting into the darkness.

"Maitland," she told him. "Counter Terror fucker. How the hell did he get here so fast?" Someone at the facility must have called him in—but it was too soon for him to be responding to the security alert. He had to have been called in response to their arrival.

"What's this got to do with Counter Terror?" Leo asked.

"Bugger all," Pierce said grimly. Maitland's involvement in her pursuit of Sebastian had been tenuously justified by the security threat that human-form shapeshifting represented, but if the only skinbinder who could create human skins was supposed to be dead... "The only reason for him to be here is if Tate could tell us something about Sebastian that he doesn't want us to hear."

"So he's our link back to Sebastian," Leo said.

She nodded. "If Maitland's people aren't the ones who faked his death, you can bet they're on the trail of whoever did." And doing their best to scrub that trail out, because to them, having control of Sebastian's abilities mattered more than getting justice for his crimes.

Not to Pierce.

She flicked the headlights off again, plunging the grounds back into shadow. "We'll see where he goes when he leaves."

Her previous efforts to track down Maitland had met with no luck; by the time she'd returned to work after her shoulder injury, the Counter Terror Action Team had been renamed, reorganised, and swallowed by other departments, its members shuffled away like the money card in a game of Three-card Monte. Trying to find anyone who knew anything about a man called Jason Maitland had only led to endless telephone loops, passed from one office to another without ever getting any answers.

But now here he was in the flesh. Pierce settled in, prepared to wait him out, but before thirty seconds had passed a sharp rap on the window made her jump. One of the gate guards shone a torch in her face, bright enough to blind her. "Is there a problem here?" he asked.

"Just making a phone call," Pierce said. She still had the phone in her hand, but she doubted the guard really cared whether she had an excuse anyway.

"Ma'am, I'm going to have to ask you to move along right now," he said. "It's policy to completely clear the access road of civilian traffic when there's an alert."

There were at least three things that set her teeth on edge there, starting with the word 'civilian': police weren't military, and prison officers working for private companies certainly weren't police. But arguing would take her nowhere useful, and it wouldn't be wise to go out further on a limb when she had no official authorisation to even be here, following up on cases that were supposed to be closed.

With the guard watching and waiting, there was little choice except to drive away.

"We'll keep digging," Leo said. "There's something here to find; Maitland's arrival proves it."

"Yeah." Unfortunately, it also meant that whatever there was to find was about to be more deeply buried.

BY THE TIME Pierce got home that night, she was too exhausted to bother to tackle her long-neglected list of household chores, which meant she had to do some hasty ironing in the morning to have a shirt for work. She switched the TV news on for background noise, half-listening until the word 'vampire' snagged her attention. Looking up to see a reporter outside a familiar-looking graveyard, she cursed and grabbed for the remote to turn the volume up.

"—victim has been identified as twenty-six-year-old Matt Harrison of Newark-on-Trent. So far there's been no official statement from police at the scene, but the date and location match the profile of past murders by the Valentine Vampire, and internet reports claim that officers from the northern Ritual Crime Unit were called to the scene."

The camera cut to an interview with one of Harrison's gym buddies, saying all the usual things that TV channels passed off as news. Pierce growled in disgust. Even if the news stations were still hedging their bets, the cat was clearly well out of the bag—more than likely released by some so-called professional at the crime scene who couldn't resist sharing the gossip. Now they were going to be rushed into giving a statement before they had their facts straight.

She was flagged down by Jill at the front desk as soon as she got to work. "Let me guess," Pierce said. "His nibs wants a word?"

"Got the impression that he wanted several," Jill said with an arch look. Pierce smoothed down the front of her dubiously ironed shirt as she headed in to knock on the door of Superintendent Snow's office.

"Enter," he said curtly, and it was still a kick in the gut to hear those imperious tones in place of Howard Palmer's voice. Pierce couldn't say she and her old boss had been close, but she'd known the man over a decade, and it didn't sit well to think he'd more than likely died unnoticed and unmourned, an inconvenient obstacle to those behind the cover-up.

As for Robert Snow... well, who was to say whether he was an innocent replacement filling the empty seat, or up to his neck in the conspiracy and watching her every move? Without knowing, there was no way Pierce could trust him.

She got the impression he didn't like her very much either, but that might just be her department's appalling statistics.

"Pierce," he said, with a face like he'd just bitten into a lemon. He was a handsome silver-haired man with an aquiline nose and military bearing, and seemed to approach these meetings as if he was a headmaster lecturing a wayward schoolgirl. "This 'Valentine Vampire' case." Snow picked the term out with a disdain that matched her own, though she suspected for quite different reasons. "Why exactly is it splashed all over the morning news before I've so much as received a report?"

She shook her head slightly by reflex, though she knew that disavowing responsibility—however accurately—wouldn't do her any favours with him. "We haven't completed preliminary inquiries or got any of the forensics back yet, sir," she said. "At this point it's still far too soon to confirm any connection to the previous killings."

"And yet the media show no such compunction." He held up a newspaper so she could read the headline: *New murder sparks 'Valentine Vampire' fears*. No doubt the tabloids were being even less constrained. "If the connection to these past murders is so tenuous, then how did it find its way out to the public so quickly?"

"We still don't know that, sir, but we'll be investigating how the details of the crime scene leaked," Pierce said. Or rather, with their lack of resources, punting it down to Nottinghamshire Police to investigate their own people and no doubt come back with nothing concrete. "All discussion of a possible connection to the Valentine Vampire murders was kept strictly between Dawson, Sergeant Mistry and myself, but it's possible someone else at the crime scene recognised the MO and spread the word."

And no doubt they could thank Christopher Tomb's bloody book for that as well. That sensationalist piece of tripe had done more to cement the public image of some blood-guzzling supernatural creature stalking the country's young and healthy than any number of news reports.

"Well, connection or no connection, I want you to make this case your top priority," Snow said sternly. "The media are already discussing the past failures of the police in investigating these killings, and I'm not about to have that happen again on my watch. Whether this is a copycat or the original murderer returning, I expect to see this killer found and brought to justice."

"Yes, sir," she said.

Easy for him to bloody say.

By THE TIME Pierce got into the office, Dawson had already buggered off back to Nottinghamshire with Constable Taylor in tow, apparently still under the impression that this was his case. Rather than pursue them, she opted to take her other constable off to York to revisit the scene of the failed raid fourteen years ago. "If we're lucky, there might still be some neighbours around who can tell us something about Leo's mystery woman." If she was the one who'd called in the tipoff about the vampire cult living there, then maybe she knew more about them than she'd said at the time.

They followed the satnav's directions into the winding streets of York. "Busy," Gemma noted, as they joined a tailback of traffic. When they arrived at their destination, a narrow terraced street with red brick houses on the right and greenery on the left, there seemed to be an excessive number of cars parked up on the grass. Pierce cursed as she spotted a news van down the end.

"Well, somebody remembers their local history." Had the details of the house been in that bloody book as well? She really ought to read the thing. A headache bloomed as she saw the odds of them performing a nice, low-profile enquiry shrivel away. With the media on the scene, everybody was no doubt already racking their brains for the most sensationally gory details they could convince themselves they 'remembered.'

A small crowd had gathered around the news van, but Pierce could see she and Gemma still stood out in their suits. A few of the gawkers might have been neighbours who'd emerged to see what the fuss was about, but many of the others looked like what Pierce might be dating herself to call 'goths': dyed black hair, Victorian fashion and caked white make-up everywhere. The uniform of your average vampire enthusiast.

And there was worse to come; Pierce held back a grimace as she got her first clear look at their destination, the house at the end of the row. No surprise it still stood empty after all these years, or that graffiti artists had taken to the chipboard that covered the door and windows, but amongst the usual tags there were some vaguely occult squiggles and less customary slogans like *we are all meat* and *blood is life*. Clustered around the low front wall were various small offerings, candles, little figurines and the like. Pierce hoped they were memorials to the victims, but suspected that she might be disappointed.

This place had become a bloody shrine for vampire wannabes.

Gemma drew her phone to take some photos of the house, unnoticed among a mob of others doing the same. Pierce hung well back from the news team on the corner, not wanting to take the chance that they'd sent someone who would know her as the face of the RCU. She surveyed the gathered crowd instead, looking for someone who seemed both old enough to have been here fourteen years ago and not too entranced by all the drama.

The road ended after the final house, continuing only as a cycle track. Pierce grimaced to see a small children's play area on the corner opposite the murder house: she remembered that sight well from the news stories of the time, every reporter worth their salt eager to get a shot of it in the background as they interviewed the horrified neighbours. The brightly coloured paint of the metal slide and climbing frames was flaked and rusted now, and as graffitied as the house.

Beyond the play area was a line of scruffy trees—and among them stood a woman.

She caught Pierce's eye with the very *still* way that she was silently observing the scene, removed from the rest of the eagerly gawking crowd. Not one of the goths, though she would have fitted among their number at first glance, pale-faced and dark-haired; she was wearing a simple grey hoodie, though, and against the T-shirt underneath Pierce saw the glint of something silver. Her eyes weren't up to the task of identifying it at this distance, but she supposed it could have been the necklace Leo described.

Leo's girl witness from fourteen years ago? Even if she'd been a teenager back then she should be older than this woman looked, but faces could be deceptive. Pierce took a step towards her, picking her way through the assembled crowd. She glanced over her shoulder for Gemma, but she'd moved away to take more pictures of the house from round the side, and there was no way to get her attention without drawing other people's.

Pierce turned back to her quarry, and saw that in the brief moment her attention had been diverted, the woman had already moved, heading away into the trees. She cursed silently to herself and hurried through the fringes of the crowd to follow.

By the time she reached the tree line herself, the woman was already some distance away across the sloping green, and Pierce almost had to jog to just to match her walking speed. "Hey!" she called out. "Police! I need to speak to you." That didn't always get a positive reaction, but a negative one could tell her something too.

In this case it got a complete non-reaction, the woman disappearing behind another cluster of trees without so much as looking back. Pierce chased after her, and found they'd reached a gravel footpath, leading to a set of metal gates with bold yellow warning signs. Pierce could see the overhead cables of the railway line beyond.

Perhaps realising she was cornered, or willing to talk now they were out of sight of the people on the street, the woman had stopped just ahead of the fence. She turned back to face Pierce with a guarded expression.

Pierce raised her hands to signal her peaceable intentions, slowing her approach to a non-threatening pace. "I just want to ask you some questions about the boarded-up house at the end of the row," she said. "Are you a neighbour? Do you know anything about the people who used to live there?"

Was this the girl that Leo had seen on the day of the raid? If it was, then Pierce thought that he must have overestimated her age back then: she didn't look like she could be out of her late twenties now. But even if this wasn't her, they still had one thing in common—she was indeed wearing a silver necklace in the shape of a bat with outstretched wings.

"Listen," Pierce said, in her most calmly encouraging tones. "My name is DCI Claire Pierce. I'm with the Ritual Crime Unit. Nobody's in trouble, I just want to—" She was interrupted by the ring of her own phone, a loud electronic blurt that shattered the relative peace of the scene. Probably Gemma, checking where she'd got to. "Sorry, if you'll just bear with me a second...." She struggled to wrestle her phone free from her overstuffed pocket.

By the time that she had it in her hand, the woman was already gone.

"Hey!" Pierce ran forward to the railway fence, looking both ways before she glimpsed a flash of a grey hoodie disappearing under the concrete bridge off to the right. She eyed the fence herself for one abortive moment, but even if she'd been stupid enough to trespass on the tracks, the thing had nasty spikes running along the top.

The woman obviously knew the area well, and Pierce stepped back from the fence with a defeated sigh. There was no way that she'd catch her now.

CHAPTER SEVEN

It TURNED OUT to be Deepan on the phone.

"Something come up?" Pierce asked, wandering fruitlessly up the hill along the line of the railway fence, though the woman was long gone.

"Big operation just nabbed a gang of thieves in Leeds," Deepan told her. "Local police had a warrant to search one of their properties for stolen goods and found a shed full of ritual artefacts. I had a look and it seems pretty legit—there's a few things that I recognise, and some of them are nasty enough that I'd rather have more educated eyeballs going through the place before we try to shift it all."

"All right, I'll join you there." It didn't look like there was going to be a lot of point in her hanging around here. "Might be an idea to grab Cliff as well." The RCU's magical analysts rarely made house calls—mostly too bloody busy and more useful to the team where they were—but while she had decades of crime scene experience under her belt, Cliff was the one who'd made it his life's work to keep up with the study of occult artefacts.

"Mind you don't let him wander in before you've checked everything for trigger runes and the like, though," she added as an afterthought. Her experience at the barn yesterday was still fresh in her mind, and Cliff was used to getting his artefacts safely parcelled up in an evidence box after someone else had done the dirty work.

"Will do, guv," Deepan said. He gave her the address, and she headed back through the trees to the boarded-up house. The news team seemed to be packing up, having reached the limits of the footage they could wring out of a long-empty house and a mob of vampire wannabes. Gemma slipped unobtrusively through the crowd to join her.

"I've got pictures of all the graffiti and the stuff left outside the house," she said. "And some of the crowd. Dunno if it's likely to be of use, though."

Pierce pressed her lips together. "Mm. Not convinced *any* of this is connected to the original killers, but they're cocky sods, so best be thorough all the same."

"Did you find our mystery woman?" Gemma asked.

"Possibly, but she did a runner. I doubt she's going to risk coming back today, but keep an eye out for anyone else wearing a necklace in the shape of a bat." She grimaced as she took in the primarily black-clad crowd with their lacy shawls and capes and corpse-white make-up. "I appreciate that's probably not exactly a distinctive marker in this mob, but do your best."

She left Gemma with the job of canvassing the neighbours, not exactly thrilled to be leaving a constable alone in the field with no backup, but seeing little choice with the way their resources were stretched. In any case, she doubted the vampire cult were likely to try anything here while the media spotlight was on the place: they were cocky, not completely idiotic.

Unfortunately. They'd managed to get away scot free too many times already; Pierce could only hope that this time their luck would run out.

*   *   *

THE ADDRESS DEEPAN had given her led her to a considerably more upmarket neighbourhood of big semi-detached houses with well-kept front lawns. If not for the police presence, her target wouldn't have stood out from its neighbours: lacy net curtains, neat conifer hedge, satellite dish on the wall. The front door and side gate were both standing open; Pierce waved her warrant card at the nearest warm body. "RCU, called in for a consult on some artefacts?"

The young PC looked blank for a moment, then gestured her towards the wooden gate. "Shed round the back. Your sergeant's out there, I think."

"Cheers." She navigated the collection of wheelie bins parked round the side of the house and passed through the gate, ducking under the overhanging strands of creeper. The back garden was less well-tended than the front lawn, a trampled path leading through the long grass to the shed that took up most of the space. It had no windows, and in place of the usual simple bolt the door had a hefty padlock, though someone had already been at it with bolt cutters.

Pierce approached the closed door, pulling on a pair of evidence gloves from her pocket. "Knock, knock, anybody home?" she announced herself before tugging it open, to no response from within.

The inside of the shed was lit by a free-hanging incandescent bulb, and had the unavoidably musty, slightly damp scent of seldom-used space. Not the safest of storage conditions for potentially volatile magical items, especially crammed to the rafters as the shed proved to be: wooden shelves along three sides were loaded with occult objects, some of which made her eyebrows rise immediately. That shrunken monkey head hanging from the corner was definitely up to no good, and she didn't much like the trio of blank-eyed dolls slumped beside it either.

A few larger pieces including storage chests, stone bowls and a cauldron were stacked in the middle of the floor—which was why it took her a few moments to spot Deepan, crouched down in the corner in front of what seemed to be an antique mirror, its ivory frame carved to resemble a wreath of thorns. The dust sheet that he'd pulled from it still dangled from his left hand, seemingly half forgotten. Pierce whistled softly to draw his attention. "Oi, oi—something interesting?" she asked.

Still no evidence that he could even hear her, and her mood flipped from mildly amused to wary fast.

"Deepan," she barked, much louder this time. "Sergeant Mistry, I am talking to you, son!" She whistled again, a piercing blast. He didn't so much as twitch in her direction. The whole of his concentration was intently focused on the tarnished surface of the mirror—though she was pretty sure it was something far more sinister than his own reflection that held him so transfixed.

Pierce edged around the obstacles to get closer to him, wary of falling into too direct a line of sight lest she end up snared by whatever enchantment lay on the mirror. Mirror magic could be nasty stuff, and it probably wasn't wise to try to move him away from it until she knew what they were dealing with. But how could she figure that out if she couldn't even look at the thing head-on?

By fighting fire with fire. She remembered she had a mirror of her own, the small square compact she'd taken to tucking into an inner pocket after a run-in with some possessing spirits a few months ago. If she knew her mirror theory, then a second reflection ought to neutralise the power of the first.

Unless it amplified it instead. Such were the joys of messing around with unknown artefacts.

But it was the least risky way of getting the measure of the situation, and whatever that mirror might be doing to Deepan, she doubted it was a good idea to let it continue. There was no saying how long he might have been crouched in front of it already.

She wasn't even sure he was still breathing.

Forcing down the unhelpful instinct to just run forward and drag him away, Pierce unfolded her own compact mirror and angled it over her shoulder to try and see, an even more awkward manoeuvre than trying to get the back view of an outfit. She couldn't get a clear look at the magic mirror with Deepan's body in the way, so she pressed closer up against the shelves at the side, jostling a line of stone jars up on the highest shelf and causing the dangling monkey head to swing ominously.

At last she got the angle right to give her a glimpse of the tarnished mirror, and in it Deepan's dully reflected face, but it was like trying to see him through a red-tinged fog. At first she thought it was a rusty tint to the mirror, but even as she watched a fresh cloud of brighter red puffed out from the ivory thorns that framed the glass, spreading through the mirror image like a cloud of octopus ink—or blood in water.

Entirely *too much* like blood in water.

Change of plan, Pierce decided. Get him away from that thing's grip, now. Still looking through the compact, she backed towards Deepan's position, bumping a shelf with her hip and flinching as a propped-up book fell sideways with a thud. The stone jars on the top shelf rocked slightly, but all that rained down on her head was dust.

Deepan didn't so much as twitch.

Pierce reached out to touch his shoulder with the back of her hand, with half-formed thoughts of safety procedures for electric shocks. His skin was warm through his thin shirt, but it was like giving a nudge to somebody unconscious: unresponsive solid meat. She gave him a harder shove, enough to push him off-balance. His feet shifted under him to compensate for the wobble, but otherwise he gave no reaction. Lights on, but nobody home.

Another glance through the compact showed that the ivory-framed mirror was already stained a vivid, bloody red. She took a grip on Deepan's shoulder, preparing to try and bodily wrench him away from it.

An urgent cough from the direction of the door made her jump and almost stumble back against the thorny frame. Pierce looked up from her intent focus on the compact to see Cliff standing in the doorway of the shed. "Ah, I wouldn't advise moving him, Claire," he said hastily. "If I'm not mistaken, that's an eighteenth-century soul mirror, and separating the victim from its hold prematurely could have very nasty consequences."

She was pretty sure that leaving him fixated on the thing would have nasty consequences too. "It's draining his blood," she said, shaking her head. Was it her imagination, or was Deepan's face already starting to look grey? "I don't know how long he was like this before I got here."

"Yes, but if we break the magical connection the wrong way, it could be like yanking out a knife."

Pierce stepped away from Deepan, ceding the field to Cliff's expertise. "Tell me you know the right way," she said.

"Hmm," Cliff said, which wasn't the most encouraging sound he could have made. Cliff was good at what he did, but he was used to thinking things through in the lab, not life-and-death fieldwork. Pierce twitched silently as he paused to think, aware that 'less haste, more speed' wasn't really an approach she'd ever had much talent for. She was only conscious of Deepan, grey-faced and rigid beside her, and that they had no way of knowing how much of his blood the mirror had sapped already.

"Need this?" She held the compact mirror out to Cliff, hoping to kickstart some sort of plan of action.

He seemed to notice it in her hand for the first time. "A secondary mirror? Ah, yes, probably a wise precaution—but don't worry, I came prepared." He was carrying a leather satchel over his shoulder, and from it he dug out a case that turned out to hold a pair of wraparound sunglasses. "Mirror shades," he said, almost apologetically, as he put them on. "Not the greatest fashion statement, I know, but remarkably useful for mirror work."

"If this works, I'll put them on the field equipment list," Pierce said tightly. She edged back into the corner to allow Cliff to pass her in the tight space. Fuck, she *hated* hanging back and watching while other people took charge, but years of experience policing many different forms of magic didn't make her a qualified practitioner. Whether performing magic required inborn talent was still a subject of hot debate, but regardless, it certainly took a great deal of patience, obsessive attention to detail, and the ability to block out all distractions.

Even if someone was dying.

Cliff gave Deepan an avuncular but absent pat on the shoulder as he crouched beside him with a creak of knees. "Don't worry, lad, I'm almost sure that I know what I'm doing." But his gaze was on the mirror, with the sort of pensive frown that better belonged on a man contemplating a difficult crossword. "Hmm, yes. Judging by the patterning, I think this might be a Schiavelli."

"Meaning you know what to do?" Pierce said.

"I hope so," he said. "Schiavelli was known for working a back door of sorts into the enchantments, so that he could reclaim control of his creations, so perhaps..."

He left off explaining in favour of doing, drawing a stick of chalk from his satchel to begin sketching symbols on the mirror. They disappeared into the glass like powder dissolving in water; watching in the reflection of the compact mirror, it took Pierce a moment to cotton onto the fact that she couldn't see Cliff's hand reflected in the glass at all, though she could still see Deepan's face there, submerged in murky red.

Had his eyes been closed before?

Cliff muttered to himself as he worked, half-heard syllables that Pierce couldn't decipher; she didn't know if it was ritual or he was just lost in thought, so she stayed silent, though her nerves were twanging.

Was the mirror surface changing as Cliff wrote? It seemed to her it had taken on a subtle new shimmer. Or was that just a stray reflection? She burned to turn around and look at the thing directly instead of through the tiny window of the compact mirror, but it wouldn't help anyone if she got ensnared too.

Cliff's chalking had grown faster, a flurry of impassioned strokes like a teacher finding sudden inspiration. Without warning he slashed the chalk across the mirror's surface, two quick strokes to make an X, and barked, "Release!"

He held still. Pierce started to twist towards him, but he held up an urgent hand to stop her, frowning at the mirror. "No..." he murmured to himself. "That's not the... Hmm." He started another frantic chain of hastily scribbled symbols, culminating in a swirling figure eight. "Release!" he boomed again, and this time the image in the mirror visibly *rippled*, like the reflection in a pond disturbed by a stone. Pierce looked at Deepan for a reaction and saw none, but then Cliff roared again, "Release!"

Deepan sagged out of his crouched position like a puppet with cut strings, collapsing toward the mirror; he would have fallen against its thorny frame if Cliff hadn't stopped him with an arm across his chest. Pierce was with him an instant later, helping to lay the sergeant down on the ground so she could take his pulse. It was there, but it was weak. She glanced up at the mirror before she could stop the idiot impulse, but it seemed to have been neutralised for now; the blood it had absorbed was oozing back out from the glass in beaded droplets, running down to puddle in the dust on the shed floor.

There was a lot of it. Deepan had no obvious wounds anywhere she could see: the mirror had drained him of it with no need for contact or trace of an injury, and if Pierce had been coming from further away or Deepan hadn't got around to calling Cliff before uncovering the mirror, they might have found him dead on the floor without any evidence of had what happened.

And he wasn't out of the woods yet. She threw the dust sheet back over the blood-stained mirror and helped Cliff to hoist Deepan up off the ground and get him away from it, looking for the first uniform officer with a radio as they got back outside.

"We need an ambulance here! Now!"

CHAPTER EIGHT

THE AMBULANCE TOOK Deepan off, but Pierce didn't get the chance to accompany it; there was still a storage shed full of artefacts to be dealt with, and it took most of the rest of the day to bag, tag and shift the contents. After the incident with the mirror, everything they didn't immediately recognise had to be subjected to various improvised tests before they dared move it, and Pierce didn't want to risk involving extra pairs of hands who didn't know what they were doing.

A call from Deepan's wife at the hospital a few hours later at least confirmed that he was doing well, no lingering after-effects expected. The good news didn't quite lift Pierce's mood. Seeing Leo last night had been a grim reminder of how easily the odds could catch up to any of them, no matter how careful and well-prepared. Deepan might—touch wood—come out of this one okay, but it was still the sort of thing that got a man with two young daughters to start re-evaluating his career path.

She was selfishly aware that if a transfer request ever did come across her desk, she'd pull out every bribe and guilt trip she could think of to get him to stay. After the number of casualties and departures her unit had seen in the last year, he was the only detective she had left whose loyalties she could be fully sure of.

Dawson was still off pursuing his own leads in Nottinghamshire, but he'd sent Eddie back to the office to cross-reference the latest findings with the old paper files. "Any joy?" Pierce asked wearily on her return, slumping into her chair with a mug of coffee.

"Er, nothing concrete yet, guv," he said apologetically. "But I've got all the details of the past scenes entered into the computer now, along with the photos and statements Constable Freeman took in York this morning, so at least it's all properly indexed and available to compare now."

"All right, I'll take a look," Pierce said, wheeling herself closer to the computer. "She still out there in York?" she asked, typing one-handed as she sipped the coffee.

"Er, no, she went to follow up on the barn scene from yesterday," he said. "She wanted to see if there was any way to get the animal corpses identified—I think she was talking to some vets about microchip scanners or something."

"Fair enough." Pierce took a skim through the statements Gemma had taken from the neighbours, but while the canvassing had been industriously thorough, it seemed that few people living on the terrace had actually been there fourteen years ago, and most of the stories they had to tell about the cult amounted to urban legends and recycled tabloid stories.

Dawson and Eddie's findings from the latest crime scene were of little more help. According to Nottinghamshire's autopsy their victim had likely died of heart failure from blood loss, a diagnosis that brought on an extra wince after today's events. Time of death was a vague enough guesstimate that it merged with the equally uncertain time of abduction; despite appeals, no one had yet been found who had seen Matt Harrison since he'd left work on the night of his disappearance, and nor had anyone come forward who'd seen him with the girl that he'd claimed to have met.

At least that was one snippet of suggested MO. Pierce checked back on the details of the previous victims. One of the men killed in 1987 had told coworkers about a new girlfriend that the police had never managed to track down; a final LiveJournal entry from one of the 2001 victims had also mentioned meeting a girl in a bar. All right then: assume a woman—multiple women, more than likely, if they were picking up men in their early twenties over a twenty-eight year period—reeling the victims in for the cult to abduct. Was that where their friend from York with the silver bat necklace fit in?

Or was Pierce just constructing patterns out of thin air? The fact that several of a given sample of young men had been talking up their recent success with women wasn't exactly compelling evidence.

She pushed her chair back from the computer with a sigh, realising it was already past time she should have been gone. "All right, unless you've found something, you may as well go home," she told Eddie, flapping a hand at him. "Maybe if we're lucky the casework pixies will come in the middle of the night and solve this for us."

"Er, yes, guv," Eddie said with an awkward smile as he stood up, not seeming quite sure how to respond to that. Poor lad was still painfully over-earnest; she hoped he grew out of that before he strained something.

He headed off home, leaving Pierce to fail to take her own advice as she gave the files one more fruitless going-over. She was conscious of the time pressure weighing down on her: going from the previous killings, they had roughly a week before the second body appeared, but the schedule wasn't fixed enough to put too much faith in it. They could easily see another death tomorrow.

Unfortunately, new evidence wasn't going to spontaneously appear just because she stared really hard at the screen. Feeling like she was conceding defeat by doing so, she logged off the computer and rose to leave.

Cliff arrived to hover in the doorway as she was shrugging her coat back on. "Are you off?" she asked him. Of all the analysts, he was the one most likely to work hours as ridiculous as hers, but she'd probably worn him out with his unaccustomed trip out to the field.

He ran a hand rather awkwardly over the remaining tufts of his hair. "Ah," he said. "Well, actually, there's a bit of a problem."

"With the artefacts that we picked up from Leeds this afternoon?" she asked, heart clenching. If that mirror turned out to have after-effects the hospital couldn't detect...

But Cliff shook his head, looking around nervously before stepping into the office. "No, I'm afraid this concerns our extracurricular research," he said in a low voice. "I'm sorry to say that while we were out, the evidence regarding the age of your panther pelt appears to have gone walkabouts. It's not just mislaid—both the physical evidence from the tests and my personal files are gone."

A chill settled over her. If the evidence had been taken from Cliff's lab, it could only have been by someone who worked at the police station—or had the connections and clout to waltz in and out of one unchallenged.

Or someone wearing the right skin.

"Did you have backup copies stored anywhere else?" she asked Cliff.

He shook his head unhappily. "I'm afraid I was trying to be discreet, and assumed it wasn't necessary to be so paranoid," he said. "A stance I am admittedly rethinking right now. But I can reproduce the results easily enough with another hair from the original pelt."

Somehow Pierce doubted it would be that easy. She pressed her lips together. "Where is the pelt right now?" she asked.

"Long-term storage," Cliff told her. "At least that ought to be considerably harder for anyone to access without the right authorisation."

Pierce made a neutral noise, far from convinced. "Should be," she said. "How about we go and take a look anyway?"

*   *   *

THE RITUAL CRIME Unit's long-term storage facility was a high-security warehouse a few miles from the station, housing artefacts from cold cases as well as seized items that were illegal to possess but either too difficult or too valuable to destroy. With the study of magic a field that was still riddled with gaps and uncertainty, it took an awful lot of paperwork to authorise the destruction of anything that could potentially increase their knowledge.

That meant that, aside from when items were on loan to academic institutions or other police departments for research purposes, the evidence warehouse played host to just about every deadly, illegal or just plain mysterious artefact that the RCU had seized in decades of policing the north of England. Pierce hoped security through obscurity really was the best defence, because there was a limit to how well a full-scale raid on the place could be repelled by a few card locks and a man called Ken with a beer gut and a walkie-talkie.

"Working late again, Doctor Healey?" the security guard asked cheerfully as they signed in to the visitors' book. "I hope they pay you overtime."

"Just a flying visit this time, Ken," Cliff said as he printed his name in the book in neat block capitals. "Chief Inspector Pierce wants to review the evidence from a previous case."

Ken nodded to her affably as she took the pen from Cliff. Pierce casually perused the previous sign-ins, but the last was Cliff himself three days ago, and the only other names on the page were other personnel from Magical Analysis, and Gemma Freeman from when Pierce had sent her to fetch some ritual blades back in January.

Not that she'd truly expected to spot anything as obvious as an unfamiliar name on the list. She tried to check if the handwriting in any of the signatures looked inconsistent with the others, but there was only so long she could pretend to take before Ken started to get suspicious.

How hard would it be to bribe or replace one of the security staff here, really? Or even to buy out the security company and take over their contract, if you happened to be a shady government agency with those kinds of resources at your disposal? Even the best security system in the world inevitably had its weak links, because sooner or later they all involved people.

Ken certainly waved the two of them through without any attempt to verify their story, and they were free to enter the main warehouse without an escort. It was a dim, chilly space with a bare concrete floor and many high, skeletal rows of metal shelves, loaded with endless stacks of cardboard boxes. In theory there was a system to their arrangement, but the practicalities of storing enchanted objects in proximity meant the system had more quirks and exceptions than it did rules.

Pierce had been here often enough to dig up evidence from one cold case or other, but it was Cliff's native territory, and she deferred to his lead. "I hope *you* know where this thing is supposed to be," she said.

"Pelts are on the storage racks at the back," he said with a nod. "I have the item number, but we don't have a great many of them in storage anyway. Since they're legal with the right licences, those that aren't part of ongoing cases tend to end up being auctioned off."

He led the way down one of the long aisles and through to the back of the warehouse, where stacked boxes gave way to items that were larger and more awkward to store. They passed a row of cursed bikes and motorbikes—a surprisingly popular crime—and many sacrificial altars of varying degrees of authenticity before they came to the collection of shapeshifting pelts. They were hung up inside zipped covers like garment bags, though the bulky furs gave the unfortunate impression of a row of body bags.

Cliff retrieved a scrap of paper from amid the loose change and crumpled notes in his trouser pocket. "Item number KZ-201412-5672F," he read after a brief squint.

They checked the row over, twice. Cliff was right—there were no more than two dozen pelts hung up on the rack, and some she could tell were wholly the wrong shape for a big cat even before she found the evidence label.

The item number that Cliff had given her wasn't anywhere among them.

"Perhaps I copied it down wrong," he said, rechecking his paper with a frown.

Pierce doubted it very much, but all the same, she went through the motions, opening up every bag to check. Inside hung the sagging, hollow-eyed forms of skinned animals: wolves, dogs, stags, bears, a *cow* of all bloody things... There were two big cat pelts in the collection, a tiger and a cheetah—neither remotely possible to mistake for the missing black panther.

It wasn't here. Their evidence was gone.

And with it, any hope of proving that the skinbinder who'd made it was still alive and out there somewhere making more.

CHAPTER NINE

IT WAS IN a distinctly depressed mood that Pierce parted ways with Cliff and headed for home. She'd missed visiting hours to see Deepan at the hospital; probably best not to inflict her current mood on him anyway. Tough to convince someone else that the risks of the job were worthwhile when she was having the sort of day where she wondered why she even bothered.

How could she hope to unravel the conspiracy surrounding Sebastian's death when the very people she was after had their sticky fingers all over the system itself? She didn't want some kind of vigilante revenge—she wanted to see the people responsible brought to justice. But who could she turn to when police channels were compromised? Politicians? That was a laugh. She could go to the press, but she needed some sort of proof first—and she'd have to gamble on finding a journalist who prized the truth over dramatic headlines.

Her cynical views on the current state of the nation's news media were not greatly helped when she turned on the TV over her takeaway and discovered they'd unearthed Christopher Tomb from whatever dark corner he'd oozed off into when his book dropped out of the bestseller lists. He still had the stupid goatee, his hair dyed a jet black that looked even more starkly false against an aging face liberally spackled with make-up to cover the lines. He was wearing a black turtleneck with what looked suspiciously like a red cape.

The caption at the bottom of the screen that read CHRISTOPHER TOMB—VAMPIRE EXPERT added insult to injury. The only part of it that was actually true was the Christopher—she happened to know for a fact that the surname he'd been born with was Brown.

Of course, being a wanker who adopted a silly name to sell books was certainly not a crime, more was the pity. But she couldn't help but feel that 'spreading details of unsolved crimes, and fear-mongering nonsense' probably ought to be.

He was spouting some complete bollocks right now, steepling his hands together with a piously thoughtful look as he gazed intently at the female interviewer. "It's possible that the break in the seven-year cycle corresponds to the vampire's hibernation phase," he said. "Threes and sevens are both powerful numbers in occultism: ritual feedings at such intervals would allow the vampire to maintain its energy through many years of sleep."

"Citation needed!" Pierce said out loud, waving her fork at the TV screen. She doubted it would have done her any good even if Tomb had been in the room; more than likely he'd have been able to produce a dozen spurious sources in a heartbeat, all part of a tail-eating chain of self-proclaimed experts who vouched for each other, not a trace of a reputable institution anywhere among them.

As if the bogus vampire facts weren't enough, he went on to get in some digs about the police being underinformed about magic and needing to consult the experts. Pierce was quietly seething by the time she turned off the TV. She was half tempted to haul the smarmy git in for questioning, though she was honest enough to admit she had no good reason to.

And the hysteria he'd whipped up with that bloody book. Pierce had never actually read the thing herself; the few choice excerpts bandied about by the media had been quite enough for her tastes, and with Tomb quickly eliminated from their enquiries and the Valentine Vampire failing to return for the expected encore, pissing herself off by reading the rest of it had slipped down the priority pile. She supposed she ought to rectify that now, just in case this really was a copycat working off Tomb's information. She was just scribbling a note to herself to pick up a copy tomorrow when it occurred to her that she might be able to get it as an eBook.

She could indeed, and thanks to a marketing department somewhere it was even half price at the moment. With a grimace, Pierce settled down with a cup of tea and a packet of biscuits to spend her evening *On the Blood Trail of the Valentine Vampire*.

To her annoyance, Tomb was actually quite an engaging writer, though he really should have been turning his skills to pulp thrillers instead of pretensions of journalism. The vivid descriptions of imagined rituals might have put a less hardy soul off her bourbon biscuits, but Pierce had a policewoman's stomach and had long since learned to eat after—and sometimes even during—just about anything. On the other hand, Tomb's depictions of the scenes where the bodies were found did more to cast her mind back through the years than reading over dry police reports, even with pictures attached.

In fact, they were rather *too* accurate. Where had he got all this detail about the arrangement of the bodies, their wounds and the clothes they'd been found in? Some of the specifics were wrong, but he still knew far more than the police had released to the public. Had Tomb somehow bribed or deceived his way into possession of one of the autopsy reports? Procedures in the 'eighties hadn't been what they were now, and nor had anti-corruption measures.

Or maybe somewhere within that over-dramatised mishmash of dubious sources and unlikely encounters, Tomb actually *had* managed to track down someone with knowledge about the cult and its activities.

Pierce was beginning to think she might just haul the bastard in for questioning after all.

DEEPAN WAS STILL off on medical leave the next day, and Dawson had apparently elected to stay down in Nottinghamshire to follow the case from there—why ask her, she was only the bloody DCI—so she deputised Eddie to track down Christopher Tomb for her.

"That book has far more detail about the crime scenes than he ought to know—I want to speak to him about where he got his information from ASAP. But don't arrange for him to come into the station," she added as an afterthought. "Set up a meeting somewhere else." There was a certain value in making people sweat with the intimidation factor of police station surroundings, but she wouldn't put it past the man to find some way to wring a publicity stunt out of it. She didn't want him claiming he was acting as a police consultant.

Gemma came in from the analysis labs waving a folder just as Pierce went to sit down. "Got some results from Ritual Materials, guv," she said. "Simon identified some herbal residue taken from our burning barn as something called..."—she had to check the file—"cold smoke powder? He says the composition matches the mix sold by a shop called Trick Box in—"

"Bradford?" Pierce said along with her, reversing back out of the seat that she'd barely sat down in. "I know it well—and I'm pretty sure they're up to their necks in *something*, even if it isn't this. Let's go and shake the place down and see what falls out." Cold smoke powder was nothing illegal, but it did have its dodgier uses, and the owners of Trick Box had never impressed her as the sort to be overly conscientious about what their customers might be getting up to.

"Any joy tracking down the source of the animals?" she asked Gemma as they drove.

Gemma shook her head in frustrated apology. "None of the corpses retrieved from the fire were microchipped, though it's possible the chips were just too damaged to scan properly. I was hoping we might be able to track down a source for the more exotic animals, but there's no zoos or animal sanctuaries missing anything on the list, so it looks like we're dealing with animals from the black market pet trade. The lynx was the most distinctive thing, but it was at ground zero for the magical blast, so there wasn't much of it left." She wrinkled her mouth. "Guess you had a pretty lucky escape there, guv."

"Mm." A timely reminder that, while animal sacrifices might not be high enough profile to get the superintendent's knickers in as much of a knot as the Valentine Vampire case, the people responsible were still dangerously ruthless in their own right. If the RCU hadn't been alerted to the possibility of a skin shop at work, it could easily have been a local Community Support Officer or even a curious neighbour who'd got to that altar and blown themselves up.

There were a lot of nasty ways that those with some knowledge of magic could prey on the unsuspecting public, so the RCU liked to keep a weather eye on any magic-related businesses in the region—never an easy task, since they tended to pop up and disappear as fast as dodgy market stalls, and often for pretty similar reasons.

Your two basic market openings in the occult field were either selling cheap, dubiously functional tat to the credulous, or dealing in one-of-a-kind artefacts that changed hands for hundreds and thousands of pounds. Dabblers didn't like to spend and experts knew better than to risk cheaping out, so any shop that managed to stay open targeting the largely non-existent middle ground was, in Pierce's view, best viewed with cynical suspicion.

Trick Box had managed to survive for the last eighteen months selling mid-range magical goods at knock-down prices, so someone either had deep pockets and a poor understanding of the sunk cost fallacy, or they were getting away with murder somewhere. Hopefully not literally.

"What's our angle, guv?" Gemma asked her as they approached the shop, tucked away between a phone shop and a pawnbroker's.

From her previous, admittedly brief, dealings with the staff of Trick Box, Pierce suspected that 'explain the situation in a civilised manner and expect full cooperation' was not going to be the answer.

"Don't bring up any details of the case," she said instead. "We'll go in like it's a standard inspection—I've got a couple of other outstanding cases I can rattle their cages over so they don't know we're after anything specific. I'll do the talking; I've dealt with them before. You just keep an eye out for anything dodgy, especially if it looks like they're trying to distract me from it."

"Am I the muscle, then?" Gemma said with a grin.

"If you like. Do your best to loom."

They pushed through the door, accompanied by the harsh blart of a cheap electronic buzzer. The inside was dimly lit, somewhat cramped and musty, as all such shops seemed to be: partly because of the nature of the goods they trafficked in, and partly, Pierce was sure, for the atmosphere. Nobody wanted to buy their magical paraphernalia from a place that looked like a computer showroom.

The owners of Trick Box had taken that philosophy to heart, and the shop had managed to look faintly grimy since the day it opened. Glass cases full of shabby-looking artefacts and books divided the space into tight aisles you'd be hard-pressed to squeeze a wheelchair down, and a sign above the counter read: *WE BUY: occult texts, magic items & ritual equipment (subject to verification)*. On the left side of the shop were racks of generic ritual equipment; on the right there were many tiny drawers filled with powders and herbs, like some kind of dubious magical Pick 'n' Mix. A stand in the corner by the door held hanging packs of candles, chalk and other *ESSENTIAL SUPPLIES!!*

There was no one in the shop this early in the morning aside from the woman behind the counter. Pierce recognised her as the owner, Helen Wilkes, a squat middle-aged woman whose solidly powerful build and stone stare would probably make most customers think twice about quibbling over the quality of service. She had a jowly face that seemed to be set into a perpetually sour expression, although that might just be the one she wore when the police showed up at her door.

"DCI Pierce," she said, imbuing the title with all the welcoming warmth of the February frost outside. "What can I do for you?" She managed to heavily imply that the preferred answer would be 'nothing.'

"Just come for a bit of a look-see," Pierce said, leaning on the edge of the counter and doing her best to keep Wilkes's attention as Gemma drifted off to inspect the merchandise. "You know we like to keep ourselves updated on what's going on in the world of ritual retail."

Wilkes sniffed. "Seems to me you ought to spend less time doing that and more on catching criminals." She looked past Pierce to give Gemma a dismissive once-over. "Another new constable, is it?" she said with a faint curl of her lip. "You do go through them."

Pierce bridled, but forced it down. She wasn't the one supposed to be getting her cage rattled here—and Wilkes couldn't know about Deepan or Leo.

Still, no point in beating about the bush. "Anybody come in recently asking for necromantic texts?" she asked, without further pretence of niceties.

"We don't sell those," Wilkes said flatly.

"Good for you. Anyone come in asking for them?" Pierce pressed.

"Not that I recall."

Somehow Pierce doubted she'd have been able to recall it even if the customer asking had left five minutes ago. But this was just the preamble, routine follow-up on open cases that were probably too cold to have a chance of turning anything up. She switched streams. "What about ritual bowls?" she asked. "Anybody been in trying to fence one with a silver rim and a rose-and-thorns motif?"

"You're welcome to go through all our receipts for pawned items," Wilkes said, her tone saying she was anything but. "We keep scrupulous records, and we always check against the lists the police release of stolen items."

"I'll take your word for it," Pierce said. A poke about in the back rooms might turn up a few items that they 'hadn't got around' to adding to said records yet, but that wasn't the game she was after today. "What about cold smoke powder?" she said. "I know you sell that."

"What if we do? It's not illegal," Wilkes said.

"Sold any recently?" Pierce asked.

"Sell a lot of it," she said with an indifferent shrug. "No reason to keep track."

"You ask people what they use it for?"

"Special effects, isn't it?" she said, shrugging again. "Smoke with no fire. Amateur stuff. Adds a bit of pizzazz to your conjuring tricks."

"Unless they add it to an *actual* fire, and then you get great billows of smoke from a source as small as a candle flame." Which was a particularly handy trick for anyone involved in say, illicit spirit-raising rituals, where smoke was one of the more convenient ways to give form to the formless, but building a big enough outdoor fire to produce it in quantity tended to be indiscreet.

"Shop's not responsible for off-label uses," Wilkes said, unmoved. "You can smack someone over the head with a coffee table. Doesn't make it illegal to sell coffee tables."

Pierce smiled without humour. That was probably about as much cooperation as she was going to get, but then, she'd expected as much. "Mind if I take a look around your stock?" she asked.

Wilkes self-evidently did, but she was smart enough not to object. "Long as you don't stay too long," she said. "Having you lot in here puts the customers off."

"I just bet it does." She took her time drifting around the shop and examining miscellaneous merchandise before joining Gemma beside one of the glass cases in the centre, where she'd been hovering for some time. Pierce raised her eyebrows at her in silent question, and Gemma cocked her head subtly towards the upper shelf. It housed a number of medallions hung on velvet necklace stands, wooden discs about two inches across.

Each was delicately etched with a stylised design of a different animal—a running hare, a hunting dog, a stalking cat—surrounded by an intricate double ring of runes. A handwritten sign in front of the stands read *Animal Spirit Charms: view the world through animal senses!*

Smoke powder used in rituals to make spirits visible. A barn full of dead animals in cages. And a collection of animal spirit charms.

Very interesting.

She turned to look back at Wilkes. "These animal spirit charms in the case here," she said. "Are they licensed?"

Unlike artefacts purporting to house trapped human spirits, it wasn't necessarily illegal to own or sell animal spirit artefacts, provided they predated the current animal sacrifice laws or had been brought in from other countries prior to the import ban.

"Licensed antiques," Wilkes said. "Got the paperwork right here if you want to see it."

"Yes, I think I would," she said. As Wilkes headed off into the back room with a long-suffering air, Pierce glanced at Gemma. "Anything else?" she asked in a low voice.

"Just these, guv," Gemma said, faintly shaking her head. "Look at all the empty stands, though," she added. There were five medallions in the glass case, but there were three other unoccupied necklace stands alongside them. "These cases are dead crowded—that's a waste of display space. So either they sold the others very recently..."

"Or they were expecting to get more in," Pierce said with a nod. Nice one. She turned back towards the counter as Wilkes came stomping out from the back room.

"Here's all your papers," she said, dumping them on the countertop with profound indifference. "Now, if that's all, I've got a shop to run."

"I'll try to keep from getting in the way of your hordes of customers," Pierce said. True, magic shops tended to do most of their trade in the evenings, but if the complete lack of customer interest the whole time they'd been in here was any indication, then it really was questionable how Trick Box could stay afloat.

But no doubt the shop accounts would be as unenlightening as this paperwork. Pierce studied a set of what looked like completely authentic licences for possession of Category C exempt spirit-bound artefacts, and probably were: she took a quick phone photo to track the licence numbers back, but wouldn't be surprised if the trail terminated at one of several dodgy issuers they'd been trying to catch out for years. Still, always best to be thorough—even experienced criminals could have a moment's carelessness, and it helped if the coppers on their trail didn't do the same.

"Antiques, hmm?" she said, flicking through more forms that certified the charms' alleged age—the evaluator had been vague, yet still somehow managed to be certain they predated any inconvenient laws. "They look pretty new to me."

"Well-kept," Wilkes said, perfunctorily; but then, Pierce didn't suppose Wilkes gave a damn what she believed. "Bought them off a collector as a set."

And there was the auction receipt; likely also a dead end, but Pierce conscientiously photographed it all the same. She'd like to seize the charms and all attendant paperwork to study in forensic detail, but the tenuous link of a legitimately sold batch of cold smoke powder and Wilkes's obstructiveness weren't enough to build a case on. The best they could do was follow up on serial numbers and signatures, and hope that this time Wilkes had been stupider than usual.

"If that's all, inspector?" Wilkes said pointedly. Pierce doubted she'd got her rank wrong by accident.

"For the moment," she said, keeping her frustration in check. "If there's anything else that needs clearing up, we'll come back."

All her instincts said that Wilkes was up to something. The difficulty was going to be proving it.

CHAPTER TEN

"If we're lucky, they'll panic and try to move those charms out quickly, or get in contact with whoever's been supplying them," Pierce told Gemma as they headed back to the car. "I want you to keep the place under surveillance—keep track of who goes in and what they come out with, both during and after business hours. I'll call Eddie out here to join you."

Ideally she would have used wholly fresh personnel whose faces Wilkes hadn't seen, but she didn't have them to spare with Deepan out on medical leave and Dawson off on a murder case. She'd win no friends by deputising assistance from the thin-stretched local forces on such an insubstantial lead; there was going to be trouble enough from Snow about the overtime if it didn't turn up case-cracking evidence. But it was the best lead they had.

Back at the office, Pierce still had time before her meeting with Christopher Tomb, so she checked out the serial numbers on the paperwork. She wasn't greatly surprised when it all came out legitimate, at least on the surface—Wilkes wouldn't have handed it over so easily if it couldn't stand up to inspection. They could chase up the issuers of the dodgy certificates, but without the spirit charms to hand, they couldn't do tests of their own to prove that the details in the paperwork were false.

She did, however, have a snapshot she'd taken of the charms with her phone—nothing that could be used as evidence, but perhaps enough to fish for some opinions. She headed next door to the research department, poking her head into the Sympathetic Magic office in passing.

"Jenny—fancy a walk down to Cliff's?" she said. "Easier to pick both your brains at once."

"Ah, exercise," Jenny said, stretching. "Almost as good as fresh air, or so I'm told by people who get out more. All right, hold on a mo." She frowned at the file before her and, after a brief flurry of typing, pushed her chair back and stepped into the shoes she'd kicked off under the desk. The low heels weren't enough to bring her up to Pierce's height as they fell into step side by side. "How goes the vampire hunt?" she asked.

"Less well than it would if we could convince people we weren't looking for vampires." They'd already had numerous alleged sightings of giant bats and people reporting their neighbours for being pale and working the night shift. She sighed. "Too little bloody evidence, just like all the other times." A serial killer case was big enough to get them rush work from regular forensics for once, but even with the advances in fingerprint-lifting techniques and DNA testing over the years, Nottinghamshire Police had yet to turn up anything of use from the scene. "I'm beginning to suspect our killers are less into gothic eveningwear and more into forensic overalls."

"Well, if there's no news on the vampire front, what did you want to pick our brains about?" Jenny asked as they arrived at Cliff's lab. He looked up as soon as the door opened for once, no sign of the usual headphones in his ears.

Of course, the horse had already bolted out of that barn door, and she doubted more alertness on Cliff's part would have stopped their evidence going walkabouts. The people they were up against were too brazen and too powerful to catch out with standard security measures.

Hence her ulterior motive in bringing Jenny in to speak with them, though she did have some police business to raise first. "Animal spirit charms," she said, bringing her hands together. "What can you two tell me about them?"

Cliff gave a thoughtful frown. "Well, that rather depends," he said. "What kind of charms?"

"This kind." Pierce brought up the photo on her phone, and the others craned over to peer at it; reflections in the glass had obscured the details of the runes, but the shot at least gave an impression of the basic look of the things.

"Hmm." Cliff rubbed his upper lip thoughtfully. "Well. Hard to be sure without getting my hands on them to examine them properly, but at a glance, they look like they're single-use charms, probably activated by a specific touch or incantation. The circular pattern of runes is the giveaway: it's effectively a containment circle, holding an inherent enchantment in check until the circle is broken."

"And how would someone have gone about enchanting the medallions?" Pierce asked. "By, perhaps, performing some kind of blood sacrifice?"

"It would certainly be a viable source for the kind of magical energy required," Cliff agreed. He shot her a look. "But that would, of course, be very much illegal."

She matched the expression. "Our seller says these are licensed antiques, naturally."

"Oh, I doubt that very much," Cliff said, peering at the phone again. "The wood's all wrong. And frankly, you'd be unlikely to see these made of wood at all, not if the enchantment was meant to be kept contained for any length of time—metal or carved stone would be more likely, perhaps bone."

Pierce nodded, pressing her lips together. "That's about what I thought, but you can't hang a conviction on it," she said with a sigh. Or prove that Wilkes had been aware that her so-called antiques weren't the real deal. "And we can't seize them to prove that they're dodgy without evidence that they're dodgy." It would certainly be outside of the RCU's budget to buy one of the things outright, in the unlikely event Wilkes would be willing to sell to them.

She turned to Jenny. "Animal senses from a charm—seem legitimate?"

Jenny frowned a little, pushing her glasses up. "Well, it's possible, though most of the enchantments I've heard of rely on using some part of the animal carcass as a focus, like with shapeshifting skins. I suppose you could conceivably use a blood ritual to transfer the focus via the blood..." She shook her head. "This is really more Cliff's area than mine." Then she brightened and snapped her fingers. "Oh, but you know who you should ask? Phil Havers at RCU Oxford. He was always talking about writing a book on human-to-animal transformations."

"Shit, Phil—yeah, should have thought of him." Pierce gave herself a mental kick. Phil Havers was a former colleague of hers who'd transferred down south about eight years back; so far as she knew, his much-discussed book was no closer to materialising now than it had been when he left, but his magpie approach to gathering shiny-looking reference materials might be of some use.

She moved as if to leave, then with a pretence of casual afterthought: "Oh, and while I've got you both here, what do you say about grabbing a bite to eat after work? The rest of my team's buggered off in all directions, and I had some ideas about using divination rituals to find enchanted objects that I wanted to kick around when we're not on the superintendent's time."

Or more precisely, some ideas about Jenny using her knowledge of divination to help them find their missing panther pelt that she didn't want to share in a room that secrets had already leaked from.

Cliff looked blank for a few moments before he seemed to catch on. "Ah, yes, I think I know what this is about," he said nodding. "Yes, of course."

Jenny blinked. "Well, I obviously missed my Illuminati meeting," she said. "But colour me intrigued. Sure, I'll be there, provided work doesn't blow up in the meantime."

"Ah, thank you, I hadn't had anybody jinx my day yet," Pierce said.

SHE PUT IN a quick call to Phil down in Oxford before it could slip her mind. "Phil! Not caught you hip-deep in intestines again, have I?" she asked.

"I should be so bloody lucky," Phil grumbled. Pierce could swear his Yorkshire accent grew broader the longer that he spent down south. "Hip-deep in paperwork, more like. While your lot are off chasing vampire serial killers we're playing hot potatoes with London on the world's most doomed antiquities case. I swear every other bugger implicated in this one has an uncle in the House of Lords and plays golf with the Chief Superintendent."

"You're the one who left us for the glamour of the gleaming spires," Pierce said unsympathetically. "I'd say you're welcome to transfer back any time you like, but we're all bloody brass and no constables up here as it is. I'm still sharing an office with the DI they tried to replace me with—I think somebody up there's hoping I'll blink first." They couldn't shuffle her off towards retirement if she refused to take a hint; so far they hadn't pushed it, probably reasoning that at her age they could afford to wait her out.

She sighed and scrubbed a weary hand over her well-greyed hair, feeling the arthritic ache in her bad shoulder that never entirely went away. Exhausted as she was these days, they might not be far wrong.

But: work to do. She sat forward in her chair. "Got a case involving animal spirit charms, allegedly endowing heightened sensory abilities," she said. "Any chance you've got anything in your reference library that might be of use? Seller claims they're antiques, but we're thinking animal sacrifice ring: found one of their abandoned workshops, but the altar was destroyed before we got a good look at it. Cliff reckons the charms are a one-shot activation deal—I can email you a pic of what the things look like, though it's not the greatest quality."

"Hmm. A little sideways from my field, but send away," he said. "I did have a few contacts in your neck of the woods, though I haven't spoken to them in years. I can shake a few trees for you, see if anyone's still up them."

"Cheers, Phil," she said. "Anything you can get us would be good." Because right now this case felt as close to a dead end as the bloody Valentine Vampire.

Speaking of which... She checked her watch. "Anyway, I'll send you what we've got—sorry I can't sit and chat, but I've got to go and see a prat in a cape about a book."

THE COFFEE SHOP where Christopher Tomb had agreed to meet her was the kind of pretentiously expensive joint where everything had unnecessarily fancy names and the menu listings featured more buzzwords than useful information. It was the sort of place that coppers usually only frequented in desperation, generally preferring their caffeine boosts to be served up fast, cheap, and readily portable.

Tomb, however, was apparently a regular; he made a point of greeting the barista by name and engaging her in chitchat about her family that Pierce wasn't convinced the tired-looking woman particularly welcomed. They ordered their drinks and took a table in the corner.

"So, Chief Inspector Pierce," Tomb said, with a broad, white-toothed smile as he held a chair out for her. "I believe it was Inspector Pierce when we met before, wasn't it? I always thought that you'd go far."

He wasn't quite as heavily made up as he had been on the TV last night, but she definitely got the impression he'd spent more time artfully styling his appearance this morning than she did in the average month. At least he'd ditched the cape, thank God, though he was wearing a billowy white ruffled shirt that wasn't much less dramatic.

"And I believe it was Christopher Brown," she said pointedly as she pulled her chair in.

He gave a small, self-deprecating grin. "Ah, well—it's important to present oneself in a way that gives people what they want to see, isn't it?" he said. "We all do it in big and small ways, from dressing up for job interviews to choosing what to share on our internet profiles. You can have the best ideas in the world, but without a little artful marketing to draw your audience, how can you possibly hope for them to be shared?"

"I'm more concerned about perpetrating the image that a serial killer wants to present," Pierce said, pressing her lips together. She wasn't going to use the phrase 'Valentine Vampire'; not with this man and his thirst for the dramatic. "It's irresponsible to spread hysteria about vampires when there's nothing to suggest that these murders are anything other than the work of a human serial killer."

She glanced around a little warily, wishing she'd insisted on meeting at his house, but their corner table was at least relatively tucked away, and no one was paying obvious attention.

"Nothing?" Tomb said, raising his eyebrows archly. "Surely, Claire—may I call you Claire?" he asked, rolling on without waiting for confirmation, "—the fact the police still have yet to uncover a single lead in all this time ought to point to supernatural involvement."

"Yeah, and we still haven't found who took the last jam doughnut either, so maybe we've got pixies," Pierce said. "We don't publish all our leads." Especially when they didn't have them. "In fact, there are a lot of things we don't publish when we're pursuing an active investigation, and I'm a little concerned just how many of them seem to have found their way into your book."

"I'm flattered that you've read it," he said, steepling his hands.

Pierce might have pointed out that it was her job, but that was when their coffee arrived.

"Thank you, my dear," Tomb said, with a warm smile for the woman.

"Cheers," Pierce said, as she accepted hers, and took an immediate gulp. This conversation was already giving her a headache, if it wasn't the cloying scent of Tomb's aftershave.

She waited until the barista was back behind the counter before resuming their low-voiced conversation. "Your book contains a number of details of the past crime scenes that were never released to the general public," she said. "Mind sharing exactly how you came by that kind of information?"

"As I explained in the book, I had a number of meetings with Jonathan, a former member of the Valentine Vampire's cult," he said, sitting back and sipping his coffee without visible concern. "He was too afraid of the vampire's ability to read his mind to tell me anything of the mortal guise it wore, but he spoke of being one of several disciples promised that they would be allowed to share the gift of vampirism if they proved themselves by following faithfully. He told me that he left the group when their initiations grew too intense, but was able to describe the nature of the blood-letting ritual as he'd seen it set out in a grimoire."

That was halfway plausible, Pierce supposed—not the vampire guff, but that a cult leader might spin the story that way to hook a few true believers who would assist with the abductions and murders. On the other hand, that line about vampire mind-control was a mighty convenient excuse for Tomb not being able to bring any actual details of the cult leader to the table. "So what was this grimoire?" she asked.

"The cult has the only copy in existence," Tomb said. "Jonathan said they translated the title as *Bleeding the Heart of the Earth*, and told him that it had been written by a twelfth-century vampire who was once a monk."

Pierce would eat her hat if there wasn't some artistic licence being taken by somebody along that chain, though in fairness the twelfth-century monk could be real.

"There were details of crime scenes that you couldn't have got just from a description of the ritual," she said.

"My source told me what he could, and I filled in the rest from interviews," he said, sitting back with a slight shrug. "I take my research very seriously, I assure you."

She pressed her lips together, unconvinced. "Either you did a lot of filling in from some dubious sources, or your so-called former cultist knew far more than he was admitting about the murder scenes," she said. "He's quite likely an accessory to murder at the very least." And frankly, even if it wasn't actually illegal, failing to come forward when you had inside information about a group that had killed and planned to kill again was hardly morally unimpeachable.

Of course, if you could arrest people for self-centredness and moral failings there'd be no one out of prison—but right now Tomb's attitude was getting up her nose. "If you believed his information to be genuine, then why not try to convince this man Jonathan to share his knowledge with the police, or come forward with what you'd learned yourself?"

"I offered my expertise to the police during the last phase of the vampire's killing cycle, but I'm afraid they didn't seem very receptive to my suggestions," he said. And if he'd phrased it in those terms, she knew exactly why whichever officer had been on duty at the time hadn't been the least bit interested in humouring him. "Of course, I'm more than happy to do so again, if the RCU is perhaps more open now to employing non-police experts."

"Expertise we've got," she said flatly. Or at least, they weren't likely to get any more of it by bringing in wannabe vampire gurus. "What I want is your sources. I need to speak to this man Jonathan. It's been fourteen years since the last set of killings—surely if the cult has left him alone for this long he can risk coming forward now." Assuming that he even existed.

"I may be able to persuade him to speak off the record," Tomb told her. "But he'll need reassurances first."

"If he can offer us credible information against the vampire cult, then there are options we can discuss," Pierce said. But she wasn't about to commit to anything sight unseen. Not when this alleged source could be nothing but a fame-hungry timewaster spinning a tall tale—or up to his neck in ritual murder.

On her return to the office, she checked in with Dawson to see how the investigation was going down in Nottinghamshire.

"Forensics are pretty sure it's the same blade as before, and the same tool used for the post-mortem puncture wounds," he told her over the phone.

She closed her eyes in a brief grimace. "So this is the real deal, not just a copycat." A murder cult that had killed at least nine people already—and got away with it every time.

"Looks like," Dawson agreed.

"Forensics turn up anything else?" she asked.

"Nothing useful. Clothes the victim was found in were brand new—parents didn't recognise them, neither did the flatmates. Been trying to track down where they were bought, but it's looking like it was an internet purchase, and not necessarily recent. No prints, no DNA."

So much for hoping that modern advances in forensic techniques would crack the case. Pierce sighed. "Anything on this woman Harrison was supposed to have been meeting the night he disappeared?" she asked, changing tacks.

"Nothing," Dawson said. "Can't even be sure that she really exists—text to the flatmates was sent at eleven thirty-six, which is two hours after the last sighting of Harrison on CCTV. Could easily have been the killers who sent it."

"So we've basically got a whole lot of nothing concrete." The problem with the Valentine Vampire case all along. Those who killed in groups were usually let down by a weak link somewhere along the chain, but this cult appeared immune to slip-ups. It was clear their leader kept a very tight hand on the reins—possibly even via some form of magical monitoring or control.

They were fast, they were clever, and they seemed to get away with abduction and murder without leaving a single trace.

But Pierce was damned if she was going to start believing in vampires.

CHAPTER ELEVEN

HER CLANDESTINE MEETING with Jenny and Cliff took place at an Indian buffet place close to the RCU's storage facility—and also, Pierce hoped, far enough outside the usual cafés and pubs where her team were semi-regulars to avoid prying ears. Cliff had the foresight to bring the satchel containing his ritual kit, which caused Jenny to raise her eyebrows, but she followed their lead in keeping the chatter light until they were all settled back at their table and the waiter had brought them their drinks.

"All right, then," Jenny finally said, dragging her seat forward. "I'm guessing this is about something a bit heavier than joint-authoring an article. What's going on?"

"I'm afraid," Cliff said, broad face atypically pinched and troubled, "we've had a bit of a serious issue with wandering evidence."

Pierce gave her a summary of events, conscious that even if nobody seemed to be actively listening, their conversation was still far from wholly private. She went from the heavy-handed interference of the Counter Terror Action Team in the shapeshifter case, something most of the station had been aware of, to the more classified details of that case involving human-to-human shapeshifting skins, and her suspicions about the murder and substitution of Superintendent Palmer.

"Christ," Jenny said, staring into her glass of orange juice as she swirled it, as if wishing she'd opted for something stronger instead. "If they can impersonate senior members of the police at will..."

"I don't know if they can do it in the long term," Pierce said. A reassurance to cling to, though it might be a false one. "The one case I saw of a human skin in use"—she paused to swallow and breathe out, trying not to think of the murder of a young constable on her team—"degraded pretty quickly." Peeled away to reveal a stranger's face before her eyes, in a vision that would be bound up in her nightmares for years to come, alongside the rest of the horrors her work had thrown at her. "But that was..."—another deep breath—"probably made in haste. They removed their version of Palmer from the station quickly, but that may have just been fear that the impersonation wouldn't hold up."

"It's a complex question," Cliff mused, rubbing his chin as he gazed off into the distance. "A well-made shape-shifting skin should last almost indefinitely—there are museum examples that have survived for centuries, though of course no one's actually worn them to see if they work. But there's been a lot of debate in the literature about the difficulty of producing working ape skins—it's possible the source animal's intelligence may be a factor in the success of the initial skinbinding ritual, or that perhaps there's a form of rejection at work, where the more similar the transformation is to the wearer's natural form, the more likely the body will revert of its own accord."

Jenny was leaning forward, and Pierce could see they were in danger of slipping into an academic debate. She cleared her throat. "Regardless of how they did it, these people clearly have the capability to walk into police-controlled facilities and seize any evidence that would incriminate them."

"And you want me to find out where it wandered off to?" Jenny surmised.

"The test results are almost certainly gone," Pierce said. "But a panther pelt's a difficult thing to sneak out of the storage facility without a trace—and a valuable artefact to destroy without good reason." Skinbinders who could make truly high-quality pelts were rare, and for that matter, panthers weren't exactly crawling out of the woodwork either. "It's possible it's still in there somewhere while they wait for an opportunity to move it out. With the amount of crap that's stored in there, we'd have to strip the place bare to find it... unless you know a quicker way."

Jenny took her glasses off to clean them as she thought. "Well... I did do some research into the enchantments on shapeshifting pelts after you brought me that case in October," she said. "I might be able to whip up a divination that'll show you if the pelt's somewhere nearby. If they've already moved it halfway across the country, though..." She shrugged apologetically.

"Well, let's see what we can see," Pierce said.

THERE WAS A different security guard on duty this time, but this one also knew Cliff by name and waved them in without quibble. The lack of curiosity was convenient for their purposes, but also made Pierce suspect that any impostor with a decent fake ID would have faced little challenge from the guards.

They followed Cliff through the echoing aisles to the rack of shapeshifting pelts they'd gone through the night before. Pierce checked them all again, nonetheless, since if there was one thing decades of police work had taught her, it was that mind-boggling stupidity was always a depressing possibility. But no, the pelt still wasn't here. She turned to Jenny. "All right, then. Your show."

Hers and Cliff's, though Jenny was directing; Pierce could only restlessly pace the aisles, useless in the painstakingly slow business of ritual setup. She made a full circuit of the warehouse, scanning the rows as if she might spot the pelt draped across a shelf somewhere, and then returned to where the others were working. Cliff had produced a roll of white cloth from his satchel to lay out on the floor, and by now it was covered with charcoal lines and curves, complex sigils set within the loops of a curling pattern that formed a kind of pointer arrow aiming away from the rack of pelts and out into the warehouse

Within the loop at the tip of the arrow was set a simple glass dish piled with silver powder. Jenny was just tapping the last of it loose from the canister with a frown of concentration, Cliff shielding the edges of the dish with his latex-gloved hands; both of them holding their breath to avoid scattering the powder. Even the smallest smudge across the design could break a line or alter the shape of a sigil, with potentially disastrous effects.

At last Jenny seemed to decide she had as much powder poured out as she was likely to get, and sat back, wiping sweat from her forehead with the back of her arm. Cliff stood up and stepped away with an audible click of his knees.

Pierce decided it was safe to speak without making them jump. "How are we doing?"

Jenny rose and stood back to survey their handiwork. "I think we're about good to go," she said. "There are a few more runes that I could add for extra reassurance, but at this stage, the more complex we make it, the more chance there is that we'll fudge it. As it is, I'm bodging about three different things, so there's every chance that it won't work as intended."

"What's the intention?" Pierce asked, moving closer to study the setup.

Jenny swiped at her forehead again and then gestured vaguely towards the rack of shapeshifting pelts with the same arm. "We're going to use the whole set of pelts as a focus for the tracking spell," she said. "Christ knows what effect that's going to have on the strength of the spell—in theory it should boost it, but the trouble with massive power boosts is that sometimes they become massive overloads and everything goes haywire."

Pierce nodded, having seen a number of attempted rituals go that way in the supposedly safe environs of the police station. Working spells on or around artefacts that were in themselves inherently magical could have all kinds of unpredictable effects, often destructive. And this place was packed to the rafters with them—secured to the best of their abilities, but often they just didn't know enough to be sure how.

"Still, it's probably our best chance of success," Jenny said. "If we just used an individual pelt, or hair samples taken from the pelts, we run the risk of narrowing the focus to the point where it won't find anything since it'll be seeking an exact match rather than shapeshifting pelts in general. And we may *need* the power, considering the amount of magical background noise there'll be in here."

She looked around at the site of their ritual. "Unfortunately, since we haven't got the floor space or the tools to build a circle that will enclose all of this, I've had to adapt the ritual geometry from a nice, safe, well-contained circle to a pointery-thing without any outer boundaries. So not only is it possible that I've screwed up translating the ritual design and it just won't work, but if it *does* go boom, it will go boom pretty messily, right in our faces."

"This is boding well," Pierce said.

Jenny snorted. "Oh, I haven't finished yet," she said. "The *other* thing I'm bodging is that this is traditionally done with a candle flame. Unfortunately"—she pointed up at the ceiling— "sprinklers."

"Not a good idea," Pierce agreed, while Cliff looked faintly ill at the very thought. Odds were such a tiny flame wouldn't be enough to agitate the smoke detectors high above their heads, but a warehouse full of vital evidence, in the form of thousands of irreplaceable, priceless magic artefacts, was not the place to go taking a chance.

"Not a good idea," Jenny echoed. "So, we're improvising again." She gestured to the dish of piled silver powder, and reached under her collar to tug off the necklace she was wearing. It was a divination pendulum that Pierce had seen her use in a couple of rituals before, a faceted amethyst crystal that came to a point. Pierce had a pretty low opinion of pendulum-based divination—subject to human arm wobbles and confirmation bias, they were distinctly suspect, magic-wise, in her view—but at least she knew Jenny had the training to know what she was doing.

"Pendulum and powder," Jenny explained. "It should, in theory, produce a similar effect to using actual smoke, but it's not going to last anywhere near as long." She nodded her head at the heap of silver powder in the dish. "If all goes well, we'll see some signal leading us to the nearest shapeshifting pelt, but once all the powder's used up, it will disappear."

"So how long before it's used up?" Pierce asked.

Jenny shrugged.

"How long is a piece of string?" Cliff said with a wry smile.

"Long enough to be useful for something, hopefully," Pierce said. She took a deep breath. "All right. Let's get this show on the road, then." Even a brief indication of a direction would help to narrow the search—or, more likely, the lack of any indicated direction would prove the pelt was long gone and not worth searching for.

Or simply be a sign the ritual hadn't bloody worked. Always a frustrating lack of certainties with magic—and this improvised ritual was a longer shot than most.

But it was the best shot they had.

Jenny sat cross-legged on the floor, closing her eyes and breathing evenly as she let the pendulum dangle from her fist above the dish of silver powder. When its subtle swings had gentled to near imperceptible, she opened her eyes.

"Like calls to like," she said out loud, her voice echoing in the empty warehouse, and followed it up with a phrase in some Germanic language, the sounds just familiar enough for Pierce's brain to briefly tangle over trying to make sense of them before she understood it wasn't English. "Essence to essence." Then the other language again; Pierce couldn't tell if she was just translating or the words in the two languages were different. "Heart to heart."

And so it went, switching back and forth through the lines of the recitation in a rhythmic chant. The air inside the warehouse seemed to thicken, the shadows around them growing deeper. Pierce had been cold before, but now the space seemed oppressively warm, as if the ritual was generating heat like a campfire.

Jenny's hand on the pendulum still appeared rock steady, and yet the weighted stone slowly began to swing, circling back and forth in ever-widening loops that reversed direction with each switch in languages. Pierce could feel a pressure in her ears and static crawling on her skin as grains of glittering silver began to rise up from the dish, spinning about the circle like leaves caught in a tornado.

The effect was hypnotic, and Pierce's attention blurred, only hooked back in as the rhythm of Jenny's words changed. "Let that which is lost now be found," she said. "Let that which is broken be whole. Let that which is unknown be known. Seek the heart, seek the essence, seek! Seek!" One more guttural phrase in that unknown language, and the pendulum lashed like a whip, snapping loose from its chain to fly across the room as Jenny cried out and clutched at her hand.

Pierce rose to her feet to run to her, but that was when Cliff called out, "Claire!" She looked down; the cloud of swirling silver had contracted into a ball of bright light and was even now streaking away towards the front of the warehouse. "Don't lose track of it!"

Leaving him to take care of whatever injury Jenny might have sustained, Pierce turned to chase after the light. She had to sprint to have a hope of keeping up, the darting light zipping away through the shelves almost too fast to follow. It was shedding material as it went, a wispy trail of silver that strung out behind it like a contrail.

The glow disappeared at the end of an aisle and Pierce

cursed, putting on a burst of speed though her lungs were already starting to burn in stressed protest. She clipped her elbow on the metal shelf support at the corner, the kind of numb jolt that would blossom to agony as soon as her brain caught up with it, but there was no time to do more than grunt with pain as she spotted the ball of light heading for the main doors. The spell had picked up something, but not within the warehouse—somewhere close? If it wasn't, they were going to lose the trail fast, because the light was already looking dimmer.

The glowing orb passed right through the warehouse doors without pause, leaving Pierce behind to face the constraints of physics as she stumbled after it and slapped the door release, glad she didn't need a card key and a code from the inside. The security guard turned her wide eyes from the streaking light to look at Pierce as she burst through. "Hey! What—?"

"Emergency police business!" Pierce panted out without a pause. "Stay where you are!" As the glow passed through the outer doors it was already little more than a silvery glimmer to the air; if Pierce fell behind, the last trace of the spell would be gone before she could see the direction of its target.

"You have to sign out!" the guard shouted after her as Pierce yanked the door open to follow. Pierce ignored her, charging out onto the road outside to look around. The evidence facility was surrounded by a chain link fence; the glow had already crossed the car park to pass through it, darting out across the dual carriageway and disappearing amid the glare of the headlights. Pierce raised her gaze up and beyond them before she could be blinded, fixing on the common ground beyond the road. Nothing out there, just a patch of scrappy grass with a few people walking dogs—

Dogs. Pierce raked her gaze over the group of dog-walkers, looking for what she was suddenly certain would be there. A dog as big as a man—big enough to *be* a man. Her eye fell on a Range Rover parked up on the edge of the grass, the hindquarters of a big black dog just scrambling up over the tailgate. There was no one there to guide the dog inside, just a reflection-blurred figure in the driver's seat, but on the second blink, it was a human hand that she saw reaching back to pull the hatch down from inside.

She grabbed her phone for a photo, but the Range Rover was already bumping down from the kerb, and all she caught was a blurry snap of the back wheels, no sign of a licence plate on the vehicle. The silver glow of the spell had faded beyond her ability to pick it out in the dark, but she was sure this was where it had been leading her. Not to the missing panther pelt—but to another, closer shapeshifting skin: a shifter keeping them under surveillance.

And she was pretty sure she knew who was behind it. The criminal operations that she'd busted liked their flashy deadly predators as shapeshifting forms: big cats, wolves and bears, exotic skins that evoked fear. But *government* people, people in the business of making threats to national security discreetly disappear, *Maitland's* people... they used dogs.

Maybe they were the ones who'd faked Sebastian's death. Maybe they just didn't want her to be able to prove that someone else had.

Either way, the fact that they were on her back meant trouble.

CHAPTER TWELVE

PIERCE WENT BACK in and smoothed things over with the security guard, implying without outright lying that the glow she'd seen race out through the reception area was down to the accidental activation of one of the stored artefacts.

"Oh, we're used to it here," the woman said, unfazed. "You get all sorts—boxes that talk to themselves, ghosts in the aisles, ice on the shelves in the middle of summer... We just call Doctor Healey down to look at things when the artefacts start misbehaving."

"I've said many times we need a more specialised storage facility than this," Cliff said apologetically.

Pierce sighed. "Yep, and after that we just need the staff and the training and the equipment..." It was a pipedream—and there was no guarantee it would have kept Maitland's people out anyway. "The panther pelt's gone," she told the others when they were beyond the reach of the guard's prying ears. "And we're being watched. Keep an eye out for big dogs and don't talk about any of this to anyone." She was beginning to regret having brought them into this at all; she needed help if she was going to sort this mess out, but it was starting to feel like her efforts were doing nothing but painting targets on more people's backs.

Still, the more of them that there were in the know, the harder it was going to be for any of them to be conveniently disappeared.

She hoped.

All the same, spotting their observers had left her decidedly on edge. She found herself watching every pair of headlights in the rearview mirror as she drove back home, looking for that Range Rover, or other signs of pursuit. Her phone rang just as she was starting up the garden path, and she eyed the unknown number warily. "DCI Pierce, Ritual Crime," she said brusquely, lifting it to her ear.

"Ah, Claire! I was hoping to be able to catch you. Not interrupting your plans for the evening, I hope." After a moment's blankness Pierce placed the voice on the other end as Christopher Tomb. "Good news—I've spoken to my contact who gave me the information on the vampire cult, and he's agreed to share his knowledge with the police."

"Great. Give me his contact details, and I hope you impressed on him that time is of the essence." Pierce fumbled through the awkward choreography of trying to unlock the door, switch on the light and retrieve her notebook without losing the phone.

"Unfortunately, I'm afraid he does have some conditions," Tomb said.

Pierce rolled her eyes to the heavens, trying but not really succeeding to keep the frustration out of her voice. "Mr Tomb, it's late, and this is a major murder enquiry," she said. "This cult has killed, and we have every reason to believe they'll kill again if they aren't stopped. We don't have time to play games—if your contact has information that could save lives, he needs to share it."

Tomb had an almost impressive way of blithely continuing the conversation, ignoring her words entirely. "He's willing to meet with you personally, but only face to face, and with me there to act as a guarantee of your good intentions." Pierce wondered rather cynically if that had really been the alleged cultist's condition, or Tomb's own effort to elbow his way into proceedings. "He's requested we meet under cover of darkness, at midnight tonight."

Well, that was a load of melodramatic bollocks. Pierce huffed irritably. To her mind this seemed more like a publicity stunt than a legitimate lead, and she was buggered if she felt like traipsing around in the middle of the night to meet some supposed informant who might not know anything useful, but professionalism reluctantly won out. There *might* be something to it, however unlikely it seemed, and Lord knew they didn't have such an abundance of promising leads that they could afford to reject anything out of hand.

"Fine," she said tightly, massaging the bridge of her nose. "Tell me where he wants to meet." No sleep for her tonight, it seemed.

THE MEETING POINT that Tomb relayed to her was the relatively unglamorous location of a pub car park on the outskirts of Leeds. Her instincts were pinging for a waste of time a lot harder than they were for an actual threat, but nonetheless she shot off a quick email to Dawson down in Nottinghamshire to keep him apprised of her movements; she couldn't have arranged more backup even if she'd wanted to, with two of her team on a stakeout at Trick Box and Deepan in no state to join her.

The pub itself was closed by the time Pierce arrived there, but there were a few cars still outside, maybe belonging to the owners, or customers who'd had the sense not to try to drive home. Pierce parked up next to a boxy old Mercedes on the end that she pegged as most likely to be Tomb's. The slam of her car door echoed loudly in the silence as she got out to look around.

Pierce was no stranger to arriving at crime scenes after dark, but usually she'd be pulling up alongside a row of emergency vehicles with their lights still flashing, the scene crawling with uniforms or people in forensics coveralls. Here, the frigid February chill had chased everyone inside, and everything seemed almost unnaturally still and silent. Even the windows of the houses across the street were largely dark, aside from the odd stray upstairs light behind the curtains.

She could see her own breath in the glow of the pub's security light as she rounded the Mercedes to peer in through the driver's door window. No one inside.

"Claire?" The voice came from the shadows of the building beside her, and she jumped before she could stop herself. She breathed out slowly before she turned on her heel, refusing to let him see how much he'd startled her.

"Mr Tomb," she said, crisply professional, though she suspected a spark of her irritation came through. She was cold and tired and extremely short on patience for whatever amateur dramatics he had planned. At least, she saw as he stepped out of the shadows, he'd forgone his ridiculous daytime getup. He wore a bulky purple all-weather jacket that didn't much suit his image but did look enviably warm.

It also made Pierce think of the Valentine Vampire's victims and the incongruously sporty clothes that they'd been laid out in, and she held back a shiver. Tomb had been eliminated from their enquiries years ago: he had alibis, and he was too young to have been the original killer—but that didn't mean he couldn't be involved somehow. She closed her fist around the comforting bulk of the radio in her coat pocket. Her team were all occupied or off-duty, but police backup was still only a shout away.

Provided she kept track of where they were going. She'd assumed Tomb's contact would meet them here, but instead the writer gestured her away from the pub and towards the park across the road, where a footpath led off under the shadow of overhanging trees. She let him take the lead, keeping a wary eye on their surroundings as she mentally inventoried the rest of her gear. Silver cuffs. Malodorant spray—not that it would do her much good unless they ran afoul of shapeshifters. The penlight on her keys.

As the pub's security light clicked off behind them, she was wishing that she'd brought a proper full-strength police torch instead. There were times when she missed her days in uniform, all the gear always ready to hand. In her role as DCI she was supposed to stand back and supervise from a distance, if not from a desk, but the understaffed RCU needed every officer they could get out in the field.

Even if they were inching ever closer to the retirement age and limits of fitness requirements, and keenly aware just how fast a supposedly simple meeting with a source could go straight to shit.

And the circumstances of this one didn't exactly fill her with confidence. The hairs at the back of her neck prickled as she followed Tomb further away from the road and the lights, feeling hemmed in by the grassy slopes running alongside the path. She didn't like that they were leaving the cars and whatever CCTV coverage there might have been around the pub; Pierce might be well outside the vampire cult's victim profile, but that didn't mean that she was safe if they decided she was a threat.

In her pockets, her hands closed around the radio and the small canister of incapacitant spray. The smell, though it might fend off a shapeshifter or disperse a rioting crowd, wouldn't do much to drive off a motivated human—but a blast of any aerosol spray in the face would send most people reeling away for a few vital seconds if need be.

Tomb, at least, was currently keeping his distance, forging ahead at a pace that suggested he was either cold or pretty nervous himself.

Or less confident than he'd led her to believe that his supposed contact would even show up. It probably wouldn't be politic to charge him with wasting police time if this turned out to be a wild goose chase, but it made for a pleasant daydream nonetheless. Pierce was already exhausted, miserably cold, and increasingly pissed off as she followed the author through to a small open patch of ground amid the trees. In the dim light that filtered through from the next road she could just make out the shadowed shapes of children's play equipment and benches.

This had better be the meeting place with this alleged cultist, because she'd just about lost all patience for walking. "Right. Where is he?" she said.

"He'll be here," Tomb said, placatingly. "He wanted to make sure you didn't bring anyone else."

"He has a high opinion of himself," Pierce said. Never mind devoting further police resources—they were lucky that she'd come at all. She'd yet to see any evidence that this rigmarole was worth her time.

Tomb moved on towards the far side of the play area. There was a metal park bench there, just visible in the deeper shadow under the trees; Pierce squinted, trying to see if it was occupied, but her eyes weren't up to it.

Sod this. Wary of being surprised by a voice from the shadows again, she shook her keys out of her pocket and clicked the penlight on. Its feeble beam was scarcely better than the fading fringes of the streetlights, but it lit up a patch of grass before her feet. She followed Tomb, trying to decide how much time she was prepared to give this if their man didn't show.

"Jonathan," Tomb said, in a hoarse, carrying whisper. "Jonathan, are you here? I brought the DCI here, as you asked."

No answer. Instinct chilled the back of Pierce's neck, but Tomb kept moving, his footsteps and the rustle of his coat potentially masking any sounds amid the trees around them. "Jonathan?"

As he approached the bench, Pierce had to keep pace with him, wanting to be ahead of a member of the public if there was trouble. It was too still, too quiet for there to be someone waiting for them unless it was with ill-intent. "Wait—" she started to say, but that was when the edge of the weak torchlight finally reached the feet of someone sitting on the bench and Tomb hurried the rest of the way forward before she could stop him.

"Jonathan, we're—" He strangled his own words with

a startled sound, flinching back as the figure on the bench slumped sideways from his touch.

"Get back!" Pierce barked, even before she'd moved close enough for the torchlight to show what she'd already guessed.

The pallid, death-distorted face of a man who wasn't going to be sharing his secrets any time soon.

No artfully posed and cleaned-up ritual kill this time: a jagged gash had torn out most of the man's throat, and blood soaked the front of his once-white shirt. The torchlight glinted off the blood-smeared shape of a silver bat pendant, twin to the one worn by the woman Pierce had chased in York. The baseball cap he must have been wearing to obscure his face had fallen askew at Tomb's touch, perhaps resettled on his head by the killer.

The unhappily familiar stink of death rolled over her as Pierce bent to take the pulse that she knew wouldn't be there. Her fingers came away tacky with blood that wasn't yet dry, and she instinctively wiped her hand on the bench before it occurred to her that she shouldn't compromise the crime scene. She stepped back with a curse.

"Don't touch anything," she told Tomb unnecessarily. He'd already backed well away, his eyes wide in the torchlight.

"Is he—Oh, God." He must have known the question was superfluous, and he reeled away from her to bend over and retch.

It was too late to help Jonathan, if that was really his name, but even as part of her was cursing that she hadn't insisted on greater precautions for their meeting, another part was cataloguing how he might help *them*. This wasn't a staged body dump this time—the ex-cultist had been killed here. There might have been a struggle, might be evidence... and for the first time, they had a clear connection between killer and victim, a possible chain of associations to follow.

Pierce drew her radio and called the incident in, retreating to a distance as she eyed up how best to secure the scene. Public park, that was going to be a bugger, but at least it was still the middle of the night...

A flicker of motion at the corner of her eye yanked her gaze back towards the trees, and she opened her mouth to warn Tomb again to back off from the body.

But it wasn't Tomb. He was still well away to her left, stooped over and panting.

"Killer's still at the scene!" Pierce barked into her radio just before it was torn out of her hand, the dispatcher's urgent voice bouncing away across the grass as a bony body slammed her to the ground with brutal force.

CHAPTER THIRTEEN

RAKING FINGERNAILS SLASHED across Pierce's face as she twisted her head away, trying to find the breath in her winded lungs to yell for Tomb to run. She hoped the dispatcher had heard enough to expedite backup—but however fast it arrived, it could still be too late.

She fought to get free as her attacker grabbed her hair to slam her head against the ground. The body pinning her down seemed lightweight, almost skeletally frail, and yet she couldn't force the bony wrists away from her. She rolled sideways, trying to wrench herself free, but the killer clung on and dragged her down, teeth snapping near her cheek.

And this was the killer—Pierce didn't doubt it. She could smell the rank decay of death and the metallic scent of blood, strong enough to make her gag. She drove her knee into what should have been a vulnerable stomach, but she might as well have kneed the ground for the response it got: not even a grunt. The clawing hands that grappled hers were sharp-nailed and deathly cold.

Pierce realised she was still clutching the penlight, though the light had clicked off. She closed her fingers around the keys it was attached to, jabbing them blindly out towards her attacker's face. That won her a slight flinch, and she tugged partway free, feeling the clawed nails rake down her hand as she pulled away. She smashed out with the keys again, but the killer was too fast, squirming sideways from the blow and biting down on Pierce's forearm, hard.

"Fuck!" Her layered winter clothes stopped the clamped teeth from sinking into her skin, but it still hurt like hell. She awkwardly tried to hit out with the keys, but they tangled in the wool of her attacker's winter hat. She patted desperately at her pockets with her other hand for something, anything she could use...

Her hand seized on the canister of malodorant spray, jammed awkwardly against her side. Pierce yanked it out, uncaring as it dragged a probably-important scrap of paper with it to fall out onto the grass; she shoved the spray can into her attacker's face and set it off. As the stinking chemicals spewed out, the killer reeled away, releasing her arm with an angry hiss that barely even sounded human.

Pierce scrambled up and backwards, already panting with exertion. Something crunched under her foot—fuck; radio, torch, a branch? As she looked down in the darkness somebody grabbed her arm, and she gasped and almost lashed out before she recognised Tomb.

"Stay behind me," she ordered, a futile instinct when the murderer had already melted back into the darkness around them. The sulphuric stink of the malodorant spray was spreading, and she coughed out a lungful, blinking frantically to clear her eyes as they threatened to water. The only light was the little that filtered through the trees from the streetlights beyond the park, and her heart beat fast as she scanned the deep surrounding shadows.

Where was the killer?

Now the frantic thrashing of the fight was over—in seconds, though it had felt much longer—Pierce realised that her radio was still babbling police chatter where it had fallen somewhere to her left. Grab for it, or would that be the distraction that proved her undoing? She didn't know if the killer had already fled the scene, or this was just a lull before the next attack.

They needed to get back onto the road, back to the limited protection of the street lighting where at least they'd see danger coming. "Come on." Pierce tugged at Tomb's arm, causing him to stagger off-balance; he was still half in shock from the rapid turn of events. "Stay by me," she ordered.

For what dubious protection she could offer. She rubbed at her forearm, wishing there was light to peel her sleeve back and see if the bite had broken the skin even through all the layers. There had been no fangs—but the strength and speed behind the bite, behind the whole attack, was more than any normal human being could have brought to bear. Pierce would have struggled to match a younger and fitter assailant, but she was hopelessly outclassed by one who was magically enhanced.

She could only hope that amplified senses were part of the deal, because the spreading cloud of the chemical stink bomb was making even her eyes burn. The anti-shapeshifter spray was a strictly one-off deal: with that emptied, she was out of self-defence tricks.

A half-heard noise made her whirl to face the trees. Was that a hunched figure creeping after them in the darkness, or just a trick of the wind and shadows? She dragged Tomb with her, hustling across the park towards that precious pool of orange light out on the road. If they could just make it back to the streets—

Tomb's arm was wrenched away from her grip as a blur of dark motion slammed into him from the side, smashing him to the ground several metres away. Pierce barely saw it happen, only heard his panicked cry as she staggered from the force of the impact.

"Police!" she yelled reflexively. "Let him go!" She chased after the two of them, searching her pockets for a weapon or even a distraction tactic, and coming up empty. No choice but to wade in anyway—

And then one of the two struggling shadows jerked upright, head snapping round—but not towards her. Towards the road. A moment later the killer was up and running across the park, and Pierce didn't understand why until the distant wail of sirens finally reached her ears too. Still some way off, but obviously close enough for the killer to have decided the window for getting away had closed.

She'd be fooling herself to pretend that she could give chase, and in any case, she had a member of the public to see to first. She ran to where Tomb lay gasping in the grass. "Mr Tomb?" She shook his shoulder. "Are you hurt?" He didn't respond to her words, but was that injury, shock, or was he just winded? She switched names in the hope that something more familiar might snap him out of it. "Mr Brown? Christopher."

He was wheezing now as he struggled to sit up with her help, but her hasty pat-down found no obvious injuries, and she dared to hope it was just a panic attack. She glanced back in search of the killer, but the sprinting figure had already vanished into the darkness.

And then the approaching sirens swept in with deafening volume and a blaze of flashing blue and headlights, bringing a stark artificial daylight to the park. Car doors slammed and voices shouted, and more bright lights approached them across the grass.

"Police!" the uniformed officers shouted, and Pierce shouted it back, holding up her warrant card for the torches. "DCI Pierce, RCU. Murder suspect just took off over park, headed for..."—she had no idea, and could only point—"that direction. Didn't get a good look, um... dark clothes, dark wool hat, lightweight build, not very tall. Probably still covered in the victim's blood. May be carrying a knife, definitely has magical enhancements to boost strength and speed."

"It was the vampire," Tomb gasped hoarsely beside her, finding his voice. "I saw... he had pale, dead pale skin, and the fangs..."

Pierce didn't think highly of the description, but arguing was only going to confuse the search efforts. "This is a suspect in the Valentine Vampire murders, caught red-handed with a new body," she said, trying to impress both the urgency and the threat. "Approach with extreme caution, and don't let him get away!"

Her commanding tone sparked a flurry of motion, though she was more than half certain that it was already too late. There was nothing more Pierce could do to assist the chase right now, so she eased herself back down onto the grass with a gasp, panting for the breath she hadn't had the time to take in the commotion. She waved down the PC who was hovering to see if she needed medical attention, and pointed him back towards the benches.

"Body's on a bench under those trees," she said. "Make sure the scene's secured."

They might not be able to catch the killer, but at least they'd have the evidence he'd left behind.

BY THE TIME word came in from all units that their suspect had well and truly slipped the net, it was more of a bitter confirmation than a body blow. A loose dragnet of local bobbies with no advance warning stood little chance of catching up to a suspect who could move that fast, especially when the description was vague enough that just ditching a layer of clothes would see the killer free and clear. Pierce's own efforts with the malodorant spray made it a waste of time trying to bring in tracking dogs.

She let the ambulance crew examine her injuries, superficial though they were, and forensics do their best to take trace evidence. She doubted that it would amount to much: the bite wound hadn't managed to break the skin through her clothes, and while they'd tried for a saliva sample from her jacket it was probably a lost cause; if anything had transferred to her during her brief efforts at grappling with the killer, it had probably been the murder victim's blood.

Nonetheless, she handed her outer clothes over to forensics, suffering a chilly wait in a set of overalls that were strictly supposed to be worn over clothes, not instead of them, especially on a winter night like this. She'd reluctantly called Dawson in to play the role of RCU oversight, partly because she was knackered, but mainly because any further involvement from her in the on-scene investigation would provide ammunition for future lawyers.

He arrived at the scene with a five o'clock shadow edging into designer stubble and a rumpled, cigarette-scented suit that might have been fished out of the laundry, but at least he was sober and alert, which put him one up on her the way she was crashing.

"I should have been involved," he said when he found her lurking amid the police cars at the edge of the scene. "This is my case." He seemed to conveniently forget that since she was his boss, his cases *were* her cases—and he'd lost any sort of claim over it as soon as they'd connected it to the Valentine Vampire killings.

Pierce was too tired to pick a fight about it, and this was hardly the time or place anyway, with a swarm of local police and forensics bods in position to earwig. "Wouldn't have made any difference," she said instead, rubbing her neck. "Victim was dead before we got here, and the killer was magically enhanced—would have taken more than the two of us to detain him." And she hadn't expected it to be anything, hadn't wanted to justify the overtime or calling her team out in the night without due cause... It was easy to pick the decisions apart in hindsight, harder to keep perspective on whether they'd made sense at the time.

Dawson grunted in dissatisfaction, no doubt unconvinced by her verdict on how much difference he could have made single-handed, but at least he let the subject go. "I'll deal with this from here," he said. "No reason for you to stay."

He was right, and it might have been kindly meant, but she bridled even so. "Fine," she said tersely. "Keep me updated." Pretty empty words when it was the middle of the night and there wasn't much that would justify waking her up.

At least he'd done as she'd asked and stopped by the station to pick up her spare keys so Pierce could get back into her car after her other set had been taken in evidence. She was finally able to change into the spare clothes that had been sitting in the boot this whole time and make her weary way back home.

She drove home slowly with the radio up loud, wary of icy roads and her tiredness. She'd had days this long far too many times in her career—even more of them when she was lower down the ranks—but they still seemed to get harder year on year. This, she knew, was where getting too old for the job was eventually going to bite her: not in the physical demands of the moment, but the need to get straight back on her feet and keep going for hours afterwards.

Well, at least tonight she finally had her chance to sleep, though she doubted it would come easily. Her eyelids might be heavy as she let herself in through the front door, but her heart was still thrumming in her chest with the speed boost of spent adrenaline and the cup of coffee she'd blagged to keep her warm. She supposed she could try taking something that would knock her out, but she didn't want to risk being groggy in the morning.

What the hell time was it anyway? Pierce shouldered through the door into the dining room, squinting at the mantelpiece clock in the light spilling through from the hall as she shrugged off her coat.

Something struck her as off.

She couldn't say immediately what—she just knew that the house, its contents rarely touched outside the small disturbances of her daily routine, was in some subtle way not how she'd left it.

She was already turning towards the living room when the light inside it clicked on in a sudden, blinding blaze.

"DCI Pierce. We need to talk," said Jason Maitland.

CHAPTER FOURTEEN

PIERCE WAS ALMOST glad of the dulled reactions that meant she didn't jump as much as she might have. Instead she finished taking off her coat and draped it over the back of a chair before reaching out to turn the dining room light on, reducing the advantage that Maitland had given himself by standing in the lit doorway.

He looked exactly the same as he had when he'd first marched up and taken over her crime scene five months ago: bland good looks and a generic haircut in a sharp suit and a long black cashmere coat, his shirt buttoned to the collar and tie still tightly knotted despite the hour. He could have vanished into any crowd of thirty-something businessmen on a train platform without a single distinguishing feature to set him apart from the herd. She wondered if that was some kind of hiring requirement.

Whoever it was that he actually worked for. The so-called Counter Terror Action Team that he'd previously claimed to represent might have a tenuous justification for horning in on her cases, but they sure as hell couldn't break into her house.

"Mr Maitland," she said, when she was sure her voice was as steady as it was going to get. "I don't recall inviting you in." She didn't recall having noticed any tampering with the front door lock, either; she could have missed it in the dark, or he could have broken in round the back, but somehow she doubted he'd gone to any such measures. The spare keys she was using had come from her desk at work: no doubt he could have had his people copy them any time that he pleased. Maybe all the way back in October when she'd been hospitalised after the skinbinder case.

Her skin crawled at the knowledge that his people had almost certainly been in here, searching every private space for any evidence she might have secreted away from her investigation into Sebastian's activities. The fact it had undoubtedly been a wholly impersonal search, every detail logged to make sure that things went back exactly where they'd been taken from, somehow made the whole thing worse, not better.

"I apologise for the intrusion," Maitland said smoothly, not a trace of any such actual apology in his tone. "I'm sure you can appreciate that it's necessary to avoid drawing attention to any meeting between the two of us."

"I'm not sure I appreciate why it's necessary for us to meet at all," Pierce said. She would have liked to showcase her lack of intimidation by going about her routine as if he wasn't there, but her only actual plan for the night had been going to bed; instead she moved through to the kitchen so he would have to follow and poured herself a glass of water at the sink. She watched Maitland approach her as a dim outline reflected in the darkened windows.

"I'm afraid I have to ask you yet again to cease your investigations into the late skinbinder Sebastian and his activities," he said. "You know as well as I do that it's vital that no one find out he accomplished a magic feat that most believe to be impossible. Continuing to investigate a closed case after the man is dead is only going to draw attention to it."

Pierce turned back to face him, raising her eyebrows in challenge. "I was investigating one of his pelts that came into our possession as part of an unrelated case. Are you confirming that there's a connection?"

He smiled thinly, as if humouring an embarrassingly bad joke. "Chief Inspector, there's a limit to how far you can get by being purposefully obtuse. Skinbinding is a difficult art. Those who practise it are rare, and those who are willing to skirt the legal restrictions are even more so. It's hardly remarkable that a talented pelt-maker would have sold his creations to other criminals. As I understand it, the shapeshifter you seized the pelt from was simply playing the role of hired thug for a group whose activities had nothing to do with skinbinding."

"You seem to 'understand' an awful lot about confidential police investigations," Pierce said. "If Sebastian is dead, what's your justification for treating legitimate investigations into the criminal use of his pelts as a threat to national security?" If that was even the excuse he was still using this week. "And what the hell kind of authority do you have to break into *my* house?"

"Sufficient," Maitland said crisply. He held her gaze for a long moment, revealing the steel behind the polished niceties. "DCI Pierce. I appreciate that you're a public servant working in what you believe to be the interest of the people, and therefore a certain leeway ought to be extended. But that leeway is rapidly running out. If you persist in behaving as if you believe Sebastian was anything other than a maker of animal pelts who was arrested for his crimes and later died, you risk drawing the attention of parties who *must* not be allowed to dig into his activities and find the truth."

"Like the fact he isn't dead?" Pierce said pointedly.

"He's dead," Maitland said, meeting her eyes with every appearance of sincerity. She didn't trust it an inch. "The knowledge of how he achieved his accomplishments died with him, and it's my job to see that it stays buried. If you continue to act against that goal, you're forcing me to reclassify your efforts from misguided to actively hostile to security."

"Whose security?" she countered. "The people that Sebastian and his supporters abducted and murdered to make those skins? The family members who'll never get closure on how or why their loved ones died and whether the killer is still out there somewhere? The innocents who were murdered to keep your precious secret buried?"

Not all of them by Sebastian and the criminal organisation that backed him, either; the dog shifters like the one she'd seen today were Maitland's people, she was sure, and she'd already witnessed one murder a woman for the crime of telling Pierce too much about Sebastian's past. She couldn't say for sure if it was Maitland's people who'd disposed of Superintendent Palmer, but neither side of whatever secretive magical turf war was going on showed much in the way of compunction. The enemy of her enemy was definitely not her friend.

All she knew for sure was that she trusted Maitland about as far as she could throw him.

"Obviously the loss of any lives is an unfortunate tragedy," he said, the words polished and perfunctory. "But closure for the existing victims has to be weighed against the probability of causing greater harm by revealing the truth. I'm working to ensure that there will be no further deaths—it's very much in your best interest to cooperate."

"Or what?" Pierce said, lacing her fingers around the water glass in her hands. "I conveniently disappear? Not to toot my own horn, but I head up a major police department. There would be some pretty tough questions to face if I went missing." The RCU might be small, but that only meant she had personal ties to everyone involved. She was the longest-serving team leader across the country's three branches, and her disappearance from the scene would draw attention no matter what the cause. "Unless, of course," she added, locking eyes with him, "you happen to have the means to replace me with a dead ringer."

To the best of her knowledge, Sebastian was the only skinbinder out there with the skill to craft shapeshifting pelts from human skin. It was a skill the world's finest had been trying to master for centuries, with no reliable proof of success. Maitland's determination to conceal an achievement no one else could copy didn't make sense—unless Sebastian was alive.

But even though he must know he wasn't fooling her, Maitland still stuck to the official line. "I'd strongly advise you to set these melodramatic conspiracy theories aside," he said. "You have nothing to support your claims, only wild speculation based on inadmissible tests. A word in the wrong ear, and you could easily end up losing your career over this kind of unauthorised investigation."

"Then that'll give me some useful information about which ears you're whispering into," Pierce said, holding his gaze. The threat was a fairly empty one when she figured she was on borrowed time anyway; if she got fired, she'd still have all her contacts, along with considerably more free time and a lot less to lose.

Maitland presumably agreed she was less trouble where she was, since he just sighed, a small flicker of humanity in his perfectly coiffed façade. "I'm quite familiar with your stubbornness by now, chief inspector," he said. "Just as I'm well aware that you're far from stupid. So let's be plain. Pursuing this will cause nothing but trouble for you and those you involve in your paranoid fantasies. Don't."

And *there* was the true threat: a matter-of-fact reminder that he no doubt knew the names and detailed backgrounds of everyone that she'd roped in to help her. Pierce stared back at him coldly, her fingers pressed white against the glass in her hands.

Maitland gave a thin smile, a small fraction away from a sneer. "I'll see myself out," he said.

She didn't give him the satisfaction of pursuing him out to the hall to make sure that he really went. It wouldn't be Maitland's style to hang around for a cheap scare.

Instead she headed into the bathroom, pretending to herself that locking the door behind her was just habit.

But as she regarded her haggard reflection in the bathroom mirror, she had to privately admit that she *was* rattled. Not by whatever retribution Maitland might have planned, but by the utterly casual invasion of her private space. She should have been getting ready for bed, but she was reluctant to change, unable to shake the feeling that someone might walk in.

It pissed her off. Pierce marched through the house turning lights on, justifying it to herself as a check to see what Maitland might have been up to while she wasn't home, though she doubted she would find anything.

What the hell *had* he been doing? How long had he been lying in wait for her to return? Walking into the living room where he'd been lurking, Pierce saw nothing that had been obviously moved, but she thought she could smell a whiff of his cologne in the air.

Think like the suspect.

Maybe he'd had someone with eyes on her all night, aware of exactly where she'd been and when she headed home, but he couldn't have been certain of the timing, so he would have been here for a while, waiting; nothing messed up your aura of omnipotence quite like being caught on the doorstep when your target arrived home.

He always looked as neatly turned-out as a Ken doll, but still, it was well after midnight and he'd probably worked a full day... why would he stay on his feet when he didn't know how long he'd have to wait? He'd want to keep an eye on the window for the light of her car, so... the second armchair, the one that she never used herself because it got glare from the window and wasn't in the right place for watching the TV.

Pierce smiled in triumph. Where a man sat, he left trace evidence behind. She went to the needlework kit that had been gathering dust in the corner since her last attempt to pretend that she had time for hobbies, and retrieved the magnifying light and a pair of tweezers. She scrutinised the seat cushions until she spotted a clinging strand that was far too dark to be from her own silvering hair. Maybe one of Maitland's hairs, a fibre from his suit or coat, even someone else's hair that he'd tracked in with him. Whatever the source, it was a trace, a link back to wherever Maitland might have been before he'd showed up here.

She knew she couldn't run it through regular forensics: even if she could find someone to do it off-books as a favour, the evidence was sure to just go walkabouts again, and she doubted that Maitland was there to find in any sort of database in any case.

But science wasn't the only thing she had at her disposal. Sympathetic magic didn't need lab tests and database comparisons to make a link—a piece of the whole *was* the link.

So if she had one small fibre transferred from his clothes... then she had Jason Maitland.

CHAPTER FIFTEEN

Pierce hadn't been convinced that she would get a wink of sleep, but she barely had the chance to lay down flat before exhaustion smothered her into unconsciousness. Unfortunately, it *was* only a wink that she managed to get. Her first bleary thought as the alarm trilled through her dreams was that it must be the phone or the fire alarm, because there was no way she'd slept long enough for it to be morning already.

She huddled mutinously under the covers for several minutes before she remembered that she'd left Dawson in charge of a crime scene and two constables on a stakeout, and Deepan was probably still going to be off work. She shoved herself out of bed to stagger through the morning routine on autopilot, and hoped that nobody was going to expect her to be human, never mind alert and with it, before well into the afternoon.

But it didn't look like the fates were going to be that kind. She switched on the TV news to keep herself awake, the Valentine

Vampire story quickly coming up in the rotation. Last night's escapades were already the new headline.

"Author and vampire researcher Christopher Tomb has related over social media the harrowing ordeal that he faced last night at the hands of the Valentine Vampire killer," the anchor said. "Tomb was assisting the police Ritual Crime Unit with their enquiries when they were set upon by an attacker that he described as inhumanly strong and fast, with dead white skin, claws, and a hypnotic gaze. Police are refusing to comment on the nature of Tomb's involvement with the investigation, but it's believed to be connected to a suspicious death that occurred in a park on the outskirts of Leeds last night. Rachel Marston is at the scene. Rachel?"

Pierce grimaced at the sight of the reporter positioned in front of a row of police vehicles. Crime scene tape had been strung around the trees, and figures in forensic overalls were still working in the background, searching for evidence that might have gone overlooked in the darkness. At least in a case as high-profile as this one they could count on the regional forces pulling out all the stops to assist, regardless of how much Dawson might have been antagonising them.

There was no obvious sign of him amid all the anonymous figures in coveralls, thankfully: he had even less patience than her for the careful hedging of words required to handle the media, and a bad tendency to make bold promises they couldn't guarantee they'd keep. But today, either he or the local DI was running a tight ship, and the on-site reporter mostly seemed to be milking the established facts and hanging around in hopes of seeing something interesting.

Pierce supposed her own plans for the morning were really much the same: she wanted to take a fresh look at the crime scene herself now it was daylight, and frankly it didn't seem like the worst idea in the world to delay heading into the station for a bit. The superintendent was bound to be on the warpath, and she wouldn't be surprised if there were reporters there too.

Dammit, who'd let Tomb run straight off to blab his story

all over the internet? Pierce would have cautioned him herself, but she hadn't wanted to there to be any suggestion of her influencing his statement—which unfortunately left him free to spout whatever bollocks he pleased about the supposed vampire. She'd barely been able to see a bloody thing when she was grappling with the killer, so she didn't see how Tomb could possibly have made out any more detail. The trouble was, he might not even be telling intentional porkies: panic and preconception could sway eyewitnesses into 'seeing' all sorts of things that weren't really there.

Pierce rubbed her arm as she stopped at a set of traffic lights. She'd have an ugly bruise where she'd been bitten, but there certainly hadn't been any skin-piercing fangs on offer. No, despite the enhanced strength she was sure it was a human being they were looking for—and human beings, no matter how clever or dangerous, made mistakes.

As she parked outside the same pub where she'd stopped last night, Pierce patted the inside pocket that held the fibre she'd taken from Maitland's chair. That little piece of evidence was staying on her person until she got the chance to deal with it.

But first, the present investigation.

She'd hoped that strolling up on foot wearing a business suit would help her sidle past the press unnoticed, but with the number of RCU cases that had made headlines—mostly bad ones—in the last year, she'd become a more recognisable face than she'd prefer. As soon as the first reporter spotted her, the others came scuttling over, scenting a possible new angle to wring more headlines from.

"DCI Pierce!" said the lucky lad in the lead, as a camera was thrust in her face. "Is the RCU treating this murder as connected to the Valentine Vampire killings?"

Sadly, 'Why don't you all sod off and let us find out?' was never considered an acceptable answer. Pierce composed her best neutral face, trying to look neither too harassed nor inappropriately cheerful. "I'm sorry, but I can't make any comment on the progress of an ongoing investigation," she said, raising a hand but careful not to look like she was trying to block the cameras. "Obviously, we *will* consider all the angles—at this stage, we haven't ruled anything out."

Sometimes she suspected her main beef with the media was simply the way they forced her to channel the sort of weasel words that she couldn't stand from other people. It sounded every bit as disingenuous to her as it must to the public, but anything with actual character and content inevitably just got ripped to pieces.

She tried to step away, but another reporter got her before she'd reached the sanctuary of the police tape. "DCI Pierce! Do you have any comment on the account published by Christopher Tomb of his encounter with the Valentine Vampire last night?"

Many, but none that she was about to unload on the press.

"We are aware of the content of Mr Tomb's account," she said crisply. In her case, only because she'd just heard it on the news, but hopefully someone from West Yorkshire Police had already been round to rap his knuckles. Unfortunately, you couldn't unspill milk, and trying to contain or refute his words now would only make a worse mess. Best to just sidestep it. "As I say, it's not possible for us to make any comment on the details of ongoing investigations."

She looked towards the camera, deciding she might as well try to wrest some control of the situation. "All I would like to add is that if anyone has any information about last night's events or the murder of Matt Harrison near Newark-on-Trent last Tuesday, we are appealing to them to come forward to the police with whatever they know. Your information could save lives."

After Tomb's publicity stunts and the media hoohah they'd be lucky to sort the legitimate leads from the crackpots, but at least it would give the news channels something to run other than her deflecting questions. And who knew, maybe there actually was someone out there who'd been planning to sit on life-saving information about a murder inquiry until a few words from a tired, middle-aged copper convinced them otherwise. Stranger things had probably happened somewhere.

Pierce left the reporters behind and headed over to find Dawson among the coverall set. From this close up he was easier to pick out, a bear of a man with his hood pulled back to reveal his shaved head. Pierce donned an unflattering coverall of her own so she could duck beneath the crime scene tape and join him. "Anything new?" she asked, pressing her lips together as she surveyed the frosty grass.

Dawson grimaced. "Not much. Looks like the assailant came up behind the bench from under the trees. We've got a size-seven boot print that may be the killer's—too small to be the victim's."

Pierce nodded. "The guy that attacked us wasn't tall—five-eight at most, maybe? Probably a bit shorter than that, but hard to say." The killer had moved fast, and knocked her to the ground before she'd had much of a chance to see what was happening. "Small, lightweight build, but very strong. And fast."

"Yeah, well, he must have come up behind the victim fast and silently—far as forensics can tell from the blood splatter, the victim turned his head but hadn't started to stand up. No obvious sign of a struggle."

Pierce pictured the scene in her head: the cultist Jonathan, arriving, nervous, sitting down on the bench to wait for her and Tomb. Some faint sound from behind him, or maybe a flicker of motion—but only subtle, a small enough thing for him to have believed that he was just jumping at shadows. He'd turned his head to look towards the trees, and...

She rubbed at the base of her neck. "Murder weapon?" she asked. The killer had come after her with his bare hands—if they were lucky, he might have ditched the weapon somewhere before she and Tomb had even arrived on the scene.

"Pathologist reckons it was a long-bladed knife." Dawson mimed throat-cutting. "Hasn't been found, but we've got the uniforms out checking bins and drains in the area."

Another reason to be glad her WPC days were far behind her. "Same blade that was used for the Valentine Vampire killings?" she asked.

He shook his head. "Size and angle of the incision was all wrong, apparently. Might have been a kitchen knife. Professional job, though—all over in one cut."

"No ritual in this," Pierce said with a grimace. Just good old-fashioned silencing the witnesses. "Any progress on identifying the victim?"

"None yet. No ID, and the bloke you were meeting with claims to have only known him by an assumed name. They're running fingerprints and dental records, but no hits so far. West Yorkshire are going through missing persons."

But it was early yet for the victim's absence to have been noted and reported—assuming there was even anyone to do the reporting. If he'd been a recluse in hiding from the cult, there might not be anybody to miss him.

Pierce scowled in frustration. It looked like they might still not have a smoking gun. The lack of a struggle meant less chance of evidence transfer to the victim's body, and if the killer had left prints on the bench or fibres on the trees, they'd be lost among any number of innocent passers-by.

Still, they'd go ahead and collect everything they could, and maybe at some point down the line it would match to something useful. She just hoped that point would come before there were more victims to process. If the cult kept to the previous pattern, they were looking at another body within the week.

And there was just enough unpredictability in that pattern that they couldn't be sure how much time they had left.

"Keep looking," she said to Dawson, as if he needed to be told. "I'm going to take a walk around the scene, see if there's anything that I missed in the dark last night."

It was unlikely she'd spot anything that forensics hadn't already bagged and tagged, but at least it gave her the illusion of doing something useful. As she picked her way across the crime scene, mentally retracing all the steps of last night's scuffle, she could already feel the pressure of the headache building up behind her eyes from lack of sleep.

Multiple deaths, and still nothing they could track back to

the killer. Pierce could almost see how her old DI had been tempted by the vampire explanation: the idea of a killer who could turn to mist or moonlight was a whole lot easier to take than one who just kept ahead by smarts and luck.

But she didn't believe in vampires. There was a human killer at the head of this cult, she was certain—and human beings had lives, they left traces, they were in the system *somewhere*. She just had to figure out where.

But she wasn't going to find those answers stalking around a park that younger, sharper eyes had already been combing for hours. With a sigh, Pierce had to admit that she was achieving nothing here she couldn't have covered with a phone call, and hanging around any longer was really just delaying the inevitable bawling out she was due from Superintendent Snow.

Not keen to risk another brush with the media, she headed away across the park instead of retracing her steps, the same direction the killer had fled in when backup arrived last night. She ducked under the crime scene tape on the other side and divested herself of the claustrophobic overalls, absently handing them off to a hapless PC standing nearby as something caught her eye.

A woman lurking by the bus shelter a little way away, watching all the police activity. Nothing criminal in that, despite the early hour: crime scenes always brought out the gawkers, especially ones big enough to have made the morning news. But something in the woman's profile, a momentary flicker of familiarity as she turned away to head off across the road—it was her, Pierce was suddenly sure. The woman with the bat necklace who'd run from her in York.

A necklace that matched the one worn by the murdered cultist. Even if she couldn't tell them who Jonathan really was, she had to know where he'd got that silver bat pendant and what it meant—and Pierce was betting that she knew much more than that.

Ignoring whatever response she got from the PC, she started off along the footpath after the woman. She didn't want to break into a run with the news crews still skulking in the background, but she strode as fast as she thought that she could get away with, breaking into a full-blown trot by the time she reached the road. The woman had already crossed over, on the verge of disappearing down a back alley between two empty shops.

"Hey!" Pierce called after her, voice at a pitch that she hoped wouldn't quite carry back to the media in the early morning quiet. The woman obviously heard her, pausing in her stride but not quite turning to look round. "Wait! I spoke to you before. You were at the house in York, weren't you? You were there fourteen years ago." The woman made no acknowledgement, but Pierce thought that she stiffened minutely. "Did you know the man who died last night?" she asked. "Maybe you know who it was that killed him. If you talk to us, we can protect you."

It probably seemed like a hollow reassurance after what had just happened to their last would-be informant. The woman was still standing, unmoving; she hadn't run—but she hadn't turned either. Pierce stepped out into the road, careful to use slow, unthreatening movements. "Look, even if you're worried that you may be implicated, our top priority is saving lives," she said. "We can—"

A BMW came rocketing around the corner, too fast, honking with no apparent effort to slow as the driver saw Pierce in the road. She scrambled back behind the white line with a curse, resisting the urge to offer a hand gesture that wouldn't look good for the police.

By the time he was gone, the woman with the necklace had vanished, hammering away down the alley.

"Shit!" Pierce dashed across the road after her, but she was no match for the younger woman. By the time she rounded the bollards at the mouth of the alley, the woman had already disappeared from the far end. Pierce followed her down to the storage yard at the rear, but it was empty: she had to have gone into one of the buildings, or over the fence at the back. It was high, but the line of recycling bins in front of it would provide a stepping stone for the sufficiently determined.

Pierce didn't risk her dignity by trying to reproduce the feat. She was already puffing, and as their chase in York had proved, if the woman wanted to stay ahead of her, she could.

But her appearance at a second scene couldn't be a coincidence. She knew *something* about this whole mess. The question was, had she been lurking to pluck up the courage to come forward to the police... or to report their activities back to the cult?

With a sigh, Pierce turned to head back to the crime scene. Either the woman would come back of her own volition, or she wouldn't. All Pierce could do was give her description to Dawson, and head into work to face the music for a string of failures.

CHAPTER SIXTEEN

PREDICTABLY, SUPERINTENDENT SNOW was not pleased. About anything, so far as Pierce could tell, up to and including her continued employment.

"Everything about the way you conducted this late-night meeting was reckless and irregular!" he said, as she stared fixedly at the wall of newspaper clippings just behind his head. He hadn't offered her a seat, and despite her exhaustion she wasn't about to ask.

Besides, he had a point—albeit one that was only apparent in hindsight. Following leads off the clock with no backup would be deemed reckless if it went wrong, but if she'd set up a full-scale police operation for a tip that hadn't panned out, she'd be standing here on the same carpet hearing about how it had been wasteful and unnecessary.

Although in that case, no one would be dead.

"Agreeing to meet this man late at night without any police support or attempt at securing the scene—that's not just cutting corners with procedure, it's ignoring it entirely. Why wasn't he brought into the station?" Snow demanded.

"Those were the source's own conditions, sir," Pierce said, since, 'thought it was most likely bollocks, sir,' wasn't going to fly as a response, and probably wouldn't have even back when she'd reported to Howard Palmer. "He was reluctant to speak to police, and I judged it better to accept his terms than risk not getting vital information."

"Well, you judged wrong!" he said. "Do you appreciate *why* we have approved procedures for these matters, Pierce?"

There was an opening best not stepped in if ever she'd heard one.

"It's not, as you seem to think, to 'cramp your style,'" he said, pronouncing the words as if he'd read them in a magazine article about the youth slang of today, "or because anybody particularly delights in coming up with ways to make the job more difficult. It is so, in the event that anything *does* go wrong, we can know that everything was handled as well as it could have been. When police officers—or entire departments, for that matter—under my authority decide to 'wing it' and make up their own rules, it leaves *me* fielding questions about actions I neither approved nor received any notification about!"

"It was a judgement call, sir," she repeated, too tired to find her way around a more conciliatory approach. All she could do was stick to her guns. "The RCU has limited resources to bring to bear, and without further information I didn't see any justification to call in support from other parts of the force."

"Yes." Snow shuffled his stack of paperwork unhappily and tapped it on the desk to straighten the edges. "And speaking of the RCU's limited resources, why were constables..."—he hesitated for a beat, but she gave him points for successfully pulling the names to mind—"Freeman and Taylor apparently tied up with a stakeout for another case entirely while this was going on? I told you to make the Valentine Vampire your top priority."

"Time-limited opportunity, sir," Pierce said, meeting his

gaze now she was back on firmer ground with a case they hadn't managed to fuck up yet. "The gang behind these animal sacrifices have proved that they're willing to kill indiscriminately to protect their operations, and this is our best chance to catch them on the hop. I wanted trained RCU eyes in place to spot any suspicious behaviour."

Snow pressed his lips together in a grimace: sceptical, she suspected, but as long as she gave him justification that he could sell on, he would probably let it go—and 'gang' was always a useful PR buzzword to be able to throw around.

"Yes, well," he said. "You're fortunate that they had something to report to show for it, or else your judgement in these matters would be called into even greater question." He briefly pinched his nose, frowning, before folding his hands together and recovering his poise. "From now on, I expect frequent reports on your team's movements, yours included— preferably *before* you get involved in any more poorly-planned escapades. The eyes of the world are watching closely on this one, and I don't need to tell you how bad the fallout will be if the Valentine Vampire isn't caught this time around."

"Yes, sir," Pierce said.

SHE HADN'T EVEN had a chance to check in with her constables before being hauled into the superintendent's den, so it was happy news to her that the stakeout on Trick Box had actually turned up something. When she returned to the office, they presented her with a series of photographs of an unmarked white van that had apparently made a late-night visit to the shop's delivery entrance.

"Wilkes returned to the shop shortly before one in the morning," Gemma told her. "The white van arrived and parked by the delivery entrance at approximately half past. One man, not the driver, got out and was let into the shop by Wilkes." She showed a couple of photos, though they'd be of limited use in identifying the man until they had a suspect in the frame: burly build, swaddled against the cold in a heavy coat and black woolly hat that by luck or design made a clear glimpse of his features difficult.

"Suspect stayed inside for under ten minutes before returning with a package that he carried back to the van, which then left." There were photos of that too, but it was difficult to make much of the vague bundle the man was carrying in the dark pictures. Gemma was grinning, however. "Couldn't see what it was, but I had Eddie go in early this morning and ask some silly questions about joining a magic group in the area," she said. "Told him which display case to look in and he said there's no sign of the animal spirit charms any more."

"Too hot for Wilkes to handle," Pierce presumed. No doubt the shop owner had falsified paperwork to show that they'd all been sold to a collector just yesterday, bad luck, chief inspector, sorry you've wasted your time... She turned her attention back to the van pictures, glad to see a visible number plate. "Have you checked into the vehicle yet?"

That was Eddie's cue to look up from his computer, blinking earnestly. "Um, trying to find out more about the owner now, guv," he said. "It's registered to a Vanessa Hills of West Bradford, aged seventy-two, but we're looking at the son-in-law, Michael Miller—he gave her address as his place of residence when he was questioned in connection with an artefact smuggling case about nine years ago. No charges brought, as he only had the one illegal piece in his possession and the investigators couldn't prove intent to sell or that he was aware of its real nature."

An all-too common story; if Pierce had been involved in that past case, it had since vanished into the mental blur of any number of similar investigations over the years, and the name rang no bells. "Anything else on Miller?" she asked.

"Still digging at the minute, guv," he said. "But he runs an internet business buying and selling ritual supplies—I've got an address for their warehouse."

That sounded promising, though they might struggle to get a search warrant on the tenuous connection. Still, an unannounced visit right on the tail of some dodgy business could sometimes fluster people into revealing things they didn't intend. "All right, then," Pierce said. "You try to get hold of Vanessa Hills, see if she can tell us anything about her son-in-law's current whereabouts, and we'll go and have a gander at the warehouse and see what's to be seen. Tell Dawson to let me know if anything new comes in on the vampire case."

Snow could go on about prioritisation all he liked, but if there was one thing she couldn't stand it was sitting idle, rereading the same files over and over and waiting for new information to come in. Forensics might come back with something useful from the murder scene, but until then, they might as well get on with some actual police work.

MILLER'S WAREHOUSE WAS tucked away in an unoccupied corner of a shabby industrial estate. On this grey February morning the whole site was quiet, only a handful of the units in use and the few parked vehicles standing amid seas of empty spaces. They left their own car in front of a carpet shop and approached on foot; sometimes it was useful that two women in business suits didn't register with most people as being police.

And as she and Gemma rounded the corner, Pierce could see their luck was in: whatever Wilkes had told her suppliers last night had clearly convinced them that a hasty clearout of the premises was required. The shutter was up, and a trio of men were loading boxes and equipment into a lorry labelled *Miller Supplies*—and the white van they were looking for was parked right beside it.

A casual passer-by probably wouldn't have spared much curiosity for the tarp-covered crates, but to Pierce's eyes they looked an awful lot like they could have been cages. She heard no obvious sounds of animal distress as the trolley wheels rattled over the rough tarmac, but she doubted the men who'd mass-euthanised the animals back at the barn would fret too much about the health risks of keeping them sedated for transport.

Pierce snapped a few surreptitious shots of the men and vehicles, hoping it would pass for checking something on her phone. That was the van, all right—but they didn't have it directly linked to a crime, only to a rather suspicious late-night visit to Helen Wilkes. Hopefully she could get her suspects to incriminate themselves with a little luck and bluster.

So she put on a smile and the apologetic air of a woman who'd just stopped to ask directions as she approached the lorry, hoping to get a glimpse inside before they cottoned on.

"Hi, excuse me," she said to the heavy-set man who was just jumping down from the rear of the lorry. "Do you work here? I was wondering if you might be able to help me." She tried to steal a glimpse into the back of the lorry, but to her frustration the cages were still covered. "I just had a few questions."

"Can't, sorry, on the clock," he grunted, stepping around her as she blocked his path. "You'll have to speak to someone else."

"All right, no problem." She wheeled about and strode towards the open shutter, prepared to see how far she could get on sheer chutzpah.

Not far, as it turned out; the man grabbed her arm to stop her with unnecessary force, and she winced as his fingers crushed the bruise from last night's bite. "Oi! Private property," he said as he hauled her back.

The gig was up, but Pierce could see that Gemma was busy trying to get a look into the van, so she did her best to distract his attention with her warrant card. "DCI Pierce, Ritual Crime Unit. Is this your warehouse, sir, or are you—?"

That was when one of the other men stepped out from under the shutter with a startled shout: "Oi! Get away from there!" Pierce recognised Michael Miller's shaggy blond hair from the web page Eddie had shown her earlier.

The man who'd grabbed her swung around to follow the cry, and spotted Gemma peering into the windows of the white van. "These bitches are with the police!" he shouted to his friends.

"Charming," Pierce said, but she wasn't going to complain if he wanted to incriminate himself by shouting warnings. "Now, if you don't mind, how about all of you come over here so we can have a nice, civilised chat about the animal sacrifice laws and how they pertain to ritual artefact licensing?"

But it looked like even an uncivilised chat was off the table as Miller clutched at something underneath his shirt, shouting "*Anima!*" A cloud of silver smoke poured out from between his fingers, billowing out to form the ghostly outline of a rearing bull with fiery eyes; the shape lingered in the air for a heartbeat before collapsing in on itself in a cloud of fluttering ashes.

For a moment, she could swear that Miller's eyes glowed fiery red.

And then he charged after Gemma with a new, startling strength, slapping her away from the van with a casual backhand that was almost enough to lift her off her feet. She staggered backwards into the wall of the unit behind her. "Hey!" Pierce barked, yanking her radio out, but the first man grabbed her arm and twisted sharply, wrenching her bad shoulder as he tore it from her hand. "Fuck!" She clutched her shoulder, ducking away from him as he hurled the radio away across the car park.

She darted a glance towards Gemma, cornered by Michael Miller against the wall. She seemed to be just about fast enough to keep dodging his magic-enhanced blows, but one lucky hit would end the whole thing fast. There was no way she'd be able to call for backup herself. Pierce scrambled onto the road after her radio.

As she did, she saw her own attacker yank another of the charms out from under his T-shirt. "*Anima!*" The wooden disc crumbled away to ashes in his hands, the smoky shape of the spirit form pouring out like gas released from a smashed bottle. Despite herself, she was distracted from her goal for a beat to watch it form. Not a bull this time, but something smaller, sleeker, canine. A wolf? A fox?

A greyhound.

She barely had time to take in the implications before the man's eyes flared red. "Shit!" Pierce turned and lunged for the radio, just a few feet away, but the man surged past her, shoving her away. As she reeled backwards, staggering to keep her balance, she heard the lorry engine rumble to life. Miller had made it into the cab, starting the engine without bothering to try to close up the back.

Pierce looked around for Gemma, felt the kick of fear as she saw her down on the ground—but she was already climbing back to her feet, hopefully no more than bruised. As her gaze slipped past Pierce to the warehouse shutter she gasped out urgently, "Guv!"

Pierce followed her gaze to see the third man making a break for it—and cursed as she realised she could smell something burning, the first coils of a less supernatural kind of smoke drifting out from inside. Destroying the evidence just like at the barn. She moved to intercept the runner, but the man with the greyhound charm charged at her from behind, knocking her sprawling with a glancing elbow strike.

She couldn't match his speed or strength, but he had no apparent plans to fight her, leaping past to chase after the departing lorry. It was only just pulling away, big tyres bumping carelessly over the kerb, but it still should have been a struggle for a man on foot to catch up. He made it in two long strides and a leap, landing well inside the back with a metallic clang and turning to yank the doors shut behind him. Gemma scrambled out of the way of the lorry as it swung through a wild turn to escape the cul-de-sac.

The third man, left behind by his escaping colleagues, was now making for the van. Pierce forced herself up from the ground, every muscle protesting the move, and staggered forward at a stumbling wheeze, yanking her silver cuffs out from their pouch.

The man reached the van ahead of her, but he had to slow to tug the door open, and his panicked fumbles gave her the chance to catch up. She slapped one cuff around his wrist, but he wrenched free from her grip and whipped her in the face with her own cuffs. She reeled back with a shout, momentarily blinded by the eye-watering crack across her cheekbone. As the man turned to kick her away, Gemma came rushing up, shoving the van door halfway shut on him before he could get in. Cursing, he scrabbled under his shirt with his free hand for one of the charms.

Before he could activate it, Gemma seized him by the wrist, and between them they turned him around and got the handcuffs on him. "This is police brutality," he said, his face pressed against the side of the van.

"Yeah, yeah. Tell it to the bruises on my bruises," Pierce said, rubbing her cheek. She looked round for the lorry, but it was well away—they'd have to call it in and hope there was someone close enough to catch up before Miller and friend ditched it. The smoke pouring out of the warehouse was already thickening alarmingly, and Pierce had a bad feeling they weren't going to retrieve much more evidence in there than they had from the barn.

But at least they'd made one arrest and confirmed Miller's involvement, so this hadn't been a complete disaster.

CHAPTER SEVENTEEN

THE MAN THAT they'd arrested was younger than the two who'd escaped, and probably fairly low down the totem pole, judging by the ease with which his colleagues had abandoned him. On the plus side, that meant he'd probably have less to lose by spilling his guts to the police.

Unfortunately, he had yet to be persuaded of that, so Pierce had opted to let him sweat for a bit while they did their best to reel the others in without his help. One thing he *had* given them, albeit unwillingly, was the charm pendant that had been taken from him on his arrival at the cells. She'd had it sent up to Cliff in Magical Analysis before going in to attempt to question the prisoner, so she headed up there now to see what he'd made of it.

For once, Cliff had some company in the Artefacts lab, in the form of his young lab assistant Nancy. She usually did the admin work and ran the more routine tests on days when Cliff was out of the office—either it was all hands on deck today, or

Cliff was nervous about the prospect of more evidence going walkabout if he left the lab unattended.

The thought was a sobering reminder of Maitland's invasion of her home last night, and Pierce patted her pocket, making sure she still had the envelope with the evidence he'd left. She was going to have to find some way to process that without going through the police labs—or involving Cliff and Jenny. She didn't want to bring any more trouble to their doors than she had already.

As it was, Cliff was already more twitchy than she was used to from him, jumping at the sound of the door and breaking off his conversation with Nancy. She looked up as well, and gave Pierce a bright smile. "Hiya, boss," she said. "Heard you had a busy night *and* morning."

"I have a busy everything," Pierce said. The week had long since blurred into one vague, headachy morass that didn't feel like it had included much sleep. "Any excitement here?"

"Ah, well, it's a bit early to say," Cliff said. "Standard forensics have just released some of the effects from our vampire cultist, but we've yet to do much in the way of tests." He gestured to the lab table where he and Nancy were standing, scattered with a small assortment of items: an expensive-looking watch with a leather band, a silver ring with a square amethyst stone, and the silver bat necklace, now carefully cleansed of the blood that had been spilled on it last night—human blood was never a wise thing to leave coated on potentially magical jewellery.

"The watch looks pretty ordinary," Nancy volunteered. "It's a nice one, but it's not engraved or anything, and there's no stitching on the band or whatever. It's probably clean."

Cliff nodded along with her assessment. "It's unlikely to have had any sort of enchantment placed on it, though of course we'll test it nonetheless," he said. "The jewellery is a more likely suspect, but I'm afraid it will take a bit of time to process, since we don't know what, if anything, we're looking for."

"Pretty sure the necklace has some kind of significance," Pierce told him. "Not sure if there's any magic to it, though."

It could just be a simple badge of membership, given out to the chosen few in the cult. "What about the charm seized from our arrestee this morning?" she asked, changing tracks.

"Ah, yes, the animal spirit charm." Cliff brightened. Leaving Nancy with the cultist's effects, he moved over to another bench, retrieving the wooden medallion from inside an evidence bag. He held it up in one gloved hand to display the carved design. "I don't know if you had the chance to take a good look at this earlier, but anyway, this rather nice little pictogram of a rabbit—or possibly it's a hare, I must admit my knowledge of zoology is lacking—"

"So there *are* limits to your talents," Pierce said. Nancy grinned in the background.

"Oh, many, sad to say," Cliff said, shaking his head. "But anyway, regardless of whether this *is* a hare or a rabbit, I believe the actual design of the carving is unimportant: purely aesthetic, or perhaps an aide-mémoire. What's important is the enchantment bound into it—perhaps, as Jennifer suggested, with the animal's blood as part of the sacrificial ritual. This ring of runes is, if you will, the magical equivalent of a rope tying back a tree branch: as soon as the ring is broken, the enchantment is loosed."

He turned the medallion over. "Now, this is the part we couldn't see in your earlier photograph, and it's really rather clever." In the centre was another carved sigil, surrounded by wavy lines that radiated out towards the rim. "This here is a perfectly simple little trigger rune, a less destructive baby brother to the one that you set off at the barn. It causes the wood to smoulder away, beginning at the outer edges, and thus destroying the ring of runes that holds the enchantment in check. Hence, you can unleash a powerful pierce of magic that should take hours to perform with just a touch of this rune and a single word."

He smiled, and closed his hand around the disc. "But obviously, we don't want to do that. Since I know how you frown on having evidence go up in smoke."

"We've had enough of that in this case already," Pierce said.

"As you say. So, I propose a slightly less destructive test," he said. "I did some research last night into sacrificial bindings, and I've found a ritual that was used in blood oaths for secret societies. Members would carry the society's sigil, but to prevent falsification, the mark was ritually infused with the bearer's blood. The ceremony itself has, sadly, been lost to the mists of time, but we do have the instructions for the verification ritual to confirm the mark's legitimacy. It should show us whether a blood ritual was used in the crafting of this charm."

"That would be a start," Pierce said. It wouldn't outright prove the blood came from an illegal ritual, but it would certainly support their case, and 'magical analysis confirmed the presence of blood' was the kind of nice, straightforward explanation that you liked to be able to present in a courtroom. "Will it give a clearly visible result?" A colour change that showed up in photographs would go down much better than nebulous waffle about signs they couldn't reproduce.

Cliff shrugged his shoulders. "*That* I'm not too sure about," he admitted. "The source text just said we'll see 'the true sign stand clear of the false.'"

"Helpful," Pierce said with a sigh. Even when they were legitimate, occult texts were all too often a cryptic mishmash of second and third-hand accounts from people too deeply immersed in the subject to recognise what ought to be spelled out. "How much of a faff is the ritual?" she asked.

"Oh, it's relatively straightforward, as these things go. In fact, if Nancy's happy there..."—busy taking notes at the lab table, his assistant gave them an absent thumbs-up—"I was just about to take a stab at it now. You're welcome to watch."

Pierce hung back out of his way as he fished a many-times folded piece of paper from his trouser pocket, flattening it out to reveal cramped pencilled notes. Squinting frequently to consult it, he gathered a miscellany of items from the equipment trolley and the cupboards at the side and began to set things up. It took long enough that Pierce was on the verge of discreetly slipping back out when it seemed he was finally happy with the arrangement.

The equipment he'd gathered together was a mix of the arcane and the pragmatically everyday. A small bronze cauldron with a band of runes around the rim sat atop a foil tray covered by a grille, rather like a disposable barbecue. Instead of charcoal, however, it was filled with a careful arrangement of twigs and leaves taken from bags that were labelled with the types of trees. He'd doused the wood in some kind of oil, with a cloying, vaguely perfumed smell.

The cauldron itself he filled with a measure of blood poured out from a bottle he retrieved from the fridge at the back of the lab. "Pig's blood," he explained, with a sidelong look.

Pierce raised her hands innocently. "Didn't ask."

To that, after another period of squinting intently at his notes, he added pinches of herbs and powders from various canisters, and then another kind of incense oil. Even cold, the mix of scents was nauseating, making the air in the room taste somehow greasy.

Finally Cliff hung the medallion from a clamp stand above the cauldron, and poured a careful ring of salt around the whole arrangement. He stood back, checked his scribbled notes one last time, then dusted his hands and beamed at her expectantly. "Right. Shall we see what we can see?"

Nancy turned round from her worktable and tucked her hands in the pockets of her lab coat to watch the show, either eager to learn or readying herself to duck. Pierce, who'd also had some experience of supposedly harmless divination rituals—especially those involving flames—stood well back, with one hand on the door handle.

Cliff lit a wooden taper with a cigarette lighter, and carefully poked it through the barbecue grill to touch the twigs laid out beneath. It didn't catch immediately, giving him the chance to pull his arm back out of the salt circle and step away to a safe distance before things began.

For several moments nothing seemed to happen. Nancy coughed, and Cliff adjusted his lab goggles. Pierce was about to ask for some hint of what exactly she was waiting for when she realised the herbal smell was growing stronger, and she could hear the faint burble of the cauldron's contents beginning to boil. Fine wisps of pinkish steam the colour of rare steak began to rise from the cauldron's mouth.

The steam thickened and spread, the tendrils coiling back on themselves as they reached the boundary of the salt circle, as if trapped by an invisible glass tube. Droplets of red-tinted condensation began to collect on the metal clamp stand and the medallion suspended from its arm.

Not condensation. At first Pierce thought the gathered droplets were just running down like raindrops on a car window—but then she realising that some of them were flowing *up*, pouring in towards the central carving of the sprinting hare like water swirling into a plughole. The lines of the design were rapidly staining a vivid, bloody red until they looked like wounds cut into flesh—and yet the containment circle of runes that ran round the outside showed no such sign of the phenomenon.

Proof, she guessed, that the enchantment had been made with a blood binding.

Pierce was so intently focused on the medallion that she jumped when Cliff's voice spoke above the sizzling of the cauldron. "Well, that certainly seems to be a positive result." He retrieved a film camera from a cupboard to take shots of the medallion from both sides. "Now, I'm not sure how well these will come out with the steam," he cautioned. "The ritual specifies that the effect fades, but not how quickly, so hopefully it will linger long enough to properly record."

He reached for the handles of the boiling cauldron to lift it away from the fire. As soon as his arm passed over the boundary of the salt circle, the steam flooded outwards in every direction, as if released from a popped bubble. Pierce covered her face with her sleeve, but the steam thinned out as Cliff carried the cauldron away to place on a mat by the lab sink, and she decided she probably didn't need to open the door to vent the room. Just as well—the superintendent wouldn't be pleased if another of Cliff's tests set off the fire alarm.

At least the steam didn't seem to have harmful effects—or so she thought, until Nancy gave a startled squawk from across the room. "Uh, Doctor Healey?" she said urgently. "I think you should look at this."

Pierce turned to look too, and saw that Nancy was standing well back from her own lab bench, where she'd been documenting the items taken from the dead cultist. Apparently the cooling steam from the cauldron had reached far enough to affect them, because droplets were already collecting on the bat necklace, forming faint shapes that Pierce was quite sure hadn't been there before.

Cliff polished his slightly steamed goggles with the sleeve of his lab coat. "Hmm," he said peering closer. "Well, that's interesting. Could you bring that over here, my dear?"

He stepped back over to the lab table and replaced the cauldron on the fire. Nancy followed with the chain of the bat necklace held rather gingerly in her gloved hand, and Cliff hung it from the clamp stand.

In the thick of the full cloud of steam, it took only moments for the lines of a sigil to show up on the belly of the silver bat, vivid slashes across the surface like freshly made cuts. Where the lines of blood had merely soaked into the existing carving on the spirit charm, here they subtly shifted and squirmed on the surface of the silver bat, as if they were watching the same symbol being repeatedly redrawn.

It was a mark Pierce didn't know, made up of two triangles descending from either end of a line—a symbolic set of vampire fangs, no doubt—with the linking line bisected by two curves like a pair of brackets facing away from each other. A simple enough sigil, but then, she doubted it was one that would be found in any existing library of magical runes. No, this was an individual's magical mark, a symbol of power and ownership like the rune Sebastian had worked into his shapeshifting pelts.

It was the mark of the Valentine Vampire—and its presence on the pendant meant that those who wore the sign of his cult shared some kind of magical connection to their leader. That was probably how he'd tracked Jonathan down to their late-night meeting—perhaps even how he'd known he was betrayed. It gave Pierce a slightly queasy feeling to realise that Jonathan might have worn the pendant just so he could prove his bona fides, and in doing so sealed his own doom.

But that wasn't the only implication of this little revelation. A magical connection was always a two-way link. If the cult leader could track his followers through their pendants, then the police could do the same thing.

They had a magical trail that would lead them to the vampire cult. Now all they had to do was figure out how to follow it.

CHAPTER EIGHTEEN

It was an impatient wait for Cliff to declare the bat pendant clear of known curses before they could risk handing it over to Jenny for a tracking ritual. Pierce grabbed a hasty lunch in the canteen and put a call in to Gemma to see how things were going back at the warehouse.

"They've let forensics inside now, but we're taking it slow," Gemma told her. "I want to check for more trigger runes before we move anything."

"Probably sensible." The locals might whine about their forensics people being tied up, but she couldn't spare any more RCU personnel to speed the checks right now.

"They were definitely keeping live animals here, too, guv—there were still a few left inside when they torched the place." Pierce could hear the note of dismay in her voice, and hoped it wasn't going to be too much of an issue; animal cruelty could hit some people harder than good old human-on-human violence, and with the number of rituals that required animal blood or body parts the RCU could be a rough ride for anyone who got too hung up on it. "Most of them probably suffocated from the smoke, poor little guys—at least it looks like they were already sedated."

But Gemma managed to keep any overt distress under wraps as she continued with her briefing. "Erm... it doesn't look like there was much else left for the fire to destroy," she said. "We've did find some woodworking tools that suggest they were manufacturing the charms here, and there's another altar setup like the one back at the barn, except this one's still mostly intact."

"Good. Make sure they get plenty of photographs and test it for blood before anything's disturbed, just in case there's another trigger rune somewhere." Proof of blood rituals would aid their case, but a good lawyer could still argue it was legally obtained animal blood, and with the altar from the barn heavily damaged they might struggle to prove beyond doubt that there was a link between the two scenes.

"Don't let forensics open or unwrap anything, even if it looks like it's free of runes," she added. "Have everything transported to Cliff sealed so he can give it all a proper going over." Gemma was competent and observant, but she was still new in the job, and Cliff knew more than even Pierce did about the many and varied ways objects could be magically booby-trapped. "Let's not lose any more evidence—or lives."

"Right, guv," Gemma said.

"Any word on the lorry?" Pierce asked.

"Found abandoned and torched down a back road about twenty miles away," she said. "No cameras. Uniform are searching the surrounding area, but they can't have got far with the cages, so odds are they switched vehicles."

"Meaning there's at least one more gang member involved," Pierce surmised. Maybe more. She sighed. "All right. Keep me posted."

She hung up and went to poke her head into the Artefacts lab. Only Nancy was still there, tapping away at a laptop. "Are we good to go on the bat hunt?" Pierce asked her.

Nancy blinked at her for a few moments' confusion. "Oh, er... we think so. They went down to the basement lab."

"Right." Pierce let the door fall closed and headed back down the stairs.

Enchanted Artefacts was the only analysis department big enough to have its own lab area for performing magical tests—and as this morning's thankfully happy accident had proved, conducting rituals in close proximity to racks of semi-identified artefacts from other ongoing cases could have some unpredictable results. Rituals other than Cliff's theoretically routine tests took place in the dedicated lab space down in the basement.

In truth, though it might be reserved for ritual use only, the small basement room resembled nothing quite so much as a repurposed holding cell, complete with a sliding observation hatch in the heavy-duty security door. Pierce checked through it to make sure she wasn't about to walk in on anything explosive, then let herself in to join Cliff and Jenny at the lab table.

Unlike Cliff's lab area, which resembled a cross between a school science classroom, an evidence lockup and an eccentric backstreet magic shop, the basement lab was more starkly appointed. A single square table was bolted to the middle of the concrete floor; there were no chairs or lab stools around it that could have been left where they might break the lines of the protective circle etched into the floor. A matching design was painted on the room's ceiling, ensuring any ritual conducted between them stayed totally contained.

In theory. A sufficiently well-designed pattern of concentric circles and protective runes would trap all but the most powerful of summoned spirits and magical effects, but it did nothing to block your common or garden explosions, fires, and projectiles. If a ritual generated enough energy to cause a blast or a small quake, it could potentially damage the containing circle from inside and allow the magic to escape too.

Pierce had presided at enough crime scenes where rituals had gone wrong to know that there was no such thing as safe, only low risk vs. high risk. Unfortunately, most of the rituals that they cobbled together to suit the needs of police work were sufficiently experimental that there was no way to rank them on the risk scale without trying them to find out.

"So what are we doing here?" she asked as she stepped in, letting the door fall closed behind her with a heavy slam.

"Ah, Claire, good," Cliff said with a smile, turning away from the table. "I was just about to come and find you—I thought you'd like to be on hand to witness this."

"Depends if it's going to explode in my face," she said, edging around the etched circle to get a good look at the setup for the divination. The bat pendant now rested at one point of a large triangular design that had been chalked out on the desktop, surrounded by many scribbled runes. A weighty yellow-paged tome rested open on the corner of the table, and Pierce could see a diagram of a similar ritual arrangement annotated with angles and compass orientations.

"In theory, we should be all right with this one," Jenny said, hauling a stack of bags and boxes from the metal cabinets at the rear. "It's always a bit of a crapshoot trying to work a divination on anything that's already enchanted, but since Cliff's pretty confident that at least one of this thing's functions is acting as a type of locator charm for our head vampire to find his cultists, there shouldn't be any negative interaction between the spells—we're basically magicking it to do something it's already designed to do."

"Famous last words," Pierce said.

Jenny lifted her gaze from the book she was consulting to offer her a crooked grin. "If you want certainties, you're in the wrong lab."

"In the wrong bloody career," she said.

"So, it *shouldn't* go messily wrong," Jenny repeated. "Enchantment-wise, we're encouraging water to flow downhill, and unless there are booby-traps Cliff hasn't managed to spot on it, the worst potential problems are either total failure, or succeeding too well. If we pick up all of the cultists and they're widely separated, we're going to have trouble pinning it down to a sensible map scale."

"How are we pinning it down?" Pierce asked.

Jenny opened up one of the carrier bags she'd retrieved from the cabinets to unveil a stack of map books. "With a slightly more sophisticated twist on traditional bibliomancy." She set out a road atlas and arranged a ring of eight incense burners shaped like open-mouthed dragons around it, checking their angles carefully with a compass. "The ritual will show us the right page, and then *this* will help us narrow it down further." She held up a silver ritual knife in its padded box.

"Oh, good, the boss always likes it when you lot start playing with knives," Pierce said.

"Rather a necessary component of the ritual, I'm afraid," Cliff said. "Since we are, in effect, attempting to hack into an existing network of magical links, we maximise our chances of success by using harmonious materials in the ritual. The principles of sympathetic magic: a silver knife to represent silver necklaces, blood to activate the blood binding."

"More pigs dying for our art?" Pierce presumed, but Cliff gave a rather apologetic headshake.

"Unfortunately, in matters such as these, exactitude can be very important," he said. "I really must advise that human blood be used."

Pierce sucked in a breath past her teeth. "Cliff, we've talked about performing human sacrifices in the research labs," she said. But more seriously, there were still plenty of issues with using even a small quantity of donated blood. "I'm not sure we have time to jump through all the legal hoops required before they'll let us do a blood ritual." Even for a serial killer case it would be a hard sell: the only approval she'd heard of since the regs had been tightened up in the 'nineties had been a case down in London involving kidnapped children and a tight time limit.

"We don't need any quantity," Jenny said, raising a finger to correct her. "Just a single drop will do. There's still an exemption for pinprick rituals provided authorisation is granted by a police officer of the rank of DCI or higher."

"In that case, granted," Pierce said. "And you'd probably better grab me a thing to sign before it all goes horribly wrong." She didn't think Superintendent Snow was the sort to be understanding about paperwork being completed after the fact. Especially since she was already being somewhat liberal about his instruction to keep him up-to-date on what they were doing in the Valentine Vampire case. Divination rituals, she was mostly sure, *probably* hadn't been included in his instruction to seek authorisation before doing anything dangerous, if only because he didn't know they ought to be.

She scribbled the appropriate arse-covering explanations on a form while Jenny made the last few tweaks and checks to her ritual arrangement. "Right," Jenny said finally, dusting the chalk from her hands. "We're about as well prepped as we can be—either it's going to work or it isn't."

She lit the ring of incense burners one by one, all with the same match and moving clockwise from the northmost, murmuring soft words Pierce couldn't quite make out. As the various perfumed scents mingled, threatening to make her cough, she felt a faint, impossible breeze stir through the air of the underground room. The match flame bent and flickered as Jenny moved around the circle, and Pierce half held her breath, fearing they'd have to stop and reset everything if the match went out before she'd completed the circuit.

But the flame held, and as she lit the last of the eight, the unnatural breeze stilled—at least, outside of the ring of incense burners. Inside it, Pierce saw the edges of the map book's pages trembling, as if blown by balanced breezes from all sides, none quite strong enough to fully lift the pages and go rifling through the book. The soft susurration of moving air was almost like a song on the cusp of hearing, a distant choral dirge in a language she didn't know.

She was so caught up on that, focused on the dragon burners, that she almost missed it as Jenny lifted the silver dagger from its case. It was overkill for drawing a single drop of blood, and Pierce winced, thinking of all too many ritual scenes gone wrong that she'd attended, but Jenny deftly touched the very point of the blade to the tip of her left ring finger, a tiny bead of red blood welling up.

Then she touched the point of the dagger against the silver bat pendant. The lines of the blood sigil appeared on the bat's belly like a brand, and its eyes, pinprick holes pressed into the silver, glowed a dull red. Pierce instinctively stepped back, as if she might somehow be spotted through those lifeless metal eyes.

She wasn't entirely certain that she couldn't be.

Her gaze was pulled away as the dragon burners all began to hiss as one, a sound more like furious animals than simple steam. White smoke billowed from the gaping mouths of the brass holders, swirling about the circle as if caught in a clash between winds. The pages of the map book rustled, lifted... began to rapidly turn, as if flipped by an impatient hand.

She saw Jenny step forward, the dagger held in her left hand by the lightest of fingertip grips on the pommel. The clouds of smoke whipped around her as the storm inside the circle raged, growing ever faster as she shouted words in Latin above the burners' hissing. As the recitation reached its climax, she raised the point of the dagger's blade towards the ceiling—and without further warning, threw it upwards into the air. Pierce flinched back against the wall unconsciously.

The dagger whipped around in a fast arc in the air, slamming down to stick point-first in the map book. The hissing of the brass dragon burners cut out as abruptly, and everything went still.

The smoke slowly dissipated, and they moved forward to see that the map book had fallen open to a double page spread covering much of West Yorkshire. The blade of the dagger had pierced all the way through the pages and into the wooden desk below, slicing a neat horizontal line through the letters of the word *Leeds*.

"Looks like your killer didn't skip town after last night's murder," Jenny said.

That was good news—but not quite good enough. "How much further can you narrow this down?" Pierce asked.

"Give me the chance for a few repeated iterations of the divination, and I should be able to pin it down to a street, if not house number," Jenny said

Pierce rounded the table towards the door. "Right. You do that. I'm going to get his nibs on board and start things rolling with Leeds police. As soon as you've got us a full address I want to be ready to move in."

After three decades chasing this cult, they finally had a chance to get ahead of the bastards.

CHAPTER NINETEEN

THE SUPERINTENDENT PROVED to be easier to persuade than Pierce had feared: Snow might not have much tolerance for the fuzzy areas of magic-based policing, but he was extremely keen for them to start making some arrests in the Valentine Vampire case, especially after last night's debacle. By the time Jenny had narrowed the location down to within a couple of streets, Leeds' finest and the local Firearms team were already prepping for the raid; by the time she called them back with an exact address, Pierce was already in the car and on her way.

She relayed the information to the head of the Firearms Support team, a man called Jim Clarke that she'd met once or twice but didn't know as well as she'd known Leo, and could only trust would follow her lead if magic became involved. "Get the street blocked off, but don't move until Ritual are there to join you," she directed. "The location could be booby-trapped, magically or otherwise."

"*We'll have bomb disposal standing by,*" he said, not making any direct acknowledgement of her mention of magic but at least not scoffing at it either. Too much scepticism could be as dangerous as panic.

Which was why Pierce had wanted to be on the scene to oversee the operation herself. Dawson had insisted on being there too, despite the fact he'd been on-shift since she'd called him out to the murder scene in the early hours; while she wasn't always thrilled with his bull-headed brand of backup, she couldn't deny that it would be useful to have someone else with the appropriate training along on the raid.

She just hoped it turned something up, because if it didn't, the cult were due to take another victim in a matter of days, and her already limping credibility would go down in smoke.

They needed a win on this one.

The address Jenny's ritual had zeroed in on was not dissimilar to the base back in York, another neglected red brick terrace where the houses were all so closely crammed together it was hard to believe that the neighbours wouldn't know everything that went on. Of course, neighbours had an inconvenient habit of minding their own business just when the police least wanted them to do it.

And of sticking their noses in at times like this. When Pierce arrived to join the entry team in the back of their unmarked van, it was in that brief period of limbo between lunch and the school run where the streets were relatively quiet; even so, this was a broad daylight raid in the middle of a city, and they couldn't afford to hang around.

But they couldn't rush in unprepared, either. "We need to be right behind you when you go in," she insisted to Clarke, a thin man with an equally thin moustache who was being difficult about her and Dawson entering the house before it was pronounced safely clear. "These people are smart, and they enjoy taunting the police. If they've laid traps, they'll be specifically set up to catch our team as they go through the house. Your people don't have the training to know what to look for."

"One little mark painted on the floor, and your brains could be on the ceiling," Dawson added.

"Fine," Clarke conceded with an unhappy scowl. "But Firearms stay in the lead at all times."

"Agreed."

The van they were currently all huddled in was parked outside a small takeaway at the south end of the street. The road was narrow enough that a second van positioned at the other end could effectively block it, and the houses stood back to back with those of the street behind, no rear exits. In theory, if there was anyone inside the house, they were pinned down.

In theory. She exchanged a glance with Dawson, stuffed into protective gear of his own and at least looking like a pretty solid barrier to any suspect trying to get out past him. Pierce was physically the weak link on this operation—but she knew better than anyone what they might be facing inside.

"We'll split the team when we go in," she said. "Dawson goes with the upstairs team, I take downstairs and the basement. Check the rooms from the doorways but *do not* proceed further without RCU okay. We tell you to stop or to retreat, don't argue, just do it. Suspects may be in possession of magical enhancements that give them superhuman strength and speed, likely have access to bladed weapons, and are practised killers."

Not much of a pep talk. Pierce glanced round at the mob of sturdy, sombre-faced officers who crowded the van and tried to think of an appropriately pithy sentiment. "This is a big one, so let's not fuck it up," she said. That was going to have to do.

She gave the nod to Clarke, he barked a few quick commands to his officers, and then the back of the van was thrown open and they poured out into the street, Pierce and Dawson bringing up the rear. As they hustled towards their target at number 7, Pierce had only the briefest instant to take the house in: concreted front yard, bars on the downstairs windows, basement window at ground level covered up by boards. Her pulse rushed in her ears. Was this the place, or just an empty house, a poorly maintained student property?

No time for second guessing: Clarke's people were already at the door. There was no glass pane to give them easy entry, but the wood looked old and battered, half the paint scratched away. One quick check to make sure they weren't about to look like idiots smashing through an unlocked door, and then it was time to pull out what they called 'the big red key'—the Enforcer battering ram.

There were doors out there that could stand up to a few slams with a lump of hardened steel, but this wasn't one of them: the second blow was practically a formality to shove the door open after splintering through it with the first. The Firearms officers poured in to the narrow hallway inside, and Dawson shoved in after them at the first shout of, "Clear!"

"Okay, up the stairs!" Pierce heard him bellow, and hoped it meant he'd scanned the hall, not just blindly charged in; she had to trust him and the rest of the entry team to do their jobs, because she couldn't be everywhere at once.

Footsteps thundered up the stairs, and she heard their shouts echoed on her radio as they slammed into each room upstairs and cleared them one by one. Then she was through the doorway herself, trying to glance in every direction at once. No lights on inside the house, the entry team flashing torches rather than hitting light switches that might have useful prints or even be wired to do worse than turn the lights on.

Pierce shone her own torch quickly about the floor and walls, seeking the threats they wouldn't know to look for: chalk marks, salt lines, any object that might be cursed or hide a trigger rune. She flicked the beam over the doorways, urgency warring with diligence. On her left, the kitchen: tiny, grimy, bare of all but the most basic fittings. On the right, a front room still unfurnished aside from a saggy sofa and a TV standing on a box. Temporary, minimal accommodation.

And there, the dark staircase leading down to the basement. Pierce ran the torch from side to side over the top few stairs: no visible lines or runes, but the light only reached down to the first bend in the staircase—the natural place to lay a trap. The stairs were too narrow for two people to descend side by side: it had to be single file.

"Ma'am, we need to clear down there," said the Firearms man beside her—Turner? Tanner?

There was no way that they'd let her take the lead. "All right, down to the lower level!" she said. "Be alert for markings on the floor or walls—stop moving if you see them." She stuck close behind Tanner as he led the descent, sweeping the torch over the poorly tacked-down carpet ahead of his feet.

The crowd of officers pressing in close behind made her feel claustrophobic, all too aware how messy a rapid retreat would be. The air below ground felt as cold as the grave, and she couldn't tell if the shiver that rippled over her was just the chill and the adrenaline or the subtle tingle of magic in the atmosphere.

Tanner made the bottom of the stairs without any disaster. "Two rooms down here!" he called. There was hardly space to justify the subdivision of the basement. The stairs came down into a small antechamber piled with junk: a clothes horse, an ancient hoover, the empty cardboard box from some large flatpack purchase. All fruit for forensics, but not their concern now; Pierce swung her torch onto the door to the next room, inward opening and left slightly ajar.

No sign of runes: she offered Tanner a terse nod. He shouldered through it, weapon raised, and swung from side to side to scan the space beyond. A moment longer than it should have taken to assess the room, and then, instead of the all-clear: "We've got a coffin." She felt the tension rise in the group behind her.

"Don't approach," Pierce cautioned, though he'd made no move to do so. This had all too many echoes of the previous disaster. "I need to see."

"Could be somebody hiding inside," he cautioned, clearly reluctant to let Pierce get too close as she squeezed in beside him in the doorway. The room beyond was small and mostly bare, a carpet rolled up and standing in the corner beneath the boarded window. There was an eye-watering smell of bleach in the unaired room.

And there, in pride of place in the centre of the floor as if set up to wait for them, stood a wooden coffin.

"I need to check it over before we open it," Pierce said. Would the cult try the same trick twice?

They were just cocky enough that she thought they might.

Tanner didn't look happy to be letting her approach before he'd checked inside it for armed suspects, but he swallowed his objections and kept pace with Pierce. She didn't let the coffin distract her from checking the bare concrete floor, the walls and ceiling, but the bareness of the room was a fairly safe assurance it was clear. Tanner kept his weapon trained on the lid of the closed coffin as she circled round it, matching her steps as if ready to bodily shove her aside the moment the lid moved.

It didn't move. As Pierce held still, it seemed to her that there was no sound inside the room except for her own breathing and Tanner's subtle shifting. The lid of the coffin looked practically airtight as she shone her torch over it. Surely no one alive could be inside?

That still left plenty of unpleasant options on the table.

Tanner tensed as she crouched down beside the coffin, but resisted any urge to yank her back. Pierce played the torch around the edge of the lid, looking for carved symbols or markings on the wood. The coffin was the real thing, as far as she could judge, plain in design but solidly constructed.

No trigger runes on the outside. If there were any inside... well, there was only one way to find out.

But that didn't mean she couldn't take precautions. She unfastened a pocket of her police vest and pulled out a non-standard piece of kit—a canister of salt that she'd picked up from Cliff's lab on her way out. Throwing salt on a trigger rune was a clumsy way of neutralising it if it worked at all—a lot like tossing a glass of water onto a fire—but it might reduce the spread of the enchantment. And frankly it felt better to have some sort of plan beyond crossing her fingers, no matter how unlikely it was to work.

She glanced up at Tanner, debating whether he'd listen if she insisted he move back into the outer room. Probably not—they both had their jobs to do. But at least she could minimise the potential damage. Pierce spoke into her radio. "All non-essential personnel, evacuate the building. We have a potentially booby-trapped coffin in the basement. May bring the place down." But they had to open it here: there was no guarantee that moving it wouldn't set off a trap too.

Tanner stayed beside her, weapon still trained on the coffin lid, but there was a shuffling exodus back up the stairs by the rest of the entry team. She listened out for all the check-ins on the radio, hearing Dawson's voice among them. The smell of bleach fumes seemed to be getting stronger, and she resisted the urge to scrub her eyes and cough.

Everybody clear now except for her and Tanner. Pierce flicked a glance at him. "Any last words?"

"I'll be pissed off if this kills me," he said.

"Fair enough." She breathed in slowly and touched her radio again. "All right. Opening coffin." She closed her eyes a moment, silently counting down from three before she eased the coffin lid up by just a few a millimetres.

No explosion—yet. Still tense, she shone the torch along the line of the narrow crack created. No visible markings along the wooden rim or the underside of the lid. Looked like it was clear of trigger runes.

But it wasn't empty: even from the small crack that she'd opened, the unmistakable stench of death and decay wafted out, overpowering the smell of the bleach. She swallowed, gripping the open canister of salt just in case she was wrong about the runes, and then in one sharp movement threw the coffin lid open.

As it clattered onto the bare concrete on the other side, she jerked, halfway through throwing the salt before she registered she didn't need to; Tanner made an abortive sound as he started to shout a warning to the pale-faced figure inside—and then realised he was beyond hearing it. The naked, pallid young man clearly wasn't going anywhere.

"Shit," Pierce said, with feeling. They'd found the cult's base all right—but they'd also found the second victim.

They were too late.

CHAPTER TWENTY

MUCH LATER, WHEN preliminary reports had been made, the house given over to forensics and the as-yet unidentified body sent off for examination, Pierce caught up with Dawson where he was taking a smoke behind one of the police vans.

"We've got them on the ropes," he said with far more confidence than she felt, cupping his lighter to shield the flame from the wind. "This is a break in the pattern. They weren't ready for us to find this body."

"*We* weren't ready for us to find this body," Pierce said. "It's only been four days since Harrison's body was dumped. The earlier killings were more widely spaced than this." There should have been more *time*.

"They're panicking," Dawson said. "Accelerating the schedule because they're scared that we're onto them. And panicking murderers make mistakes."

She grimaced. "Wouldn't hurt if they made a few bigger ones. They might not have had the chance to stage the body in their usual style, but they still managed to clear out before we got here. According to Jenny the tracking spell isn't working anymore, so they obviously had some way of detecting what we were doing."

"And it rattled them," he said. "Must've cleared out pretty bloody sharpish. They're running scared now."

Baseless bravado, in her view, but she wouldn't have minded a shot of it; it was hard to stay optimistic when the cult evaded their efforts at every turn.

But at least, now that she'd done all that she could here, she had her chance to pursue a quarry who *had* left some evidence behind. Pierce patted her pocket, reassuring herself that the hair she'd taken from Maitland's chair last night was still there. As she returned to her car she took a casual look around, but she didn't spot any obvious signs of surveillance; hopefully his people were smart enough not to lurk around the fringes of a major police operation where they'd attract all the wrong kinds of attention.

And that meant now was her best time to act.

The only trouble was, she couldn't do it alone. She needed someone to perform a tracking ritual for her—and with the usual police channels out, her options were thin on the ground. She didn't want to drag Cliff and Jenny any further into this mess than she had already; they hadn't signed up for this.

But there was someone else she'd already involved: someone who had as much motive as she did to want to see the conspiracy surrounding Sebastian's death exposed, and might just have some contacts of his own they could call on.

She started the car and headed for Leo's.

PIERCE HADN'T RISKED calling ahead, almost certain that Maitland would have some way to listen in on phone communications, but she managed to catch Leo at home nonetheless; she got the impression he didn't get out much these days. He was a perfectionist, the sort of man to have hands-on, manual hobbies, and she doubted he'd get much pleasure out of struggling through things he'd once found easy.

It was hard to decide if it made her feel better or worse about calling on his aid that he was so transparently eager to assist, despite—or maybe because of—her warnings of the dangers. You didn't work in Firearms because you liked a risk-free life.

"I might know somebody," he told her. "Probably too small-time for the RCU's attention, but she's got a good rep for finding lost property and missing pets, and she helped a friend of my wife's track down her ex."

"Where is your wife, by the way?" Pierce asked, guilty conscience in full swing. Unlike her, Leo had a family to think of.

Though it seemed right now he was comfortable with not thinking too deeply. "Late shift," he said. "If my contact can fit us in tonight, we can be out and back before she knows I was gone. I can tell her it's confidential consultation work, but the less anybody knows, the better."

"Yeah," she said dubiously. It was probably true, but it still felt shady. This kind of sneaking about had never been her nature.

Leo, by contrast, seemed positively cheerful as they headed out to meet his contact. It seemed to bring a subtle new alertness to his features to have a mission to concentrate on, that intensity of purpose she remembered from field operations in the past.

The address that he supplied brought them to an ordinary-looking house in the suburbs, where the door was opened by a harassed-looking man in a rugby shirt clutching a toddler. He offered them a polite smile. "Ah, hello—you must be Kate's seven o'clock." He did his best to nudge a plastic trike out of the way of the door with his foot. "Um, do come right in. She should be with you in a minute."

He guided them past a living room where two older kids were watching something noisy on the telly and into the kitchen, a small space rendered more cramped by a slightly too-large table and the high chair in the corner.

"All right, just take a seat," he said, pulling one of the chairs out and removing a stuffed dinosaur from it. "Let me get all this out of your way..." He gathered up letters and piled newspapers from the table one-handed while the toddler against his hip squirmed and made increasingly urgent noises around his dummy.

"Sorry to show up at such short notice," Pierce said, itching to assist him, but afraid she'd only bring the whole precarious process crashing down.

"Oh, the place is always like this, I'm afraid," he said with a rueful grin. He bumped his way backwards out of the kitchen door with the papers held against his chest. "I'll just go and get Kate for you now."

Pierce breathed out as the door bumped closed behind him. Houses full of kids had never been her scene; one of many reasons she didn't visit her sister more than she could help it. She caught Leo massaging his bad leg under the table as the two of them sat in awkward silence; she wanted to ask if it was all right after their visit to the prison, but didn't think he'd appreciate her drawing attention to it.

Before the wait could stretch too long, the kitchen door opened again to admit a plump woman with crimped blonde hair and a chunky orange jumper. "Oh, hi!" she said brightly. "You must be Rose's husband—it's Leo, right?—and this is...?" She looked at Pierce expectantly.

"Claire," Pierce supplied, not wanting to give her police affiliation away if her fame didn't precede her. She'd been interviewed on the news more than a few times, but she doubted most people paid attention to the face, only the story.

"Claire," the woman repeated with a friendly nod, and clasped her hands together. "Well, I'm Kate Winston, and this, if you squint very hard and apply a bit of imagination, is my office, so what can I do for you?" She pulled out a chair to join them at the table. "I understand you've got somebody that needs tracking down?"

"Yes." Pierce decided they were better off giving minimal details. She retrieved the envelope with the hair that she'd collected. "I think this is one of his hairs, though it might be from his clothes."

Kate raised her eyebrows, but asked no awkward questions.

"Well, unless your friend's a nudist, let's assume his clothes are somewhere near where he is, eh?" she said, grinning. "All right—hair's always a good place to start. Is he a blood relative of either of yours?" They both shook their heads. "Pity, that would have made it easier." She clapped her hands together with a smile. "But nonetheless, we shall make do. Back in a jiffy."

She nipped into the next room, and returned carrying what looked like a fabric-covered needlework box; she opened it up to reveal a collection of miscellaneous odds and sods that Pierce wasn't sure she'd have taken for a magic kit without having been told.

Kate rooted around in the bottom of the box for a while before coming up with an acorn-shaped wooden pendulum on a length of knotted string, which she polished on the bottom of her jumper for a moment. "This was my grandmother's," she said, unscrewing the top to reveal a small chamber inside. "She taught me the art of pendulum divining, just as she learned it from her mother before her. Who apparently learned it from a slightly dodgy bloke named Bob she beat at cards, but still, it's more or less a family tradition." She grinned briefly, and held out a hand. "If I could have the focus?"

Pierce handed over the envelope with the hair somewhat reluctantly, wondering if this had been a big mistake. Kate used a pair of tweezers from her ritual kit to transfer the hair to the pendulum chamber and then screwed it shut. She let a foot or so of string play out and held the pendulum suspended over the table for a moment, frowning thoughtfully. "Hmm, yes, that feels like it's got enough magical resonance... We should be able to get a good reading from that."

Pierce tried not to let her scepticism show as Kate delved into the box again and pulled out first a sheet of cloth embroidered with sigils that she laid out like a tablecloth, and then an elastic-banded deck of what appeared to be children's alphabet flashcards, complete with brightly coloured pictures of things like apples, balls and cakes.

Either she wasn't very successful at containing her reaction, or Kate anticipated it: "Trust me," she said, as she shuffled the deck of letter cards in her hands. "These things are just as good for divination as any set of ancient rune stones they try to sell you for six hundred quid on eBay." She dealt them all out face down on the tabletop as if planning to play a memory matching game, set out a few crystals and other vaguely occultish knick-knacks at points around the arrangement, then took up the pendulum again. "All right. Do we have a name for this gentleman we're looking for?"

Pierce hesitated, reluctant to give too much away, although nothing about this display was doing much to convince her this woman was in the pay of a dangerous conspiracy. She glanced over at Leo, but he was obviously prepared to follow her lead.

Oh, well: better to make a bad move attempting to achieve something than fail through timidity. "Maitland," she said. "Jason Maitland. Or at least, that's the name he gave. I'm not sure if it's his real one."

Fortunately, Kate didn't question what kind of business they might be mixed up in that involved possible false names; maybe she was used to it, if her jobs often involved tracking down wayward spouses. "Doesn't matter if it is," she said. "What does real even mean, when we talk about names? A thing is what we call it. If he's gone by that name, if people know him by it, then he's linked to it. Now, if he doesn't use it very much, it'll be a less powerful link than a name he goes by every day... but every little helps."

She began to twirl the pendulum in slow circles without further ceremony. "Right. Maitland, Jason Maitland..." she murmured to herself. "Where might you be?" She adopted a sing-song tone. "*Pendulum, swing your line, give us now some form of sign, seek the truth, circle round, tell us where what's lost is found...*"

Playground doggerel, to Pierce's cynical ears, but she kept her mouth shut as Kate continued to chant in a low murmur, eyelids falling closed. She moved the pendulum in slow, swaying circuits over the cards, passing over each in turn—until, above one of them, the pendulum gave a sharp jerk upwards as if the string had been abruptly yanked. Despite herself, Pierce leaned forward a little as Kate turned the card over to reveal a letter H, accompanied by a cheery little illustration of a hippo.

More passes, another jump of the pendulum and upturned card: A for apple. R for rainbow... Kate picked out five more cards by the same method before she made a final circuit with no visible twitch from the pendulum and set it aside with a sigh of released tension.

"Hardison." Leo tried the sequence out aloud. Too neat and logical a collection of letters to be mere random chance, but it could still be done with a stacked deck or subtly marked cards: not even necessarily malicious or deliberate fraud, but a subconscious twitch towards a letter that 'felt' like it ought to go next. Like eyewitness testimony, simple divinations all too often fell prey to the human mind's tendency to prefer a good narrative to provable facts.

"Does that mean anything to you?" Kate asked the pair of them expectantly, but didn't look terribly troubled when they both shook their heads. "Well, never mind, that's only the first stage of the divination. It might be the name of the house owner, of a business, perhaps from some kind of sign or billboard nearby..." This was starting to sound like the deliberate vagueness of cold-reading to Pierce's mind. "Now we find the distance."

The second divination involved tossing a number of carved wooden sticks and consulting a little book to translate the pattern, giving a distance of forty-eight miles, a result Pierce found even more dubious than the first. The finale that followed turned out to involve setting up a ring of candles. Specifically, tiny pink-and-white-striped birthday candles.

"Trust me, these are great for doing rituals," Kate confided. "They don't go out by themselves, and they don't set off the smoke alarm."

Apparently the RCU's research specialists were missing a few tricks.

Kate laid a compass in the centre of the circle and set a collection of semi-precious stones around it in a star-shaped pattern mimicking the compass rose. She began to move the pendulum slowly from point to point, murmuring more simple rhymes. "*North to east to south to west, seek the object of our quest; west to south to east to north, show us which way to go forth...*" She spun the pendulum through an ever-quickening sequence until one of the candles around the ring abruptly puffed out, then another, then a third...

When only one lit candle was still left standing, Kate grinned and raised an arm to point in its direction. "All righty, then. If my readings don't deceive me, your man is thataway." She pushed the seat back and stood up. "Let me just grab you a map."

Fifteen minutes later and they were back out on the road with a vaguely pinpointed region of the map and the name Hardison to guide them. They drove in relative silence, Pierce uncertain whether her professional opinion of that display—she'd pin it down as somewhere around 'well-meaning but dubiously useful'—was even worth offering. It was a long shot, but they weren't wasting any police resources checking it out, and it seemed pointlessly harsh to puncture Leo's renewed sense of purpose with a reality check on facts he had to be aware of already.

Full dark had settled in by now, and once they left the A roads for narrow country lanes it became a rare event to pass another car. The only illumination aside from their own headlights came from the windows of the odd tiny village or isolated farmhouse.

Pierce was all too conscious of the futility of their search. They weren't here with the full might of the police behind them, going door to door to ask questions of the neighbours with a squad of uniforms and authority on their side. There were two of them, one with a bad knee and the other running on too little sleep, following a lead too vague to give them any hope of spotting Maitland even if they parked outside his home address. What were they going to do, hope he looked out of a window at the right moment?

But conceding defeat had never come easily to her, so she continued to drive almost aimlessly, turning down each awkward little country lane and hoping something other than suicidal wildlife might jump out at them.

It was Leo who finally spotted something, stiffening as Pierce slowed for what she thought was a turning but then realised was just a private road. "That looked like a security fence," he said. She started to slow down again, but he shook his head. "No, keep going. You can park behind those trees over there— if this is the place, we're better off cutting across the fields on foot than driving right up to the gates."

Once Pierce shut the headlights off, she could hardly see a thing; what little moonlight was on offer scarcely filtered through the cloud cover and trees. "What did you see?" she asked Leo.

"Not sure, but it looked pretty high-security," he said. "Military, maybe, or a prison."

"If they've built one around here, nobody sent me the memo." Of course, it could just be some kind of business site, but the isolation and security pointed to something potentially interesting. Pierce still had her warrant card in her pocket; if they were wildly off-base and got stopped by some form of site security, it wouldn't strictly be a lie to say they were looking for suspicious persons—though it could definitely get sticky if anybody followed it up far enough to speak with her superiors.

All in all, probably better to avoid getting caught.

They rounded the stand of trees and clambered over the low wall that bounded the fields. She heard Leo give a faint grunt as he dropped down on the other side. "You okay?" she asked. She could just about make out the motion of his nod.

In spite of his bad leg, Leo moved into the lead, ingrained habit from his days in Firearms. As her night vision adjusted to the limited moonlight, Pierce could make out enough to tell that he was limping quite badly, but she kept her mouth shut.

They picked their way across the damp grass, heading back towards the private access road that they'd passed by. Pierce could see a faint glow in the distance ahead: security lights around the top of a high metal fence. Leo was right; the setup resembled the enhanced offenders institution that they'd visited a few days ago.

In more than one way. As they drew a little closer—Leo moving at a low crouch now despite the fact it clearly pained him to do so, and Pierce doing her best to mimic him—she could see that there were dogs roaming the inside of the fence. Big dogs: the kind that could very easily be shapeshifters.

Big dogs that could probably sniff out wandering strangers if they drew too near. Leo nudged her shoulder, veering sideways across the field towards the road instead of getting any closer to the building. He nodded at a small, discreet sign up by the gates, and she squinted at it, struggling to make out the block letters in the dark.

HARDISON GROUP. No more explanation of the business or its purpose than that, a conveniently meaningless name that could hide all manner of sins.

But a name that confirmed this was the place. They'd found Maitland's current base of operations.

Problem was, with that fence and the shifters on patrol, they didn't have a hope in hell of finding a way inside.

CHAPTER TWENTY-ONE

THEY MADE IT back to their car apparently unseen, and drove on before they could push their luck too far.

"If that's where they're keeping Sebastian, we're going to have a job getting inside to prove it," Pierce said. It would take a full-scale police raid, and even if she could somehow justify it to her superiors, Maitland's people would surely know about it well before it happened. Hell, for all she knew her superintendent was one of them.

"We'll find a way in," Leo said. It felt more like a declaration than a prediction, but she didn't challenge him. Lord knew one of them should probably keep some optimism.

As for her... she was just tired. She'd made it home, shovelled her way mechanically through a microwave dinner, and was seriously contemplating taking an early night when her phone rang. She was tempted to ignore it, but when she checked the ID it was Phil Havers calling her back. She lifted it to her ear with a sigh.

"Phil!" She did her best to keep her exhaustion from her voice. "Anything on those animal spirit charms?"

"Nothing in my notes, I'm afraid, but I made a few calls to my old contacts up in your neck of the woods, and I've found someone who thinks he might have had your sellers sniffing around. Adrian Shore: he's an artefact dealer in Huddersfield, fairly well-known in the biz—you've probably heard of him, though he keeps his nose too clean to get much police attention."

"Rings a vague bell," Pierce agreed. Odds were Phil had met the man back when he still worked for her, but she couldn't dredge up any details this many years later.

"Well, he had some people make him an offer the other day he thought was suspect—he said they seemed pretty eager to offload a set of antique charms, then got shirty and started talking about having other buyers waiting when he wanted additional expert verification. He's a cautious bugger, our Adrian, though, so he didn't bite."

"Sensible of him," Pierce said. "But we might need him to take a nibble on it after all. We've made one arrest, but so far the bloke's not talking, and we know there are at least two or three other gang members still out there. If we can get them to bring the illegal charms to an agreed meeting point, then we might be able to nab them all in one go." She wandered through the house in search of a notepad and pen. "Right. Got a contact number for Shore?"

Phil gave her the relevant info, and she updated him on the progress of the case so far. "Sounds like you're close to sewing it up," he said. "How goes the vampire hunt? Saw your DI on TV earlier—he sounded pretty confident."

"Oh, bloody hell, again?" Pierce winced. "The man needs a muzzle. No, it's going... well, let's just say it's going." She felt like she was chasing one of those lizards that just shed its tail and scampered off when you thought you'd finally caught it. And with the apparent acceleration of the time scale, they had even less time to get their acts together before the cult committed their third kill and went to ground for seven years again.

Or for fourteen. Pierce pressed her lips together. That missing interval still didn't sit right with her. Oh, Christopher Tomb could talk all the guff he wanted about vampire hibernation phases, but she was certain they were looking for human beings performing a ritual—and rituals generally required slavish adherence to their patterns to build power. She sat back in her armchair, resting her feet on the footstool.

"Hey, Phil, when was it you transferred down to Oxford? About the end of 2007, wasn't it?"

"Thereabouts," he said. "Yes, it must have been, because remember they were shortstaffed after that business with the goat demon at Hallowe'en."

"Yeah." Pierce cringed a little, guiltily glad that one hadn't happened on her patch. "God. Poor old Henry."

"Hell of a way to go," Phil agreed with a rueful sigh. "Sammy Sykes was never the same, either—he did stay on for a few months to oversee the transition, but you could tell his heart wasn't in it. Not that I blame him."

"No." For a few moments they were both silent, aware of the weight of all the colleagues they'd lost over the years to injury, burnout or worse. The longer you spent in this game, the more the numbers mounted.

Then Phil cleared his throat and audibly pulled himself back together. "Anyway, um, why'd you ask?" he said.

"Well, I was just thinking, it must have been about the time the last set of Valentine Vampire killings was due, the one that never materialised." She distinctly remembered arguing with Superintendent Palmer over whether they could really spare personnel to relieve Oxford with more murders on the horizon, and why London branch couldn't do their bloody bit for once. "Since our killer cult is back in action, I have to wonder if they ever really went to ground at all. Maybe there *were* murders back in 2008, and we just failed to connect them to the pattern."

If the cult were willing to change up their methods now to keep the heat off, then maybe they'd done it before. Leaving the bodies staged in graveyards was just grandstanding, not a necessary part of the bloodletting ritual: perhaps having been spotted dumping one of the bodies had encouraged them to play safe for a while.

Phil was clearly following her line of thought. "You think they might have crossed the border into Oxford's jurisdiction?"

"It's possible," she said. "Oxford was still in a complete muddle at the time, with the whole goat demon business and the change in personnel—if the cult struck much further south than their usual hunting grounds and changed up their MO for disposing of the bodies, then the RCU might not have linked the deaths to the Valentine Vampire case. They might not even have reached our attention at all." If the bodies had been burned or allowed to decay undisturbed long enough to hide the signs of ritual cuts, they'd most likely have been pursued as normal homicides.

"I can have a poke about," Phil said. "See if there are any unsolved murders or missing persons from the time that fit the victim profile."

"Please," Pierce said with a sigh. "At this stage, we still need all the help we can get."

AT LEAST DEEPAN was back at work again the next day, although she was still dubious about allowing him to do more than man the computers. "I'm fine, guv," he insisted. "Totally recovered."

"Yeah, well, you can sit there and be fine at a desk for a while," Pierce said. "What's the latest from our scene in Leeds?"

Frustratingly little, as it transpired. The young man from the coffin was still unidentified as yet: Leeds were looking into university students who'd failed to attend lectures, but that was a tough group to narrow, and it probably wouldn't tell them anything when they did have a name. The house where he'd been found had been rented out as student accommodation on a slightly dodgy cash basis from a landlord who'd apparently seen nothing, making that another dead end.

Forensics had found a few prints, but none of them had come up with matches so far, and Pierce had a feeling they wouldn't: the people behind ritual killings like this were rarely the sort of repeat offenders who were in and out of the system. These murders weren't acts of vengeance or aggression or even cold-blooded attacks on enemies—they were just the means to an end, the dispassionate slaughter of human beings to provide fuel for a magical ritual.

And the killers were getting away with it, far too well for her liking. Until they had an actual suspect to compare those prints to, it was looking less and less likely that the house in Leeds would yield anything useful.

Pierce let Dawson keep the job of overseeing the investigation, and turned her attention instead to the lead Phil had given her on the spirit charms case. She called up Adrian Shore, who turned out to have a nasal voice and a rather jittery telephone manner, or else he was just rather nervous about speaking to the police. He was definitely eager to protest his innocence, though she hadn't called it into question.

"Well, obviously, um, I didn't recognise the gentleman—that is, I wouldn't normally deal with anyone offering such flimsy provenance for articles of a potentially, um, restricted nature, and if they knew my reputation for honest dealings I'm sure they would never have approached me..."

Pierce cut through the stream of nervous self-justification. "We appreciate that, Mr Shore. You're not under any suspicion—these people know their operation has come to the attention of the police, and they're undoubtedly keen to offload the merchandise any way they can." God bless criminal greed, the force behind many an idiot decision to hold onto incriminating evidence rather than lose money by destroying it. "The fact they're desperate enough to start approaching honest dealers like yourself is actually good news for us, because it means that with your assistance we can catch them red-handed."

Shore didn't seem enormously thrilled at the opportunity. "Oh, er, well... obviously I support the police completely in, er, in bringing an end to these barbaric magical practices, but I'm not really sure how much assistance I can actually be..." He trailed off with the vagueness of a man hoping someone else would politely supply his excuses for him.

Unfortunately for him, Pierce was quite happy to bulldoze through social niceties. "You really wouldn't have to do very much at all, sir," she pressed. "There'll be plenty of police on hand to deal with everything—all we need is for you to let them know you might be interested in buying and get them to bring the merchandise to your shop so we can arrest them and seize it."

Odds were Miller and co. would be hoping to sell off their whole stock of charms in one go, and bring the entire gang along to escort them. It would be a chance to arrest the ringleaders and get their goods off the street all in one tidy scoop.

If Shore played ball. She couldn't compel a member of the public to assist an operation with anything more than persuasive arguments and a bit of emotional blackmail, and emphasizing the fact that these weren't just dodgy dealers but dangerous men who ought to be locked up seemed likely to be more counterproductive than anything.

Shore was already squirming as it was. "Well, I, um, I'm afraid I was really rather emphatic in rejecting their offer before"—Pierce found that hard to believe, considering how wishy-washy he was being in dealing with hers—"so I'm not sure that they would believe such a fast turnaround..."

As the shopkeeper *ummed* and *erred*, Pierce was more than half expecting him to wriggle free with belated claims he had no way to reestablish contact, but either he was made of sterner stuff than she'd given him credit for, or the prospect of lying to the police unnerved him even more than assisting them with a sting operation. "Well, er, I suppose I could attempt to set up a meeting..." he eventually said weakly.

Pierce pounced before he could back out again, and then it was all over bar the practical arrangements

* * *

THE OPERATION TO arrest Miller's gang was a much smaller-scale affair than the previous day's raid; they'd have a pair of Firearms Support officers standing by to assist the uniforms, but armed only with Tasers this time—with luck, the gang had already burned through the most dangerous of the spirit charms they had to hand and even that level of force wouldn't be necessary. Pierce was hoping a simple show they were surrounded would be enough to make them come in quietly.

They certainly seemed to have realised they were in a tight spot, setting up a meeting with Shore within a matter of hours; she had to scramble to get the op organised and her team in position before Miller's gang arrived to scope the place out themselves.

The shop, dubbed *A. A. SHORE—OCCULT BOOKS AND CURIOSITIES*, occupied a yellow-brick Victorian building, the ground floor fully converted but the upper still retaining some rather nice arched windows. Of slightly more use to the police was the larger archway leading through to the yard behind, these days a private car park closed off by a metal gate. They tucked the garishly marked Armed Response Vehicle and its occupants behind it out of sight, where Gemma Freeman and half of the arrest team would also lie in wait. Pierce and the rest of them would be upstairs. All Shore had to do was meet with Miller's men for long enough to confirm they had the goods, and then excuse himself upstairs to let the police take over.

A simple plan, which limited the number of things that could go wrong, if not how quickly and easily they could do so. Miller might be paranoid enough to have had eyes on the street hours early and spotted the police moving in, or Pierce might have overestimated the gang's urgency and they'd only send a lackey with one sample charm. Or—and this was currently her biggest worry—Shore might panic and throw the whole plan off.

In person, he didn't quite match the image that she'd formed over the phone. Pierce would have pictured small and twitchy, possibly with a bowtie: in fact, he was quite a big man with broad shoulders and a mane of greying curls, and a firm if slightly clammy handshake, which might have been just nerves. She'd also been wrong about the bowtie, though he did have a gold waistcoat.

"Just go about your business as normal," she advised him, as he joined them upstairs for the fourth or fifth time and peered nervously out of the windows. "They may send someone in to check the shop is clear before they approach you, so you don't want to arouse suspicion by disappearing up here all the time."

Shore nodded, swallowing convulsively. "Yes, of course, you're right, um, I'll just..." He looked around the box-filled stockroom blankly for a moment, hands twitching spasmodically as if seeking something useful to grasp, before shaking himself and heading back downstairs.

The sergeant corralling the team of uniforms that she'd been loaned, a solidly-built bloke called Smithy with a face that looked like it had been through some rugby matches, appeared distinctly dubious. "You can practically hear that bloke's knicker elastic twanging," he said. "We'll be lucky if he doesn't blow the whole thing before we even get down the stairs."

Pierce wasn't much happier, but as officer in charge she probably shouldn't outwardly agree it might go tits up. "We're not asking him to recite the works of Shakespeare," she reminded them. "All he's got to do is answer the door and ask them to show him the goods. They're probably expecting him to be nervous." An obvious first-time buyer of illegal goods from hardened criminals had legitimate call to be jittery.

Too legitimate for her liking. Sweating in the stuffy air of the stockroom, she mentally crossed her fingers that 'tits up,' should it occur, wouldn't put Adrian Shore in the way of any of that harm she'd assured him he wouldn't be in.

That was the trouble with the interminable wait before a bust went down—nothing to do but go over the plan and air all those second thoughts.

Until time abruptly ran out.

Gemma's voice, amid a crackle of static on the radio: "*White van approaching now, guv. I think it's them.*"

"All right." The tension tightened in her stomach. "Stay out of sight until I give the word." She released the radio and nodded to Smithy, resisting the strong but stupid urge to move to the window to look out for herself. An unexpected shadow at the window when Shore was supposed to be alone could definitely scare Miller off.

Smithy gestured to his team to take up their positions at the top of the stairs. Today Pierce would be bringing up the rear; she'd only get in the way of the strapping young constables, unless Miller's crew pulled out some extra magic beyond the charms they'd already been briefed about. Her main role outside of advisory was just going to be making sure the shopkeeper stayed out of the firing line if things turned nasty after all.

"Right," Smithy said to his team, "get your tutus on, girls, because it looks like it's showtime. From now on it's silent running—keep your lips zipped, don't knock stuff down, and try not to fart. And yes, I do mean you, Kev." Grins all round, but they settled into obedient silence, listening, waiting.

For an eternity, nothing happened. Then, finally, the jangle of the bell above the shop door, almost making her jump. Pierce tried to make sense of the footsteps: two men, maybe three? Good. Hopefully the whole of the gang was here.

She didn't think Shore was quite so happy to have them show up in force; she winced at the thin, reedy quality of his voice as she strained to hear the group talking downstairs. "Er, hello, um, are you here about the, er, sale items we discussed on the phone?"

He didn't just sound jumpy; worse, he sounded forced, talking overly loudly like an actor trying to project his voice to the back rows of the theatre. But he only had to hold it together through a few more words of the script... She gritted her teeth. *Take the bait, take the bait...* All they needed was confirmation that Miller's crew had the goods on them.

"Got the money?" a lower, rougher voice demanded bluntly. Was it the man with the greyhound charm from outside the warehouse? She couldn't be sure without getting a look at him.

"Er, yes, of course. In cash, as—as you requested, very, um, understandable. But I need... that is, I must ask to, um, see the merchandise before... You have it with you? I must insist, um..."

In his nervous babble he was over-egging it. Fuck. Even without having eyes downstairs, Pierce was sure she sensed a shift in the mood of the room below, and judging by Sergeant Smithy's sudden tension he could feel it too. Things were teetering on the edge of going bad, but all they needed was one word of confirmation...

Instead, there was a thick, dangerous silence as Shore's voice trailed off, and then a sharply unhappy curse from the man who'd asked about the money. "This stupid fucker's wearing a wire or something," he said. "Let's get out of here."

"No! I, um, I..." Shore spluttered, but Pierce didn't wait to hear if he could somehow talk them round again. Smithy was already on his way down the stairs, jerking an arm at his team to follow, and Pierce grabbed for her radio as she hurried after them.

"Romeo Charlie Bravo team, move in, move in!"

For better or worse, it was showtime.

CHAPTER TWENTY-TWO

"Shit, there's police in here!" somebody shouted downstairs, and Pierce heard them scramble for the door as she thundered down the shop stairs on the tail of four younger, fitter officers.

"Police!" Sergeant Smithy shouted at the head of the pack. "Everybody stay where you are. You! Put that down on the ground and back away from it." There was the splintering crash and attendant clatter of some heavy piece of furniture being shoved over in the shop, and somebody swore.

Pierce was caught in a logjam at the foot of the stairs when a hoarse voice shouted, "*Anima!*" She cursed and grasped at her radio again as a brief flare of silver-white light cast its glow through the doorway.

"Charms are live!" she barked into the radio. "Get the Taser team in here!" The second prong of their trap wasn't in position yet, and this could get ugly fast.

"Upstairs!" Smithy ordered, and a panicked looking Adrian Shore was manhandled into Pierce's space. She squeezed back against the wall to shove him up the staircase past her.

"Just stay upstairs. We've got this under control." Blatant lies, but the truth wouldn't do much to calm him, and Miller's gang were surely focused on escape rather than vengeance for the setup—provided he stayed well out of the way.

"My stock..." Shore said rather plaintively over his shoulder as another, more glassy crash sounded amid the scuffling beyond.

"It'll be covered—go!" She'd do her best to see that someone paid the poor sod's damages after she'd put him in this situation, but that couldn't be her main concern right now.

As she broke through into the main room of the shop, she saw that Smithy and two others of his team were all wrestling with one man, and not successfully: Pierce recognised the burly bloke she'd clashed with at the warehouse as he hurled one of the constables aside to crash painfully against a rack of coat hooks. She was betting he was the one who'd set off the spirit charm.

"You all right, Jordan?" Smithy called after the swearing PC. Even as the young man nodded, gasping, the suspect seized his chance to make a break for it, elbowing Smithy in the stomach. The sergeant doubled over with a groan, but just about managed to keep his grip, and Pierce decided that scene was semi-under-control. She looked round for the other gang members.

The fourth PC from her team was facing off against a new face to her, short, dark and skinny. Looked like the constable had him in hand, one cuff already snapped around his wrist and a restraining grip on his free arm to make sure he couldn't reach the medallion round his neck. Good. She cast about for Miller.

He was backing away into the rear of the shop with his arms wrapped around a wooden box about the size of a briefcase. No second exit that way, but Pierce still moved after him, wary of a bid to destroy the evidence. "Put the box down on the ground and step away!" she ordered him—but that was when the burly man successfully broke free from Smithy and made his bid for escape. Pierce lunged after him, but he was too far away and too fast, already almost at the door—

Just as it slammed inwards, the bell tinkling incongruously as the two Firearms Officers burst in with Tasers at the ready. The man skidded to a halt, probably more from sheer surprise than in response to their bellowed "*Police! Freeze!*"

Miller showed no such hesitation, taking advantage of the distraction to snatch up a heavy stone-carving from a nearby display and hurl it out through the shop's end window.

The builders clearly hadn't splashed out on laminated glass: the window shattered in a spectacular spider's web around the hole as the stone figurine punched through it. Miller shoved his way through after it, widening the hole with a few blows from the box in his hands and then holding it up over his head to shield himself from the rain of glass shards.

He was halfway out onto the street by the time Pierce caught up to him; she grabbed for his trailing leg, but he kicked out at her and she flinched away from the falling glass. As she tried to follow him out, he swung at her with the wooden box and she had to duck away again.

"We need people out on the street!" Pierce yelled back to her team, but they were struggling to contain the other two gang members in the cluttered space, everybody too closely entangled to risk using the Tasers, and she wasn't sure if her words registered above the general chaos.

She climbed through the broken window after Miller, elbows knocking more glass free as she wrapped her arms over her head. She stumbled, misjudging ground level, slapped reflexively at the window to try to keep her balance and almost fell right through.

Miller swung the box at her two-handed before she'd recovered, smacking her own arm back into her face. There was a sharp crack as pain blossomed through her nose, and she was sure he'd broken it until the latch of the wooden box in his hands bounced open, spilling the medallions out across the street.

"Shit!" Rather than abandon the goods and just run, he

dropped to the ground to grab for them. Pierce drew her hand away from her bloody nose to grab her cuffs.

"Leave it!" she barked at him, stepping on one of the charms to cover it. "You've got nowhere to go, so—"

Miller surged up out of his crouch into a rugby tackle, knocking her backwards into the car park sign at the edge of the kerb. The impact clacked her teeth together, and she couldn't tell if the taste of blood in her mouth was just from her nose or she'd bitten her tongue. She didn't have a hand free to check it as she had to bring them both up to defend herself from Miller's efforts to crack her head against the sign, no chance to get the cuffs on him.

He still had one of the charms in his hand, and Pierce snatched for it, prying the wooden disc loose from his grip but unable to yank it away from him with the cord wrapped round his fingers. He shoved at her again, and as she tried to angle her head away from the metal pole behind her she staggered out into the road. She turned her ankle coming down from the kerb, her grip on the medallion slowing her fall until her weight wrenched the cord out of Miller's hand. As she hit the tarmac, her cuffs clattered away from her.

Miller came after her, reaching inside his jacket for one of the charms—or who knew what else. Pierce was still on the ground, nothing to defend herself with except the wooden disc in her hand, too lightweight to use as a weapon.

At least, not any conventional weapon. Pierce hadn't had a chance to get a good look at the charm, but she'd seen them in action, she knew how they worked... and most importantly, she knew the activation phrase. She clutched it tighter in her palm, covering the trigger rune that Cliff had shown her on the back.

"*Anima!*" she gasped.

All at once the wooden disc flashed hot in her hands, crumbling away between her fingers like ashes. Before there was even time for the heat to scorch her skin it was no more than dust pouring from her palm.

In its place she held a spreading ball of cool silver light

that raised pins and needles as it brushed over her skin. She glimpsed a sinuous feline shape twisting amid the smoke...

And then the effect hit her nervous system with a jolt like biting down on a metal fork. Pain like an ice-cream headache stabbed right through her brain as all her senses screamed protests at once, as if somebody had found a bank of mental volume switches and flipped them all up to the maximum.

Traffic noises, roaring so loud in her ears she looked around for the car that must be about to run her down. Her vision felt like it had been stretched into widescreen, details at the corners of her eyes as sharp as right in front of her face. The brightness seemed to have been turned up until the colours bleached out, the *No Entry* signs and green wheelie bins of the alley across the road blending into the same murky yellow as if she'd suddenly been struck colourblind. She could smell the stink of the bins as if she'd shoved her head right in them, mingling with the pungent scent of dog or fox urine and choking traffic fumes.

It was a disorienting blare of excess information that hit her like a mix of migraine aura and nauseating motion sickness. She'd almost forgotten Miller completely until movement at the corner of her vision grabbed for her attention like a flare.

As he kicked out at her again Pierce rolled away, muscles responding before her brain had the chance to remind her that she couldn't move that fast. She could; her limbs felt fluid and loose, as if someone had oiled all her joints with WD-40. She was back on her feet and twisting around to meet him before he'd even caught his balance from the kick.

She felt feverish, buzzing as if she'd overdone the caffeine, everything coming at her amped up and intense, yet oddly dreamlike. She could smell Miller's deodorant and the faint scent of his cooked breakfast clinging to him; see his every move telegraphed in the subtle shifts of his gaze and posture. She could hear the crashes and shouts coming from back inside the shop as if the fight was happening inches from her ear.

Miller took a wild swing at her, but she leapt back before it even came close. Instead of following up, he darted back towards the pavement and the spirit charms scattered across the ground. Pierce lunged and grabbed his wrist just before he seized one; in the corner of her eye she saw her handcuffs glinting where they'd fallen halfway under a parked car. She was stretching to reach them before she realised her deceptive new sight made them seem a whole lot closer than they were.

But she was also stronger and faster than she expected to be, hauling Miller off his feet as if he was a toddler. She snatched the cuffs up and twisted to snap one round his wrist before he'd even straightened up. He cursed and lashed out at her with his free hand, but she barely felt the blow, effortlessly capturing that arm too and locking it into the cuffs. She pinned him to the pavement, wincing slightly as he hit the ground with a much harder thump than she'd intended; the strength and speed the charm had given her was all out of whack with the force her brain said she *should* need against a man of his size.

A figure ran into her expanded peripheral vision, and she was spinning, adrenaline burst ready for the fight, before she could make enough sense of the distorted colours to recognise a police uniform.

"All yours, constable," she said, not sure if she was speaking at the correct volume as she let him step in to take charge of Miller. She was glad to hand him off, not sure he should be in her custody when she was this out of it from the charm. She hoped she hadn't done him any actual injury; the circumstances would make it hard to claim excessive force, but she didn't like the thought she wasn't fully in control— and even in an emergency, unauthorised use of an enchanted artefact wouldn't look too good on a report.

It didn't feel that brilliant, either. Pierce pressed the heel of her palm to her splitting head and squeezed her eyes shut to block out the distortion. The sounds of the rest of the team dealing with the other two prisoners still echoed in her head, though it seemed to her that the urgency of the scuffle had calmed. Everything under control, she hoped.

Aside from her burgeoning headache. How long did the effect of these bloody charms last, anyway? It couldn't be that long—there was only so much magical juice you could wring out of even a blood sacrifice—but the effects were definitely distracting.

"Guv?"

The soft voice calling for her attention sounded like the bark of a drill instructor. Pierce pinched the bridge of her nose as she turned to see Gemma Freeman coming towards her, the enchanted sight leaching her face of natural flesh tones to make a kind of jaundiced, bruised yellow. It gave Pierce the unsteady feeling of being on the edge of a faint, where her vision went wobbly just before it turned to black.

"We've got all three of them, including Miller," Gemma reported. "No major injuries, and we didn't have to use the Tasers." It was good news, but Pierce couldn't concentrate when it felt like the volume on the world was up too high. "You all right, guv?" Gemma asked.

"Set off one of the charms," she said, by way of curt explanation. "I'm fine, just the migraine from hell. You can handle the aftermath here."

She was going to have to, because right now Pierce needed to find somewhere dark and quiet to curl up.

CHAPTER TWENTY-THREE

AFTER A BRIEF once-over by a first-aider who was in no position to do more than monitor the basics and affirm that she didn't seem to be dying, Pierce endured a miserable car journey back to the station—the only available compromise between heading home alone with nobody to monitor her, or to a hospital where they'd surely have no more clue what to do with magical side effects than the first-aider had.

Home alone would have been her preferred choice if they'd let her, and if there hadn't been too much work to take the day off; within moments of arriving back at the busy police station, she was wondering if she shouldn't have insisted anyway. Having no private office of her own, she holed up in the Ritual Materials lab; empty, with Simon on one of his many days off. It had the advantage of being relatively quiet and devoid of distractions, but the disadvantage of a number of chemical smells and uncomfortable chairs.

Though Pierce suspected anything would be uncomfortable

right now. Everything smelled funny, felt funny; every tiny movement snatched at her attention. Even sitting in Simon's lab with the door closed, she could hear the sounds of typing and shuffling of papers in the adjacent offices, as if everybody had switched to clackety old typewriters and started throwing heavy books around. She could hear Eddie speaking on the phone in the RCU office down the hall, on that maddening cusp of hearing where she couldn't ignore the susurrus of his voice but couldn't quite make out the actual words.

After the first half hour of trying to tough it out, she took some painkillers, but they were no obvious help: it wasn't a headache making her oversensitized, but the other way around. She should probably just give the day up as a loss and head home after all, but the idea of a second car journey didn't appeal much more than staying here, and besides, an inconvenient headache didn't change the fact that they were running out of time on the Valentine Vampire case; she ought to be on hand in case anything new came up requiring her attention.

Which didn't mean she was precisely happy when something *did* come up.

The footsteps in the carpeted corridor outside all sounded so close that it took her a moment to realise that this set *were* actually coming her way. The click of the door was like a gunshot, and she squinted in the bright blaze of the corridor lights. It took her a moment to even recognise Eddie, ginger hair rendered a dull straw colour to her modified sight.

"Guv, we've had a call on the Valentine Vampire tip line," he said. "Woman who says you spoke to her by the railroad tracks in York."

It took a moment for her to switch her beleaguered brain into the right gear. "Leo's witness from the last raid. The woman with the silver bat necklace." She'd come forward after all.

Eddie nodded solemnly. "I remembered you asking me about that, so I thought she might be the real thing. She claims she used to be a member of the vampire cult and she might be able to help you find them now."

"What's her information?" Pierce asked, frowning in an effort to focus through the lingering daze.

His mouth twisted apologetically and he tugged nervously at his shirt. "She won't say over the phone, guv," he said. "Says she wants your personal guarantee of protection as the officer in charge—she won't speak to anyone else."

"God, everybody thinks they're a negotiator these days." Pierce huffed unhappily. The charm's effects had yet to show signs of wearing off, but this was too urgent to risk any delay— or chase off a potential informant. "All right, set something up, ASAP," she said. "Better bring Dawson in as well—he's the one been keeping up with the case."

And she might need him for backup if her brain wasn't back to normal by the time of the meeting.

She grimaced as a further wrinkle occurred to her. "I'd better go and clear all this with the big cheese. He's not going to be thrilled to have a cultist dictating terms after what happened with the last one."

Fortunately, it seemed that either their recent successes or the fact she was actually asking permission instead of forgiveness for once put Snow in a more cooperative mood.

"Very well," he said, folding his hands and giving her a stern look over his glasses. "Agree to this woman's terms—but this time there'll be no Lone Ranger antics. There *will* be at least one other officer with you at the meeting, and you *will* keep a backup car standing by ready to move in, just in case this vampire cult goes after your witness again."

"Yes, sir," she said, happy to let him believe he'd won a concession.

The woman, who'd identified herself as Violet—a name Pierce didn't suppose was much more authentic than 'Jonathan'—had agreed to meet them in a little café not far from the boarded-up house in York. To Pierce's relief, the headache was abating as they headed out—either she was adjusting, or the effects of the charm were slowly wearing off—but all the same, she opted to let Dawson do the driving.

"I can take this," Dawson said, glancing across at her as he drove. Pierce suspected she looked either stoned or pained as they zipped down the dual carriageway with her vision still set to widescreen. She thought her colour vision was starting to come back, but it was subtle, like trying to make out hues through tinted sunglasses. She couldn't tell if her other senses were going back to normal, since all she'd been able to smell since she'd got in the car was Dawson's cigarettes, and the engine noise was a roar in her ears.

She realised she was drifting again, which couldn't be doing much to convince Dawson that she was with it. "I'm fine," she said, belatedly. "And our source has said she'll only talk to me."

"I'll wear a wig," Dawson said. He shrugged. "It's a power play. Wants some attention from somebody with a bit of rank. Doubt it's going to matter to her who."

"That's flattering," she said dryly. "And no, I'm fine. It's wearing off." She was more or less certain that was true, and besides, she wasn't about to sit this one out. She didn't trust Dawson to ask the right questions of an informant who'd already proved she was cagey about talking to them at all.

They left their uniform backup parked discreetly down a side street a short way away from the café: out of sight, but within radio hailing distance if things got nasty. Pierce hoped. She couldn't help but remember just how fast their attacker at the park had moved.

And no amount of haste was going to do them any good if Violet was dead before they got there.

She pushed the what-ifs aside, and instead tried to put her expanded senses to good use as they drove towards the café. Nothing obviously suspicious that she could see—the streets were quiet apart from a pensioner walking a slow-moving Scottie dog and some workmen half-heartedly building a brick wall. But then, it was broad daylight this time: maybe that would be enough of a deterrent to keep the killer away.

Or maybe it wouldn't, if he was keeping close enough tabs on his disciples' movements to recognise something amiss. Shit, she should have had Eddie tell the woman not to wear her bat necklace to the meet. But it was too late now—and at least if the cult leader did make a move, it would be their chance to nab him.

Maybe they should have brought more backup after all...

Dawson pulled up outside the café, a small corner building on the end of a row of terraced houses. A sign proclaimed it *Melanie's Café & Sandwich Shop*; it looked like the sort of shabby little place that guaranteed either the best cooking in town or food poisoning. The blinds were angled half-closed, and Pierce would have been dubious that it was even open, if not for the sign on a string hanging inside the door. Maybe Violet had picked this place for the privacy.

She let Dawson take the lead, still scanning the streets for threats. The woman with the Scottie dog was watching them from across the road, but only with the kind of bland indifference that suggested they were marginally more interesting than watching the dog pee up a wall. The workmen were now out of view, but Pierce could still hear the faint *clinks* and *thuds* of bricks being shifted. All apparently quiet. She followed Dawson through into the shop.

The dimly lit interior was as cramped as the outside had led her to expect, with just about room for three tiny, two-person tables lined up opposite the sandwich counter. The middle-aged woman indifferently wiping it down with a cloth glanced up at them briefly, but offered no greeting before getting back to her task; there was a half-closed door behind her that was marked EMPLOYEES ONLY, though Pierce was dubious about the need for the plural. They seemed to have the place to themselves.

Until the door fell closed behind her, and a whisper of movement from the corner made her spin. She saw that there was a fourth table in there after all, tucked in behind the door and next to the bin. Sitting in the corner seat with her back to the wall was a dark-haired woman Pierce recognised well.

"Violet, I presume?" she said, pulling out the chair opposite her, and trying not to wince too obviously as the metal legs scraped on the floor. She was grateful the blinds in here were down, blocking out the worst of the sunshine, but the food smells were overpowering, and not in a good way. The cuts of meat on the sandwich counter stank like a slaughterhouse, the bin smelled rancid, and the vinegar bottle on the table stung her eyes and nose like chemical fumes.

"DCI Pierce," the woman said with a small nod. She had a low, soft voice that Pierce suspected she'd have had to strain to hear if it wasn't for the silence of the café and her boosted senses. Her previous impression held: Violet didn't seem old enough to have been the woman Leo claimed to have seen outside the booby-trapped base. Maybe she was a relative of that woman: a sister, even a daughter. Cults did encourage recruitment, after all.

Or maybe she was very well-preserved. How much of the effects of the blood ritual did their vampire killer share with his followers?

Pierce's gaze dropped to the silver bat necklace around her neck; as if in nervous response, Violet lifted the pendant from her chest to fiddle with it, winding the chain around her hands. She seemed calm on the surface, but her face was very pale, and Pierce couldn't help but suspect that her choice of seat hadn't been random chance, tucked away in the corner here with her back to the wall and the exit close by. Her eyes kept flickering between it and the employee door that must lead to the kitchen and the flat upstairs.

"Got another name to go with that?" Dawson asked, dragging a chair over from one of the other tables to join them. Pierce was uncomfortably aware of the woman behind the counter listening in.

"Yes," Violet said tartly, and didn't offer it. "Do *you* have one?"

"This is Detective Inspector Dawson," Pierce said, before he could steamroll ahead with his questioning. She was already beginning to regret bringing him along; his brand of forceful interrogation was hardly likely to be a help.

Or maybe it would. She was having trouble getting a proper read on Violet: nervous gestures, but a calm expression.

Maybe magical youthfulness robbed you of expression much as surgery did.

Or maybe Pierce was just reading too much into tiny movements that she wouldn't even have noticed without the effects of the spirit charm. She forced herself to focus. "You said you had some information for us?" she said, still wary of talking too directly, with the woman at the counter listening in.

Violet either noticed or she'd had the same thought. "Can I get that coffee now?" she asked, and the woman left the counter with what seemed a rather sullen lack of response, heading through into the kitchen behind to set some whistling, burbling coffee machine noises in motion. Pierce grimaced, the headache she'd only just shaken off digging its claws in again.

But at least the noise of the machine gave them a moderate degree of privacy. If Violet truly had something too important for public consumption to share, then they'd have to talk fast to persuade her to come into the station.

Pierce tried to concentrate on the woman before her, and not the noises from the other room. "You said in your phone call that you could tell us about the vampire cult," she pressed.

Violet nodded, fiddling with the bat necklace again and looking down at the plastic-covered café table. "I... was very young when they found me," she said in a low voice. "They made promises: eternal life, strength and speed beyond your wildest dreams, and freedom—freedom to be whatever, *do* whatever you wanted. They made it sound like something very beautiful." Her pale eyes gazed into the distance.

"Till it got ugly," Dawson said bluntly.

She gave him a sidelong look that seemed almost annoyed, as if she didn't appreciate having her monologue hurried along. "They... made me do things I'm not proud of," she said finally, returning her gaze to the tabletop. "I wanted to get away, but I didn't know how. Until the police came, and the vampire disciples fled and left everything behind. Left *me* behind. I thought it was over and I was safe. Until I saw on the news that they'd killed someone else..."

She was painting them a picture, but one frustratingly lacking in detail, and Pierce couldn't help but worry that the woman making her coffee was going to come back in and cause her to clam up before they'd even got anywhere.

Dawson had even less patience for faffing about than she did; Pierce let him take the lead so she could step in to play good cop if needed. "These disciples. You got names? Descriptions? Addresses?" he pressed.

"The disciples took new names when they were reborn in service," Violet said. Typical cult bollocks, and Pierce tuned her out for a moment as a stray noise from the kitchen caught her ear over the cappuccino machine. No, not the kitchen: a wooden creak that could have come from the stairs. Was there someone else in the building after all?

Or it could have been the roof or the gutter shifting. Dawson didn't seemed to have heard a thing: probably couldn't, with the coffee machine burbling away. Or maybe there was just nothing to hear. Pierce tried to drag her attention back to the here and now.

"What about the ringleader, this so-called vampire?" Dawson demanded. "What name did he go by? Could you describe him to a sketch artist? Give us something to work with here. You said you had information that could help us."

Violet gave a private smile, looking at the tabletop. "I could give you a description, but it wouldn't help you find him," she said, shaking her head. "He has the power to mesmerise his victims—he can look however it suits him to look."

"Yeah?" said Dawson, unimpressed. "Can he mesmerise cameras?"

Before Pierce could decide whether to rein his sharp tone in or back it up, there was another sound from the floor above, this time the distinct click of an opening door. She snapped her head back as if her charmed sight would somehow allow her to stare right through the ceiling. "Who's upstairs?" she demanded.

Dawson hadn't reacted to the noise, but he followed her lead, pushing up from his chair. "Who else is here?" he asked Violet sharply.

"Just Melissa," she said, her face creasing with a fractional frown of confusion. "Unless her husband is home...?"

Dawson strode over to the kitchen door and shoved it open. "She's not in here," he said.

"Perhaps she needed something from upstairs," Violet said. She still seemed oddly, almost serenely calm, considering the way she'd bolted the last two times Pierce had seen her. Pierce felt her nerves kick up a notch.

"Check it out," she told Dawson. He shot her a sceptical look, probably thinking she was paranoid, or trying to get him out of the way, but he didn't argue, heading through the kitchen to the stairs. The silence left in his wake was oppressive, Pierce disregarding Violet for a moment to listen intently. Something didn't feel right here... Was that another sound, hidden under the noise of Dawson climbing the stairs? She reached for her radio, just in case.

"I'm sure it's just Melissa," Violet repeated, distracting Pierce from her efforts to listen. Something about that name nagged at her: Melissa, Melissa... The name of the café had been *Melanie's*, not *Melissa's*.

Which meant nothing, of course. Shops changed hands, names acquired reputations worth hanging on to, Melissa wasn't necessarily even the owner...

But something smelled off. *Literally* off: above and beyond the smell of coffee emanating from the kitchen, the rancid odour underneath seeped through. A mix of butcher's shop with a slight hint of decay; she'd thought it was her enhanced senses overreacting to sandwich meat and food waste from the bins, but the longer she sat here...

A definite scuffling thump from the floor above, and Pierce was on her feet without a thought, lifting the radio towards her mouth. "All units to *Melanie's Café* on—"

Motion at the corner of her eye. With the enhanced reflexes from the charm, Pierce was moving even before it had fully registered.

Which was the only reason her throat wasn't slashed open as Violet leapt across the table, knife in hand.

CHAPTER TWENTY-FOUR

THE KNIFE FLASHED past her cheek, close enough to shave if she'd had the whiskers to lose. A part of Pierce's brain inanely registered that it was probably the same blade that had killed Jonathan.

He might have been questioning his association with the cult, but it was clear the woman Pierce was facing now had done no such thing. She'd lured them right into a trap.

There was a violent crash from above, and a masculine grunt of pain: Dawson, either hurt or getting the better of his attacker. Pierce didn't have the time to work out which: Violet was coming at her with supernatural speed. Even with the lingering magical boost from the cat spirit charm, Pierce could barely stay ahead of the slashing blade.

She ducked a swipe at her face, but it was a feint. The backhand blow that followed it just clipped her shoulder, but still sent her staggering across the room to crash into a table. As Violet leapt after her, Pierce tried to scramble out of the way, legs tangling with a chair. She shoved it into Violet's path, but she just leapt up onto the seat, grabbing a handful of Pierce's coat to yank her back with steely strength.

She was too fast, too strong... and this struggle was all too familiar: not just the unnatural strength, but the skinny frame that produced it. The attacker from the park. Pierce cursed as she realised that despite everything, she'd let unreliable eyewitnesses lead her astray. She'd known enough to disdain Tomb's description, but still echoed his unthinking assumption they were looking for a man.

This woman had been right there at the scene of Jonathan's murder, she'd been at the base in York when it blew up; Alan Waite had even seen her when he'd witnessed the body dump. She was no mere disciple of the killer: she had to be the Valentine Vampire herself.

But Pierce wasn't going to get the chance to share that revelation with anyone if she didn't get out of here alive. She twisted to wrench her coat free from Violet's grip, but the move left her off-balance as she jerked back to avoid a lightning knife strike, and she went crashing to the floor. The last gasps of the spirit charm's enchantment gave her the flexibility to kick out at the legs of Violet's chair and knock it over, but the effects were fading fast. Her field of view was narrowing, shades of red and green flowing back into the world as the shadows deepened.

Even as she tried to push herself up from the floor, her body seemed to grow massively heavier, joints locking up as if the stiffening of years had set back in all at once. Violet leapt sideways from the falling chair to land on her feet, and it was all Pierce could do to scramble to her knees in time to meet her. Another backhand slap sent her reeling across the shop.

She blundered into the door and grabbed for the handle, but Violet was back on her in a heartbeat, narrowly missing her with a swing that ripped through the paper menu on the door behind her head. Pierce yanked the door open and tried to duck around it, but she was only halfway out when Violet grabbed her arm to haul her back in. The move wrenched on her bad shoulder and she cursed, shoving the door at Violet to try to force her back.

The blow from the door's metal frame didn't seem to faze her, but then a crash from the floor above distracted them both. The pained-sounding curse that followed it could have been Dawson's, but with her hearing back to normal Pierce couldn't quite be sure.

She was in no position to run to his rescue either way. Pierce took advantage of the distraction to rip her arm free and pull it back through the door, slamming it shut after her. The sound of sirens wailed loud in her ears, and she risked a frantic glance over her shoulder to see the backup car just screeching up.

But she couldn't spare much thought for the pair of wide-eyed coppers scrambling out to join her. She was on the wrong side of the door to keep it closed by leaning on it, and she couldn't hope to win a tug of war contest—but as Pierce looked back through the glass, Violet only smiled coldly and reached up to shoot the bolt across.

"Shit!" Pierce immediately reversed course, trying to shove the door open, but it was too late. Violet stepped back from the glass, disappearing back into the building towards the stairs.

And Dawson was still trapped inside.

Pierce stepped away from the door as her backup, Sergeant Horton, reached her side. "Need to get through that door right now, sergeant," she said urgently, bracing her hands on her thighs as she tried to catch her breath. "My DI's still in there with our ritual killer and at least one of her cultists." She looked up at the upper windows of the building, but couldn't see a bloody thing from here.

"Shit," said Horton, a ruddy-faced man of few words. "Right, put that window in," he ordered the constable beside him. He turned back to her as the PC broke out his baton. "There'll be another car here in two minutes."

"I don't think he's got that long," she said, grimly shaking her head. "Suspect's armed with a knife, and has enhanced speed and strength." Dawson was a big lad, still carrying plenty of muscle along with the middle-aged spread; but while he might hold his own against a couple of cultists if they weren't magically enhanced, there was no way he could face off against Violet alone.

She wasn't sure that she and two uniform coppers would exactly do much to swing the balance, but all the same, they had no choice—no time to wait for more backup.

Pierce shielded her face with a flinch as the blond constable—Nicholls, that was his name; probably best to remember it if they were going back in there together—smashed his way through the toughened glass of the door with his baton. He knocked the window in and groped around for the bolt. "Got it, sarge," he said after a moment, and slid it back across. He pushed the door open, baton held at the ready as he scanned the corners of the shop's front room. "No one down here, looks like."

He and Horton led the way through past the cramped kitchen and to the narrow staircase at the back. "Police!" Horton yelled as they thundered up to the flat above and slammed through the door. Pierce gagged immediately at the stink of death: a woman's blood-soaked body, poorly wrapped in a sheet, had been carelessly dumped on the sofa. The shop's unfortunate real owner, probably.

With her eyes drawn to the corpse, it took her a second more to spot the woman Melissa crouched behind the sofa. Pierce opened her mouth to shout a warning to the others, then realised she was chained to the pipes by Dawson's silver cuffs. "Not our main target—go, go, go!" she ordered the men with her.

"Stay down!" Horton barked at the woman as they passed. She snapped her teeth like an animal, spitting curses at them.

As they reached the door at the far side of the room, it flew open, and a man charged out towards them with a snarl. Pierce glimpsed a bald head and deep-set eyes before the man threw himself at Horton, screaming and scratching and trying to headbutt and bite him. Horton staggered backwards and PC Nicholls dived into the fray, the two of them bearing the man to the ground.

Pierce shoved her way past the struggle and into the room beyond. Violet had Dawson cornered, slumped on the floor behind the bed; he still had his arms raised weakly in self-defence, but she could see that his shirt-sleeves were stained with blood.

"Drop the knife!" Pierce barked as Violet spun away from Dawson to face her. In answer, the killer hurled the knife at her: a tumbling, unaimed throw with little chance of striking home, but Pierce ducked away from the flashing blade by instinct. Violet turned towards the bedroom's end window and slammed her palms against it, smashing the frame right out of the brickwork to crash down onto the street below. With an easy leap she swung herself out through the gap, reaching up for the gutter to pull herself onto the roof.

"Shit!" Pierce rounded the bed, but by the time she got to the window Violet was already out and away. "Suspect's escaping over the roof!" she shouted over her shoulder. But from the crashing and cursing behind her, the others still had their hands full trying to restrain the bald cultist. The wail of distant sirens told her more backup was coming, but there was no way it would get here in time.

"Go after her," Dawson gasped behind her.

"Not out that bloody window, I'm not," Pierce said, crouching over him. Even if she didn't wedge herself in the gap, Winnie-the-Pooh-style, she doubted she could trust the plastic guttering and old, ill-anchored tiles to hold her weight for long enough to scramble up on top. She could run back down the stairs to try to give chase at street level, but there was no way she'd keep up.

And she had a higher priority right now. An alarming amount of blood was already seeping through Dawson's thin shirt, and there was a wheeze she didn't like to his breathing. Christ, why hadn't she insisted they wear stab vests?

She grabbed her radio. "We need an ambulance to the scene at Melanie's!" she shouted into it. "Officer injured!"

Violet had escaped them yet again—Pierce was damned if she was going to let her add another murder to her tally.

But that might well be out of her hands.

*   *   *

IT WAS SOME hours later when a considerably grimmer and wearier Pierce made her way back to the office. No news yet on Dawson's condition: the ambulance had arrived promptly and he'd still been conscious when they loaded him in, but stab wounds to the abdomen were nothing to mess with.

Violet, as she'd suspected, had already vanished into thin air by the time a proper search got underway; at least now they had a description to circulate, and hopefully some useable prints from the café that would link her to both Jonathan's murder and the house in Leeds.

And they'd arrested two of her cultists. Pierce doubted that they'd get any cooperation there, but just getting them off the streets was still a win: they were accessories to murder at the very least, even if Violet performed all the ritual kills herself. Pierce hoped that these two were the only disciples she had—she might kill just as readily without them, but she'd have a much harder job doing it without leaving a trace.

All the same, Pierce was in no mood to look on the bright side, and neither was the superintendent.

"Your department limps from one disaster to another!" Snow snapped in disgust, his nostrils flaring. He was agitated enough to be on his feet today, towering over her. "Your pursuit of this case has been a shambles from beginning to end: murdered informants, leaks to the media, members of the public endangered, procedures disregarded... and now it emerges that the serial killer outright *invited you to a meeting*, and yet not only did she slip through your fingers once again, she put one of our best men in hospital doing it!"

Pierce forbore from pointing out that he'd signed off on their plans himself. Much as she'd like to snarl at him, sitting here in his nice clean office measuring gut feelings against textbook guidelines, it wasn't as if he was even wrong: she'd been the one on the front-line of the case, and he'd relied on her for a read of the situation. She couldn't help but feel that somehow, some way, she should have smelled a rat much earlier.

She let out a slow breath, trying to keep her temper at bay. "This was clearly a deliberate ambush aimed at hampering the police investigation," she said. "We've come too close to catching her on multiple occasions this time round—this was a panic move."

Snow didn't look impressed. "Close, Chief Inspector, may count for something when it comes to my daughter's maths homework, but we don't give points for effort in police work. The fact is that this woman remains on the loose, and is extremely likely to kill again soon—assuming she hasn't done so already."

Pierce wasn't sure if that was actually a jab at Dawson's uncertain condition, but that was where her mind went anyway. She might not be fond of the man, but that wouldn't make it fester any less to have another member of the RCU die on her watch—in fact, it only made the self-reproach weigh heavier. She was all too aware that she hadn't made even the cursory attempts at getting to know the man that she had with her two new constables; she knew his first name was Graham, not that his dismissive demeanour particularly invited using it, but she wasn't even sure if he was married, if he had kids, or what interests he might have beyond smoking like a chimney and gunning for her job. It wouldn't make much of a eulogy.

Of course, when a fellow officer was downed in the line of duty, whether permanently or otherwise, there was one thing you could always do for them: make sure that you got the bastards behind it.

"We have two members of the vampire cult under arrest," she reminded Superintendent Snow. "Possibly the only followers that she still has. We've closed down one of their bases, we've got a description and prints, possibly even DNA this time. She can't evade us for very much longer."

Or so they had to hope.

CHAPTER TWENTY-FIVE

CULT MEMBERS WERE rarely an easy nut to crack when it came to persuading them to see the sense in shopping their accomplices, but Pierce had hoped the pair they'd pulled in might at least rant and rave about their cult's teachings and give her some clues. It seemed even that might have been over-optimistic.

"They've been non-responsive since we brought them in," Sergeant Horton told her over the phone. "Not just playing difficult; practically catatonic—we just had the doc in to look at them, and she doesn't think they're faking."

Brilliant. "Some kind of drug?" Pierce asked with a grimace.

"We've had our eyes on them the whole time," Horton insisted. "If they took anything, it was before the arrest. Reckon this is one for your department."

He might just be passing the buck for the suspects going downhill in his custody, but he was more than likely also right: either the cultists had done this to themselves with some kind of magical trigger, or the control that Violet had over the group extended to more than just tracking their whereabouts. Balls. Pierce should have insisted they be checked over for tattoos and stripped of any suspicious jewellery the second that they'd been restrained, but she'd been preoccupied with Dawson's injuries and the search for Violet.

She sighed into the phone. "Right. I'll send some people over to check over the prisoners and their effects, see if we can figure out what happened." It was doubtful in the extreme that there'd be any way to reverse it, let alone that they'd find it in time for it to be useful. "Let me know if their condition changes." She hung up and made her weary way back up the stairs to the RCU office, where the remains of her team were assembled.

Deepan looked up from his computer as she pushed through the doors. "Just got off the phone with the hospital, guv," he told her. "Looks like Dawson's going to be okay—they want to keep him in for a bit, but it sounds like his injuries were relatively minor."

"Good." That was one weight off. "Unfortunately, it seems our two cultists we just arrested have gone magically mute. I want you and Eddie to get over to York and find out why. I'm going to head in to the hospital, see if Dawson's got anything to report he didn't tell us at the scene." It was doubtful, but at least it gave her a work-related pretext to blunt the awkwardness of visiting a man she couldn't pretend she considered a friend.

She arrived at the hospital within visiting hours, and Dawson was in a regular ward, so she had no hassle getting in. That said, she almost managed to miss the man himself, not expecting him to have another visitor already. It was only the familiar voice that snagged her attention, halfway down the row on the opposite side.

Pierce narrowed her eyes at the sight of her DI in low-voiced conversation with a tall, blond man in a business suit. Who was that? Not a doctor, she was fairly sure, but he didn't look enough like Dawson to peg him as a relative, either: much slimmer build, with finer features and fairer colouring. Could be a friend or neighbour, she supposed, but if so he'd arrived awfully quickly—and Dawson had never struck her as the type to broadcast a brief hospital stay. He was more the sort to stubbornly tough things out alone till he keeled over.

But then, what did she really know about the man and his life outside work? For all she knew he'd had to call a friend and ask him to feed the cat.

Or maybe he reported to somebody other than her, and had all along. Maitland's people definitely had some way of keeping tabs on what was going on within the RCU, and she'd had her suspicions about Dawson from the start—though it was hard to be sure if that was anything he'd done, or just her dislike of the man.

Before she could make up her mind whether to risk trying to eavesdrop, Dawson's visitor rose from his seat to go. It seemed to Pierce that he gave a distinctly wary look around the ward before leaning forward to murmur some inaudible parting comment to Dawson; the two exchanged brief nods, and then he left.

Pierce wasn't sure if Dawson had spotted her yet, but judged it best to march straight over to him just in case.

"Not interrupting, am I?" she said, tilting her head after the departing visitor. Dawson didn't answer, just raised his eyebrows. Pierce helped herself to the recently vacated chair. "Friend of yours?" she pressed.

He gave a noncommittal grunt that could have been deliberate evasiveness or just his usual brusque manners. "They tracked her down yet?" he asked, not bothering with any attempt at pleasantries.

Pierce gave up and turned to the case, shaking her head. "Looks like she got away clean," she said. She doubted he'd appreciate any sugarcoating of the situation.

Dawson grunted, grimacing slightly as he adjusted his position in the bed. "Should've gone after her," he said.

"Yeah, well, if I'd gone out that window, there'd be two of us in here, and she'd still have got away," she said. She nodded at his hospital gown. "What are they telling you?"

"Didn't manage to skewer anything major," he said. "I should be back in the office tomorrow."

Having had the joy of her own personal stab wound before now, Pierce doubted that was the official prognosis. "Don't push yourself," she said. "We can manage without you for a couple of days without the department coming to its knees." Or more pragmatically, they were so terminally understaffed at the best of times that being one down could only do so much to make it worse.

"We've got a major case on. I can handle it," he said, forehead furrowing.

Pierce stayed noncommittal, far from convinced, but in no position to reject the help.

All the same, she couldn't help but wonder exactly why he was quite so determined: just a dose of the usual macho crap and his desire to get the credit for the Valentine Vampire case—or because he wanted to be back in position to report on her activities to Maitland?

PIERCE MADE HER excuses soon after, fairly sure that further attempts at friendly chit-chat wouldn't have been much fun for either side. The rest of the day's investigations were a similar waste, serving only to underline that Violet had well and truly vanished, her cultists weren't likely to be talking to anyone anytime soon, and no, forensics hadn't come up with anything since the last few times she'd hassled them. She went to bed at the end of the day battered, frustrated and nursing a brutal reprise of her earlier headache.

The next morning she got a phone call from Phil Havers before she'd even left to go to work. "I spent the night going through the old files," he said. "I think you're right—your killer *did* hop the border into Oxford's jurisdiction back in February '08. I've got two likely bodies found near Kettering and Peterborough. Haven't managed to dig up a third, but it could have missed RCU attention entirely, or fallen between the cracks." RCU cases on the borderlands between jurisdictions had a bit of an unfortunate tendency to get bounced back and forth while they argued over who could least spare personnel to make the trip.

Pierce consulted her rusty knowledge of those parts of UK geography that weren't usually her problem. "That's... over Cambridgeshire way?" she hazarded.

"Thereabouts."

And Matt Harrison's body had been found down near Newark-on-Trent, which was really quite far south in relation to the other killings, mostly clustered around the bases in Leeds and York... She needed a map.

"All right, thanks, Phil," she said distractedly, clamping her phone in place with her shoulder as she bent down to rifle through the detritus of old newspapers and takeaway menus that cluttered her living room bookshelves. "You may have just been a big help. Send me whatever you've got on those two murders, okay?"

"Will do," he said. "I'll keep looking out for a third. And good luck—I know this one's been hanging over you a long time."

"Yeah, like a bloody vulture," Pierce said. She seized upon the spiral-bound spine of the map book and tugged it out, sending a cascade of papers to the ground. "All right. Talk to you soon."

She carried the map book over to the dining table, and with the aid of much cross-referencing of map pages and consultation with her notes, eventually managed to plot out the locations of all the known body dumps. Most were clustered in a loose ring around the Leeds-Bradford area; the 'nineties killings had taken place in Lincolnshire, but both they and the recent dump near Newark could have been taken as a wider extension of that ring.

Add in the two murders further south in Oxford's jurisdiction, and all of a sudden it started to look like a different picture. Like there might, in fact, be another focal point, somewhere around the Lincolnshire-Leicestershire border. She drew a loose triangle connecting the three most southerly sites, and found it centred on... well, a whole lot of nothing much, really; the only thing of note at this map scale was a stretch of the A1.

Pierce frowned, wondering why that rang a faint bell in her head. Someone had mentioned driving on the A1 recently, she was sure, but her brain refused to dredge the context up. Maybe just her team discussing the drive down to Newark-on-Trent? No, she was pretty sure it had been something she'd read. A detail from one of the old case files? She racked her brains, but couldn't place the reference.

She was in her car, halfway to work and grimly contemplating whether she really wanted to hear what was on the radio news, when the memory finally clicked. Christopher Tomb's book—he'd described being taken to a barn off the A1 where the cult had supposedly conducted initiation rituals. At the time, it hadn't particularly stood out among numerous other dramatically rendered incidents and encounters, all vividly described but suspiciously short on specifics—names, locations and dates—that would allow for any sort of verification.

Of course, on that first read-through she'd also been operating on the assumption that what legitimate information Tomb did have to offer had probably been cribbed from an inside source in the emergency services. Knowing he really had made contact with a former member of the Valentine Vampire cult put a different spin on things. The details might be heavily embellished, but perhaps the barn really did exist—and perhaps it had been in use recently enough that there would still be useful evidence to be found there.

It was a long shot, but at this stage, any lead was worth checking out.

When she arrived at the office, she skimmed through the case files Phil had forwarded. Easy to see how the connection could have been missed—no one down in Oxford had been on the alert for more Valentine Vampire killings, and these two were a step away from the usual MO. One body had been dumped in the woods and set upon by scavengers before it was found; the other effectively dismembered, the presence of ritual cuts noted, but the overall pattern overlooked.

Violet and her cult of killers had been careful that time out, apparently spooked that the police had come close to tracking them down the last time they'd been active. But when their precautions had worked, they'd probably decided the close call had been a fluke and gone back to the cocky showboating, returning to their old hunting grounds, displaying the body of their first kill in a way that was sure to grab everyone's attention.

Sometimes you caught the clever ones because they wanted you to *know* that they were clever. Violet had showed her hand too many times, and now the net was closing in.

Recent events would probably cause her to go to ground again, but right now she had a limited window for a third killing to complete the ritual. If she was relying on the magic to maintain her supernatural strength and youth, she wouldn't want to abandon the ritual part-finished—it was quite possible she *couldn't*. Magic was a hell of a drug, and withdrawal could be lethal. After a good three decades or more of living on magical energy, there was no telling if she'd even survive without it.

So she needed to kill again, soon—and hopefully, with her resources severely curtailed, she'd be backed into returning to one of her old boltholes, where they stood a chance of tracking her down.

"I'm going to see Christopher Tomb again, and find out if he can give me more on the locations where he met with this man Jonathan," she told Deepan. Without calling in advance this time: if this really was a lead, she didn't want him blabbing it all over the internet and potentially tipping off the killer. "You follow up on the Oxford murders—see if you can find any evidence of another killing around the same time that might be our third victim, or anything that might indicate where the cult were based when they were operating down there. Violet's already lost two bases and some if not all of her most loyal followers—she can't have an unlimited number of places left to go."

She moved to leave, then ducked back into the office with an afterthought. "And if Dawson comes in, tell him I said to go home."

"Right, guv," he said, with obvious scepticism. She didn't think Dawson would listen either, but at least if she was going to be out of the office, then worrying about his potential loyalties didn't have to be her problem for a while.

PIERCE DROVE OVER to the address that they had for Christopher Tomb, a semi-detached house not too far from the park where Jonathan had met his end. She knew it was the right place from the car parked out in front, though the cheerful redheaded woman in cycling gear who answered the door gave her pause.

"Chris!" the woman called back into the house. "Someone for you." She gave Tomb a quick peck on the cheek when he appeared at the door, looking remarkably normal in grey jeans and a navy blue jumper. "Right, I'm off on my ride. See you later." The woman gave Pierce a polite smile as she slipped out past her and went round to the garage to fetch her bike.

"Ah, Claire," Tomb said, with a dip of the head. "What can I do for you?" He seemed to have recovered his poise after the shock of the altercation at the park.

"Your book," Pierce said without preamble. "You mentioned being taken to a farmhouse off the A1 by a member of the cult. Thanks to some new information that's come up, that site is now of interest in our current investigation. Do you still have the address?"

"New information?" he asked, with an ingratiating smile.

She'd only said it to cut off the smug finger-waving about having disregarded his evidence for so long, and now she immediately regretted it. "The details are confidential, I'm afraid." Like some earlier details she could mention, but the lecture on loose lips was probably best left until after she'd got the information that she needed. "The address?"

"I'm afraid I honestly couldn't tell you," he said, a glib apology she didn't trust for a minute. "It was a long time ago, and Jonathan insisted on doing the driving himself so that I could stay hidden until he was sure that none of the others were there. He never told me the name of the place we would be visiting."

That was plausible, but Pierce was certain he was holding something back, probably envisaging making some grand discovery himself—and cocking up the police investigation in the process. "Any details you can remember would be helpful," she said evenly. It probably wouldn't have hurt to butter him up and imply he'd get some credit for the assistance, but she didn't think she had it in her. Not after how many lives had been lost already.

"Oh, I can do better than that," Tomb said, smile widening. "I may not be able to give you the address, but I'm certain I could guide you there from the road if I was to accompany you."

She should have predicted that. "All right, well, I'm sure you can do that just as easily from some street-view pictures on the internet," she said. The last thing she wanted was Tomb along to interfere in the investigation—worse, waiting for him to confirm the location in person would mean a delay in getting forensics to the scene; she couldn't very well drag an entire team along on a wild goose chase waiting to see if he came up with the goods.

"I'm afraid not," Tomb told her, all contrived regret. "You see, the aura of a place is very important to my mental vision of it. I remember that the farm had a sense of foreboding evil about it that I would certainly know again if I visited it in person, no matter how much it might have outwardly changed. I can't guarantee you I'd be able to do the same from a photograph."

Pierce didn't believe a word of it, but really, what could she do?

"All right, Mr Tomb," she said, pressing her lips together. "It seems we're going to have to take a road trip. But be warned, if you're wasting police time in the middle of an extremely urgent murder investigation, there *will* be consequences."

Possibly for her as well as him. Time was running out entirely too fast.

CHAPTER TWENTY-SIX

AFTER AN HOUR in the car with Christopher Tomb, Pierce was beginning to think the trip was more likely to trigger a murder investigation than solve one. Not only did he seem to be incapable of leaving any moment of silence unbroken, but what he was rambling on about was her field of expertise, and most of what he said was utter bollocks. She had to bite her tongue repeatedly to avoid snapping at him or giving away details of the case. She still needed his cooperation to find this place.

Assuming he wasn't just leading her up the garden path, something she became steadily less sure of as the drive went on. Maybe she should have assigned this duty to one of the constables, but she was sure Tomb would have been even more difficult if he didn't think he was getting the high-level attention he deserved.

And even being stuck in a car with a complete prat at least offered some illusion of accomplishing something, making some kind of progress. Being back at the office doing the paperwork while others pursued potential leads would only have driven her potty.

Having tuned Tomb out some time ago in sheer self-defence, Pierce was caught off-guard when he finally offered something relevant. "I think we need to come off at the next exit," he said, sitting up in his seat as they passed a Little Chef. "This looks familiar—in fact, yes, I think I'm starting to sense the aura now..."

Pierce let that pass, busy pulling in front of a lorry with rather less warning than she would have liked in the light rain. She raised a hand in an apology at the foghorn blast from the driver, guiltily glad she wasn't driving a marked car.

She only got a brief glimpse of the road sign, a list of village names she didn't know. Tomb seemed to be fairly confident, though, directing her left at the end of the slip road to pass back under the dual carriageway. The road they'd pulled off onto was much narrower, hedged in by steep slopes covered in spindly saplings and bushes, and they'd left most of the traffic behind on the main road.

The road surface along here was cracked and potholed, and Pierce had to slow down further and nudge the windscreen wipers up a notch as the rain began to ramp up in earnest. The slope of the land gradually evened out, but the hedgerows only drew in closer to the road, joined now by high firs that closed off even more of the surrounding view. The few turnoffs they passed were mostly unmarked gravel tracks leading away through the fields.

They'd driven past several that all looked much the same when Tomb said abruptly, "This is it."

Above the ragged hedgerows Pierce could just make out the mossy corrugated roofs of farm buildings. The site was closer to the road and coming up faster than she'd anticipated; she'd hoped for the chance to approach more stealthily and poke around, but it didn't look like there was anywhere she could park without being spotted from miles away.

Nothing for it but the front door approach. Pierce drove

between the open gates to park up on the gravel beside the two buildings. There was no sign of any other vehicles, and she couldn't help but be aware of how long a shot this was. Even if this *was* the place that Jonathan had brought Tomb before, there was no guarantee the cult had used it in the last seven years, or that Violet would have chosen to come here now. Hell, for all she knew Tomb could have made the incident up entirely and just brought her to the first likely looking abandoned barn in the region rather than admit it.

If so, he was committed to putting on a performance regardless. "This is the barn that Jonathan showed me," he said. "He told me this was where the disciples brought him when he was first recruited. They drank the blood of farm animals together and promised him eternal life if he would swear himself over to the service of their leader."

"Uh-huh," she said neutrally. She supposed it sounded plausible enough: a few less murderous blood rituals to gauge new recruits' responses, see how many lines they could be persuaded to cross after they'd seen a few demonstrations of supposed vampiric powers and been promised they could have them for themselves—though from what had happened to the two cultists that they'd arrested, she doubted Violet was the sharing type. "All right. Stay in the car, and keep your phone ready. If anyone but me approaches, lock the door and call the police."

The place seemed to be completely abandoned, but she was taking no chances.

Pierce opened the door and stepped out into the driving rain, half wishing that she'd brought some backup with her, half glad she hadn't been able to bring a full team to what looked to be yet another dead end. She'd probably used most of the year's budget for joint operations in this week alone.

And they still didn't have the Valentine Vampire in their custody to show for it.

The rain was hammering off the metal roofs of the buildings, splashing back from the puddles gathering in the ruts of the gravel drive and plastering her hair to her head. The lee of the main barn to her right would have provided a little shelter, but she moved away from it at first, towards the smaller shed ahead of her. It stood open to the weather, seemingly unoccupied but too dark to be sure. This time she'd come prepared with a proper full-sized torch; as she clicked it on, she drew her phone with her other hand to give Deepan the details of her location.

"Doesn't look like this place has been used in a while," she told him, shining the torch around the inside of the shed. It seemed empty, but there were a few big old rusty metal drums that had once held who-knew-what. She rounded them to peer into the rear corners: nothing but some old sacks and impressive spider's webs. "But still, see what you can dig up about the ownership, now and over the last thirty years. I don't know what the road is, but there's a sign here says the place is called Manor Farm."

"Will do," he said.

"Any progress on forensics?" she asked, hunching against the rain as she moved back out towards the much bigger main barn. It looked like a once-larger entrance had been bricked in, a small metal door set in the middle of the mismatched brickwork. She tugged at the handle, but was unsurprised to find it locked. A quick glance back at Tomb to make sure he was staying put in the car as ordered, then she moved around the side of the building.

"Nothing from yesterday's scene," Deepan told her. She had to press the phone right to her ear to hear him over the sound of the rain on the roof, the corrugated metal sheets rattling uneasily in the wind as if debating whether to choose today to rip free. "But they managed to ID the second victim as a university student called Alex Wagner. I sent DC Freeman to speak with the parents, but I doubt that they're going to know much. He was living in halls."

"Younger than our previous victims?" she asked as she picked her way through the waterlogged mud.

"Nineteen," Deepan confirmed. "Youngest before that was twenty-one."

Hmm. Hard to say if that was significant or sheer chance, though it might be another point in favour of the hypothesis that Violet had been getting wary, changing up patterns and preying on easier meat. Whatever good it did them to know that this late in the game.

She reached another door around the side of the barn, this one seemingly original to the building. She doubted the rotten old wood could stand up to a tap from an Enforcer ram, but a search warrant could be tricky to arrange just on Tomb's claims. It was looking like he'd dragged her out here in person on a massive waste of time.

All the same, she gave the cast iron ring pull a tug. The door shifted in its frame, but didn't open. She gave it a second, harder yank, on the theory that if it just happened to come open in her hand it would surely be her duty to check inside and secure the scene. Sadly, whatever bolt or latch held it closed was made of sterner stuff than the wood, and though it gave a strained creak it didn't seem as if was likely to give. She sighed and let it go. "Looks like I'm not going to be able to—" She broke off as a dull banging noise reached her ears. "Was that at your end?"

"Was what?" Deepan asked. Rather than answer, she took the phone away from her ear so she could listen. More muffled thumps, like something—someone—knocking on a distant door, or kicking at something solid.

It sounded as if it was coming from inside the barn.

Pierce stepped back to check that Tomb hadn't left the parked car, but couldn't see into the passenger seat from this angle. It couldn't be him making that noise; she'd most likely have seen him get out.

She thumped on the barn door herself, raising her voice. "Hello? Is anyone inside? This is the police." If Violet was here, she'd probably heard the car approaching anyway, and besides—Violet would have no reason to be banging and kicking.

A flurry of more urgent thumps. Her pulse quickened, and she raised the phone back to her ear. "We could have a live victim here," she told Deepan. Or it could be a trapped animal, or a particularly deceptive breeze... She shouted through the door again. "If you're able to speak, please respond. This is the police!"

Was that a muffled cry from within? She couldn't hear anything clearly over the clatter of the rain against the metal roof. She hammered on the door once more, and was rewarded by more distant thumping.

Shit. It could be someone trapped inside, perhaps gagged and restrained or in too much of a bad way to call out. If Violet was now working alone, she might have left her victim temporarily unguarded while she retrieved supplies for the ritual. Or she might be in there even now, unable to interrupt the magic in full flow to deal with police interlopers.

Either way, Pierce had a duty. She was out here without backup, hadn't even checked in with the local police since Tomb had been so purposefully vague about where they were going, but there could be a life in danger, and there was no time to wait for assistance to get here.

"I'm going in," she told Deepan. "Figure out whose jurisdiction I'm in and get me some backup out here—and make sure you warn them what we could be dealing with." RCU assistance would be better, but the rest of her team were a good ninety minutes' drive away, and RCU Oxford weren't much closer.

"On it, guv," Deepan said, sparing her the arguments and questions. Good lad. Pierce ended the call and tucked the phone away so she'd have both her hands free to tackle the door.

However she was going to do that. No convenient windows to smash here: the only points of entry were the doors. The metal one round the front was an obvious no-go, but she was fairly sure she could shift this wooden one with a bit of applied force.

Unfortunately, she'd left the battering ram in her other coat, not to mention the sturdy young officer to do the swinging for her. She cast around for anything else she could use to break through. No conveniently dumped tools or bricks, no rocks any bigger than pebbles; the fenceposts that ran nearby were metal, and looked harder to break than the door. There were a few saplings behind the fence, but it didn't look like their skinny branches would be up to damaging much.

On the other hand, a thin twig might actually be more useful. Grimacing, Pierce dug through the mulch of dead leaves at the foot of the trees until she came up with one that seemed suitable, thin but not too whippy.

There was no visible lock on the wooden door, so it must be secured from inside—hopefully with a simple bolt rather than a padlock. She tugged again on the iron ring, pulling the door outwards as far as the loose hinges would allow, and fed the twig into the narrow crack that she'd created in a bid to locate the bolt on the other side. When it seemed to get wedged halfway up she thought her luck might be out, but as she jiggled the twig back and forth a bit she realised the door was held shut not by a bolt, but by a simple hook latch.

The latch was stiff enough that it still took some effort to work it loose without snapping the twig, but at last she heard it scrape free from the catch and the door bounced forward a fraction. She tugged it further open, wincing at the screech of the rusty hinges. She'd just have to hope that neither Violet nor any surviving cultists were here right now, because she wasn't convinced she could make an arrest with handcuffs and intimidation alone.

The inside of the barn was dark, lit only by the thin cracks of light that made it in around the ill-fitting roof. The high-ceilinged space was too big for her torch to highlight more than a small patch of it at once, and stacks of wooden crates and indistinct tarpaulin-covered shapes created a maze of threatening shadows around her. Off to her right was a rickety wooden ladder Pierce assumed led to a hayloft; below it ran a line of animal pens with rusty metal gates, like old barred cells.

She entered the barn at a wary pace, heart pounding as she flicked the torch about to peer into the shadows. The drumming of the rain and the rattle of the roof created a murmur of background noise that could have hidden any number of sounds all around her. More than once she jerked around to face a flicker of motion, breath catching, only to realise it was just the darting shadows cast by her own torch.

The dull knocking came again, somewhere over to the right, and Pierce swallowed, licking her lips nervously. There could be a victim in here, but she still hesitated to call out again.

She made her way in the direction of the sound at a nervous crouch, edging round each obstacle and checking every corner. Something soft gave under her foot, and she jumped away, her heart pounding, before she registered that it was just a fold of tarpaulin. She kicked it out of her way, and the tarp slithered down to reveal the low stone slab it had been draped over. The stone rose about six inches above the floor, etched with grooves that all funnelled down towards a wider channel at one end. There were heavy metal rings at the corners that looked like they were meant to anchor ropes.

Pierce had a bad feeling that it wasn't intended for anything involving livestock.

The best thing she could do with the grisly discovery was keep well away from it until forensics arrived. Pierce skirted around the stone block. She could call Deepan to confirm that this was definitely the right place, but backup was already coming, and she didn't want to risk the distraction.

That banging sound again. It was coming from one of the animal pens at the far side of the barn. She swallowed and crept closer. An irregular dull knocking—just something come loose, tapping against the brick wall in the wind, or was there somebody there?

"Hello?" Pierce said tentatively. Her own tremulous tone annoyed her, and she squared her shoulders to speak more firmly. "Is somebody there? Identify yourself. This is the police."

She thought she might have heard a choked breath, almost like a sob—but if so, it wasn't followed by any louder cry, only more of that soft tapping against the brickwork. She inched forward, cautiously shining her torch through the metal grill that closed off the pen. The inside was heaped haphazardly with straw, and at the back there was a hump of fabric that might or might not have been a human form under a blanket. "Hello?" she said again. The blanket didn't stir.

The tapping had stopped.

Pierce opened the gate onto the pen—another simple latch, though the metal had stiffened enough to make it difficult— and tugged it open, flakes of rust cascading to the ground. She moved to stoop over the shape in the blanket, drawing her phone from her pocket to call for an ambulance if it was needed, and reached out to give the huddled lump a cautious shake.

The blanket collapsed under her touch, revealing only more heaped straw. There was a creak from the hayloft above, and she started to look up—

Not fast enough to avoid the shadowy form that leapt down to meet her.

CHAPTER TWENTY-SEVEN

PIERCE HIT THE hay-strewn floor of the barn with a startled *oof*, the breath smashed from her lungs by the body that slammed into her from above. The torch gave an ominous crunch in her hand, and the barn was plunged back into darkness. The phone was still cradled safely against her chest, but before she could think to dial, her arm was wrenched viciously back and clawing fingers ripped it from her grip. She heard the impact as it shattered against the barn's rear wall.

Then the weight was gone from her back, and the pen door slammed shut with a rattling crash.

Like jail cells, she'd thought when she'd first seen the things. Oh, fuck. She'd been lured into a more literal trap this time—and the fact that she wasn't dead yet was probably only a sign of nastier plans in store.

Pierce climbed heavily to her feet, repeatedly clicking the torch in her hand but getting nothing in response. Definitely broken. She shuffled forward through the straw, groping blindly ahead until she met the metal gate that now barred the exit from her cage. She shoved at it, but was grimly unsurprised to find no give; unlike the warped old barn door she'd broken in through, this one rested securely up against the edge of the frame, and the grill was too narrow to fit her hand through. She had to wonder now if these 'animal pens' had actually been original to the barn at all, or fitted by the cult with this exact purpose in mind.

She was in big trouble.

Still, admitting that wouldn't get her anywhere. "Hey," Pierce shouted, rattling the cage again, a demand for attention. "You think this is going to get you anywhere? In a couple of minutes this place is going to be flooded with police." She wished. Deepan would do his best, but with only her report of suspicious noises to go on, she'd be lucky to have a pair of local bobbies show up when they'd dealt with their other business.

Not the sort of thoughts she wanted to be projecting right now. Act confident. "There'll be Firearms Officers called in— you're fast, but you're not going to outrun a bullet," she said. "It's in your best interest to surrender peacefully to the police before they get here. Nobody wants this to end in bloodshed."

Except of course, Violet probably did—and the prospect of peaceful surrender wasn't much of a carrot to dangle for someone who was looking at life in a high-security facility, assuming she could even survive breaking off the cycle of killings that sustained her. All the reply that Pierce got was the scrape of the barn's outer door, Violet's outline briefly silhouetted in the doorway before she pulled it closed again behind her.

It would be nice to think that meant she'd decided to just leave Pierce here and run while there was time, but more than likely she knew the talk of backup was overinflated, and was just heading out to Pierce's car to move it out of s—

Fuck! Tomb. She'd left him waiting for her in the car, and hadn't even warned him of the cult leader's true identity. What if she tricked him into getting out of the car? And even if he didn't, locking the doors wasn't much of a defence; Violet could smash her way in without raising a sweat. Would he have the time—and the presence of mind—to call 999 before she got to him?

She doubted it very much. He was going to end up dead... and there was nothing Pierce could do about it from in here.

She shoved at the metal gate again, more urgently now, but it wasn't budging. *Think*. Her phone. Violet had thrown it, it had sounded like the screen had shattered, but maybe... She got down on the ground to scrabble through the straw, trying to guess where it had fallen from the sound. There was barely enough light to make out more than the vaguest outlines of the space. If only the bloody torch hadn't broken too...

Wait. She still had her penlight. Cursing herself for an idiot, aware of the useless panic hammering away in her chest, Pierce scrabbled in her pockets for her keys. She was so frantic to activate the penlight that she flicked it on and off again before she got a steady light.

Its feeble beam could barely map the confines of her cage, but it showed enough for her to spot her phone down in the corner. As she lifted it she heard the disheartening rattle of something loose inside, but she tried to switch it on all the same, lifting it to her ear despite the blank, broken screen.

Dead. Goddammit.

Dropping the now-useless phone, she turned the penlight upwards, remembering how Violet had jumped down on her from above. There was a trapdoor up in the floor of the hayloft, presumably intended for dropping feed down to the animals below, but it would be well out of her reach even if she tried to climb up the inside of the cage door.

She was completely trapped.

In lieu of any smarter escape plan, Pierce went back to slamming her weight against the door of the makeshift cage, bracing herself against the wall and kicking out at it in an effort to jar the lock open. She suspected she was onto a losing game, up against a structure made to contain livestock that could kick a lot harder than her, but she had to try.

Amid the juddering rattles of the metal framework, she almost missed the sound of Violet's return. The sudden influx of weak daylight drew her attention back to the barn's outer door; she grabbed the bars of the door to still the reverberations and clicked off the penlight.

She could see that Violet had something slung over her shoulders, a bulky burden that she carried as if it weighed nothing; Pierce's heart jolted as she recognised the unconscious form of Christopher Tomb hefted in a fireman's carry. At least, she could only hope he was unconscious. There was no way to be sure of his condition in the dark, but he'd yet to make a sound, and though she strained her eyes, she couldn't see any evidence of movement.

She thought that Violet would bring him over to another of the cells, but instead she unceremoniously dumped him on the floor a few steps in and went off to rummage for something in the shadows, obviously not worried he was going get up and run. When she returned to the light, Pierce saw that she was carrying a coil of rope. Her heart lurched. While rope at least implied a live prisoner, opting for it over the easier choice of the barred cells suggested she had specific plans for him.

Her mind flashed back to the stone slab with its metal rings, and she started to yell.

"Hey!" she shouted, slamming the cell door again, as Violet began to drag Tomb across the barn floor like a sack of potatoes. "Don't make this worse for yourself. Let him go! The police are coming!"

Futile words, she knew even as she yelled them, but she kept on shouting anyway, because it was better than just sitting silently by. Pierce could see little of Violet's movements in the shadows, but she heard the clink of the heavy metal rings, what might have been the drag of rope being tightened through them.

What she didn't hear was any outcry or sound of a struggle from Tomb. Was he even still alive? If she was right about what Violet had in store for him, he might be better off to have quietly died when she'd knocked him out—but Pierce doubted Violet would have been so careless enough to render him useless to her.

After all, corpses didn't bleed.

Pierce wasn't sure how well Christopher Tomb would fit the requirements of the ritual—the previous victims had been younger, fitter—but perhaps the ritual would work just as well with any blood sacrifice... or perhaps Violet was hedging her bets and hoping that two older, less healthy victims could make an adequate substitute for one young one. Pierce had to have been left alive for a reason, and it couldn't be anything good. More than likely the only reason she hadn't been first on the chopping block was that Violet had needed to pen one of them up before she could go for the other, and Tomb had a dozen years more life expectancy in him than Pierce did.

Years that Violet meant to take for herself.

Still ignoring Pierce's banging and shouting, she went about the business of stripping Tomb out of his clothes and lashing him down to the rings with practised speed. Then she rose and headed back out of the barn door. Pierce immediately drew the penlight again and shone it through the bars, trying to get a decent look at Tomb.

"Mr Tomb!" she called urgently. "Christopher. Chris. Can you hear me?" She wasn't sure waking him up for what came next would be a kindness, but she needed to know if he was going to be capable of getting up and moving.

Never mind that she was skipping a couple of vital steps in her plan.

Unfortunately, it was clear that Tomb wasn't just playing possum. Her shouts failed to raise him, and when she scrabbled around in the straw until she found a suitable pebble to try to throw through the bars, it brought no visible response. She was on her own.

Where the hell was that backup Deepan had promised her?

As if summoned by her thoughts, she heard the crunch of wheels on gravel outside—but there was no accompanying engine noise to match it. Violet was moving her car, Pierce realised after a moment, strong enough to simply push the thing along even without having the keys to it. A few seconds later there was a rusty creak and a clang that she could only assume was the doors of the second shed swinging shut to conceal the vehicle and any damage Violet might have done to it.

Shit. She was in trouble here. Pierce turned her attention to the barred gate imprisoning her, trying to find some way to squeeze her hand through. The grid was made up of small squares, big enough to take a few fingers but not her thumb with them no matter which way she tried to angle her hand, and the latch that held it locked was impossible to reach from the inside. Still, she wasn't dealing with the kind of heavy duty metal bars you'd get on a cell window; more of an extra-sturdy mesh. Maybe she'd be able to bend the bars, or somehow file away at the rusty metal...

It wasn't much of a hope, but it was something to focus her efforts on rather than just sitting and waiting for the horror to come.

She clicked the penlight back off as Violet returned, not wanting to give away that she still had it, as useless as it probably was. The slam of the metal door plunged the barn back into almost total darkness, deeper still in Pierce's cell with the shadow of the hayloft overhead. Well, good: maybe that meant her efforts at escape would go unnoticed. It felt like an almost childish level of wishful thinking, but she had to believe that she was doing *something*, or else she was probably going to lose it entirely.

She didn't try to draw Violet's attention again, and in return was equally ignored despite the small noises as she tested each of the rods that kept her caged in turn, feeling for a loose bar or one that was already bowed out of position. But if Violet didn't care what she was doing, it was hard to keep up the same indifference to the footsteps, *clinks* and faint scuffing sounds that spoke of preparations underway. Pierce's shoulders were tensed at every moment for Tomb to wake up and start panicking when he realised his predicament; for Violet to begin the ritual bloodletting in earnest.

Where the *hell* was that backup?

The sounds of the storm were increasing outside, the rain a torrential downpour hitting the roof like a shower spray, the wind howling around it. Maybe she should wish for the storm to rip the roof clean off and collapse the place: it seemed no less plausible a plan than her current futile efforts at escape. The cold was starting to numb her fingers as she pushed and pulled at the metal bars, searching in vain for a weak spot; she cursed as flakes of rust broke loose, jabbing her fingertips.

At first she thought the flicker of light at the corner of her eye was lightning; then she realised Violet had struck a match. By its tiny glow Pierce could see that she'd set out candles around the concrete slab that Tomb was tied to, and her stomach rolled. Lighting candles was usually one of the very last stages in ritual preparations, because of the risk of the flame going out at the wrong moment.

Violet's preparations were as good as done. She was ready to make her sacrifice.

Pierce realised that Violet was singing as she lit the candles, the words indistinct amid the backdrop of the storm but the tone incongruously clear and sweet. She lit the candles she'd laid out one by one, every new flame bringing a greater, unwelcome clarity to the scene. Now Pierce could see Tomb clearly for the first time, his head slumped sideways where he lay lashed down. His face looked pale even in the warm hue of the candlelight, and there was a trickle of blood at his temple.

There'd be plenty more of it soon.

And then Violet's singing abruptly stopped. Her head snapped up and she twisted towards the door, as if she'd heard something despite the storm outside.

A moment later, Pierce could hear it too: the grumble of a car's engine, pulling up right outside the barn door. The backup from the local police that Deepan had called out for her. Would they notice something was amiss? Would they even investigate, seeing her car gone, or just assume that her directions had been wrong and move on in search of some other farm? Pierce froze, uncertain whether to bang and shout now, or hold off until they came closer and were more likely to hear.

Violet held equally still, both of them waiting for what would come next. It seemed to take forever for any further sound of movement. Pierce could easily imagine the debate going on in the police car as it sat parked outside. *Doesn't look like there's anyone here... sure this is the place? Well, it's what they said, mate... Probably gave us the wrong directions, bloody RCU... It's pissing down out there, is it really worth going over there...?*

The sharp rap on the metal door of the barn made her jump. Violet sprang to her feet immediately, headed not for the door they'd knocked at but the wooden one that Pierce had broken in through. Pierce's heart lurched. Did she plan to ambush the police? She was easily fast and strong enough to take down two unprepared officers. But they'd have radios with them, and even if they didn't get a chance to use them, they'd still be missed a lot quicker than Pierce.

Which was small consolation against the prospect of yet more lives lost, and rescue being delayed for that much longer. The second that Violet was out of the barn, Pierce began to bang on the cell door and shout. "Hey! Hey! RCU! Murder suspect is coming towards you, look out!" She was on the far side of the barn from the police car, and with the lashing of the storm outside, she wasn't sure that they would hear a thing. "Hey! In here!" She rattled the bars of her makeshift cage.

If there was any urgent response outside to her yelling, she couldn't hear it—and if she couldn't hear them, they probably couldn't hear her. Pierce fell silent for a moment, trying to listen, but all she could make out were the sounds of the raging weather.

What was happening out there? Had Violet already killed whoever was outside? Or had she guided them away from the building and the chance of hearing anything, playing the innocent as she did so well? Playing it off as a false alarm, perhaps even claiming that *she* was the RCU officer who'd put in the call for backup.

How thorough and suspicious would the local police really bother to be, when they were probably already annoyed to be pulled off their beat for some vague request for help from the RCU, probably all too eager to get back in their nice warm police car and get out of this ugly weather?

Pierce renewed her shouting and thumping, though her hands were beginning to sting from the impact... but all too soon, she heard the faint sound of the police car pulling away. They were leaving. Violet had managed to convince them it had been a false alarm, or that they had the wrong address.

As the barn door creaked back open, the dull chill of despair settled over her like a suffocating weight. The local police would report back that the call for backup had been premature, that there was nothing to see at the barn and RCU were probably on their way back to Yorkshire empty-handed. Nobody would miss her now—not until maybe the third or fourth time someone on her team tried to check in and got no response, until a few more hours went by with no contact.

Until it was far too late.

Pierce watched numbly as Violet returned to the stone sacrificial altar and pinched out those candles that were still burning. The interruption clearly hadn't cost her too much delay; she simply began the sequence again, taking up her rising and falling song from before. A pattern of thirteen candles; as she lit the last, the quality of the light abruptly changed, flames rising and thinning and beginning to shine with a purple-blue light that cast long, strange-hued shadows on the walls. They lit Tomb's laid-out body and slack face, too, a harsh and unforgiving light that reminded her of the autopsy room.

Entirely too fitting for comfort. As Violet drew a narrow blade and passed it ceremoniously through each of the candle flames, Pierce silently prayed for Tomb to stay unconscious, that he was down too deep to have any awareness of what was about to come.

But once Violet raised the blade and the cutting began, it didn't take long for him to start screaming.

CHAPTER TWENTY-EIGHT

"HEY! GET AWAY from him! *Stop!* Hey!" Pierce lost track of how long she'd been yelling, throwing herself at the barred gate of the pen with all the senseless violence of the animals that it had been made to contain. Long enough for her throat to be ripped raw and her body to feel like it was stamped with grid-patterned bruises.

It didn't make the slightest impact on the woman committing ritualised murder right before her eyes—and nor did it block out Tomb's agonised cries. Violet paused after every slash of the knife to murmur more ritual words, drawing the bloodletting out with hideous slowness, and Pierce could see how Tomb cringed in anticipation, helpless to escape from the bonds that kept him lashed down to the altar.

It was going to take him a very long time to die.

It felt like it had been an eternity already. Pierce slammed against the door of her prison yet again, hoping Tomb might at least be aware that she was there—not that it was likely to be any comfort in his current world of pain. Tears stung her eyes, as much from angry helplessness as pain and distress. It was supposed to be her job to protect the public from this kind of horror, and instead she was trapped here, forced to watch it happen, because she couldn't get out of this *fucking* cage. She tried to jam her fingers through the gaps between the bars again, knowing that it was useless but refusing to just give up and watch this obscenity unfold. She had to keep on trying.

And then she heard it: another car engine approaching.

It could have been just her imagination, a hallucination born of desperate wishful thinking. Violet didn't seem to hear anything, but she was deeply wrapped up in the ritual, features rendered skull-like by the unnatural light that seemed to shine, as much from the offering-bowl of blood as from the purple-blue candles.

Another faint noise from outside—just the wind, or could it be a car door slamming?

Pierce realised she'd stopped her own thumping and hammering to listen, and started again quickly, fearful the sudden lack of noise might draw Violet's attention where nothing else she'd tried had done the same. She found a renewed volume from her parched, ragged throat as she began to yell again.

"Hey! You think you're going to get away with this? The police are going to be coming in armed!" she shouted. "You may have strength and speed on your side, but there's only one of you. Let him go before he bleeds to death! Let me out of this cage!"

She yelled out every useful bit of tactical information that she could, not knowing for sure that there was even anyone out there, or that they could hear anything she said—but gripped by a near-paralysing sense of hope. Maybe the local patrol hadn't been fooled, maybe Deepan had raised the alarm over her failure to check-in, maybe someone had seen Violet attack Tomb and hide the car...

If this turned out to be a false alarm, then it might just be it: the moment she gave in to the howling panic that lay beneath the thin veneer of anger.

Please, Pierce thought, almost prayed—but only inside her head, just in case Violet was listening after all. *Somebody be out there...*

"Let him go!" she shouted out loud. "He can't afford to lose much more blood!" She wanted to yell out the full details of their positions, but she couldn't think of any way to get the facts across that wouldn't alert Violet to what she was doing. "Put the knife down!" she cried instead. "Step away from the altar!"

Maybe she was just shouting to the wind.

Her voice was cracking, losing strength from all her futile yelling, but she did her best to keep on making noise, as much to provide cover for anyone outside as in hopes of getting their attention. Tomb's screams had died down now to a pained gasping, and she didn't know how much longer he had.

She pressed up close against the barred door of her makeshift cage as she slammed and rattled it, trying to see the wooden door she'd come in through. If the police were coming in, that would be their point of entry. The way the altar was positioned left Violet facing that end of the barn, but Pierce had no effective method of drawing her attention away, and no way to warn whoever might be coming in.

If anyone was coming in...

With every second, the initial rush of hope was seeping away. Maybe it *had* been just the wind, her imagination clutching at straws to distract her from the horror. In the brief lull in her shouting, she heard Tomb let out a stomach-churning whimper, lacking the strength now to scream as he'd done in the beginning, but still stubbornly, horribly failing to sink into the mercy of unconsciousness.

Pierce wished that she could do it herself, just let go and block it all out until the same fate came for her. The adrenaline burst had spent itself, and now it took all she had just to give the door of her cage another perfunctory shake that barely raised a rattle. The near-hypnotic humming of Violet's chant seemed to drill right through her head, sapping her energy, as Pierce watched her raise the bloody blade yet again in the cold candlelight...

And then bright light and shouting chaos exploded into the world. Pierce flinched back into her cell as a swarm of uniformed figures burst through the wooden door, shining torch beams everywhere and barking aggressive orders. "Police! Get down on the ground! Drop your weapon and down on the ground!" The invasion of shouting voices and moving lights was enough to leave her dazed, after an eternity shut in the dark with only Tomb's agony and the echoes of her own hoarse yells for company.

Violet suffered no such paralysis, springing up to take off for the other door with a speed the armed police aiming at her couldn't match. She tore the metal door open one-handed with such force that the top hinge ripped right out of the brickwork and the door fell inward at a drunken angle. She ran out into the lashing storm beyond—and into the arms of the second Firearms team stationed outside the door. Pierce heard their chorus of shouted warnings, but Violet must have decided to fight rather than back down, because the next thing she heard was a thunderous volley of gunfire.

It went on long enough that Pierce was sure Violet had somehow evaded them after all... but when the guns finally fell silent, so did everything else apart from the sounds of the storm. A moment later the words crackled through from multiple police radios around her. "Suspect is down."

"Stay cautious," another brusque voice cut in. "She may be able to take more damage than a normal human being."

Sounded like Dawson. Pierce blinked, dazed. She wasn't sure he should even be out of the hospital yet. Just how long had she been in here?

Not important right now. She called out to the officers who'd run to the aid of the injured Tomb. "Get him in an ambulance! He's lost a lot of blood." They could probably see how much just by looking in the ritual bowl. "And somebody unlock this bloody cage." The effort of speaking even those few words did her in, and she sagged against the wall.

One of the uniformed police came to release her, giving the shadows a wary scan before he let her out. Pierce didn't know whether to laugh or cry at the simple twist of the metal catch: such a simple little thing, but she'd been utterly powerless to do it from inside.

She'd been pretty bloody useless all round, it seemed.

"DCI Pierce?" the man asked, and she gave an exhausted nod, not sure that she had much voice left to share. "Do you need medical attention?"

Pierce shook her head without bothering to inventory herself and decide if it was true. Didn't look like he much believed her anyway, as she stumbled out of her prison on dizzy sea legs, feeling like one of those lab animals that staggered round in circles after being released from their cages. Normally she'd have snapped when the man beside her reached out to steady her, but right now she wasn't sure how far she'd get without the support.

A crowd of people were already hurrying to cut Tomb free from the ropes and get him prepped for transport. "How's he doing?" Pierce asked the room in general.

The woman crouching to take Tomb's pulse shook her head grimly. "He's lost a lot of blood," she said, clearly not wanting to commit to more than that. "Come on, let's move!" she ordered her team. As they hustled to lift and move him, Pierce caught a glimpse of his face, as pale and lifeless as a wax dummy. Even the small expanse of his chest still visible above the blanket was criss-crossed with still-bleeding cuts.

He might survive the blood loss, but what about the trauma, the aftereffects of whatever method Violet had used to knock him unconscious? This was nothing he was going to walk away from without scars, internal and external. Just from having witnessed it, Pierce was sure she'd have some new nightmares to add to the regular mix. God, she'd been doing this job for far too long.

She stood in a vague daze after Tomb had been moved out, aware she should probably be giving orders or at least doing *something*, but unable to sort her tumbling thoughts into anything resembling order. The candles around the bloodstained slab had now dimmed back to the warm hue of natural candlelight. Should probably put those out... no, wait, photograph them first... Her gaze kept being pulled back to the offering bowl that held Tomb's blood.

"Claire?" It was a voice she hadn't expected, and it took several moments of blank staring before she connected the bearded face before her with the less lined, less grey-haired version in her memory.

"Phil?" she said, moderately bewildered to see her former coworker standing there in a uniform vest. It only added to the sense of having come adrift. "What are you doing here?"

He waved vaguely at a group of overall-wearing figures that she didn't recognise poking around the remnants of the ritual. "Your man Dawson called in backup from Oxford branch," he explained. "Your people are on the way down, but our team was closer when the balloon went up."

Pierce was still confused how Dawson had even been here to do that, but then everything was a bit disjointed right now. She struggled to focus. "Where is Dawson?" she asked.

"Outside, supervising what's happening with the killer's body," Phil said. "He's insisting Firearms stick around and the pathologist's not happy—shaping up to be a pissing match, from the look of things."

"He has a gift," Pierce said dryly. She found herself gazing at the offering bowl again, and shook herself. Right. Better go and deal with Dawson's latest diplomatic entanglement, then.

"You okay?" Phil asked her as she belatedly turned to move towards the door.

"I'll live," she said.

More than could be said for most of the people who'd tangled with Violet and her gang of vampire cultists. At least they'd put a stop to her killing spree—but bringing the suspect in dead always felt like just another shade of failure. That wasn't justice, not really; it was just an end to the affair.

She headed out of the dark barn, almost surprised to find it was still pissing it down outside even though she'd been hearing the sounds of the storm the whole time; it was still, in fact, barely into the afternoon, early enough for her grab a late lunch without it blending into the evening meal. Not that she ever wanted to eat again, for all that some of her light-headed nausea had to be from hungry exhaustion.

A hasty forensic tent had been rigged over Violet's body, not quite fast enough to stop the blood from running in the rain. As mortal as anyone else up against a hail of bullets, it seemed, however much of an edge her magical enhancements might have given her.

If Pierce had been in charge of the bust instead of Dawson, she might have insisted on Tasers rather than firearms—but who was to say that would have been right? Maybe they could have brought the suspect in alive that way, or maybe Violet would have shaken off the effects and fled the scene to kill again. The hell of making judgement calls in the field was that you could never know for certain that you'd made the best call; only recognise when you'd fucked up.

At least this time they could be certain that they'd had the right woman.

She spotted Dawson lurking outside the crime scene tape, stealing a soggy cigarette. Either he'd won his head-butting contest with the other police units, or he'd retreated from the field; the latter wasn't usually his style, but he was looking distinctly peaky to her eyes.

"Should you be smoking that?" Pierce nodded towards the cigarette as she ducked under the tape to join him, her muscles protesting. "Or here, for that matter?" He'd still been in hospital the last time she'd seen him.

"You complaining?" he asked.

It did seem fairly churlish to object. "How'd you get here so fast?" she asked instead. "I didn't think the local police realised anything was wrong." That moment when her supposed backup had knocked and then gone away again would probably have a starring role in a few nightmares as well.

"They didn't, till I got here. I was already following you down. This is my case," he reminded her.

Her eyes followed the figures in forensic overalls. "Yeah, well, you might have to fight Oxford for it." Coming in to make the bust like this after the northern branch had no results for years, they were going to look like the heroes of the hour, and their DI was just the type to try to make hay from it.

Pierce had no energy for a PR battle. Or anything else, for that matter. "Right," she said with a heavy sigh. "If you've got everything under control here, I'm going home."

If Dawson wanted to rake through the ashes of this case for some glory, he could have it. All she could see was that it had dragged on for far too long and seen too many people hurt or worse before it ended.

But at least now it was finally over.

CHAPTER TWENTY-NINE

PIERCE DOZED A little in the car on her way back up north, giving her just enough energy to feel guilty at the thought of skiving off for the afternoon. She wasn't sure she wanted to sit at home with nothing to do but dwell on her time in the barn in any case; burying herself in routine paperwork was usually a good way to blot out the dark thoughts that followed ugly scenes, and two big cases closed in as many days had left her with plenty to tackle.

All in all, a productive week's work, she supposed, but not one she could feel all that proud of. Too many fuckups, deaths and injuries that might somehow have been avoided if she'd only handled things better. If she'd insisted that Tomb give her the address and stay behind, if she'd gone in with a police team from the start... if they'd managed to arrest Violet at the café, or after Jonathan's murder; if she'd insisted Jonathan come to the police station to meet with them, or brought a bigger escort...

Hell, why stop there? Might as well go back to 2008, when she'd failed to do the due diligence and find the Valentine Vampire's new hunting grounds down in Oxford, or 2001, when she might have done more to challenge her old DI's hasty conclusions. With the murder investigation stretching back almost as far as her own history with the force, she was spoilt for choice when it came to self-recriminations.

But at least one of their more notorious cold cases had finally been laid to rest.

"So you're certain that this woman... 'Violet'... was the one behind all of these murders, going back to the 1980s?" Snow asked when she dropped by his office to make her report in person.

"All the evidence points that way," she said. Complete certainty was a luxury they seldom got in their line of work. "She appears to be the same woman who was spotted at the original bust fourteen years ago, and given her other magical enhancements, the lack of visible aging was probably part of the effect of the blood ritual." Unfortunately, once that little detail got out to the press they'd be probably looking at a wave of attempted copycat rituals by other would-be seekers after eternal youth. The vast majority wouldn't have access to legitimate occult texts, but they could still do all kinds of harm in the process.

Snow grimaced and straightened the papers on his desk. "So we have no way of telling exactly how old this woman really was?" he said.

Pierce shook her head. "They'll autopsy, but there's no saying what the results will show." Violet might prove to have the internal organs of a woman decades older, or they might reflect her outward-seeming youth; it was always difficult to guess with magic. "Not sure we're going to be able to get any better identification, either," she admitted. Not with the uncertainty over dates and the fact that Violet must have been keeping under the radar since back when it was easier to do so.

Snow sighed and pinched the bridge of his nose. "And Christopher Tomb?" he asked.

It felt like an accusation even with his neutral inflection. Pierce tried not to flinch. "Still in critical condition. His wife's been notified." And she was guiltily relieved not to have to take that particular job; it was bad enough to have a mental image of the woman thanks to their brief encounter earlier that day.

"He should never have been there in the first place," Snow said.

"I know, sir," she said tiredly. No point making excuses, and it would have left a bad taste to shove any of the blame onto Tomb. He might have been being deliberately obstructive in an effort to get invited along, but she still should have known better than to let him accompany her into a potentially dangerous situation. And nobody deserved to suffer what he'd gone through in that barn.

Perhaps she looked and sounded ragged enough for her boss to take pity, or else he just saw no mileage in repeating a lecture he'd given once already this week. "Well, what's done is done," he said rather grudgingly, pressing his lips together. "At least the killer's off the streets, and the press are off our backs—though frankly, I would have preferred it if RCU Oxford hadn't put out a press conference about the joint operation without consulting with us first."

"You'll have to take that up with DI Dawson, sir," she said, not particularly repentant at dropping him in it. "I was indisposed at the time."

"Yes." Snow eyed her battered, dishevelled appearance. "I suggest that you go home, Pierce—and take at least a couple of days off. Your team claim enough overtime as it is without half of you being at work when you should be on medical leave."

"Yes, sir." Pierce didn't think she had the energy to argue, which probably proved his point.

She headed back up to the RCU offices, where Gemma was the only one around. "Anything come in that I should know about?" she asked as she collected her bag and coat.

"Nothing major, guv," she said, shaking her head; Pierce suspected she'd have said the same regardless.

She stood for a moment, blank with tiredness, certain she must be forgetting things, important or trivial. "Everything squared away on the spirit charms case?" she asked.

"So far," Gemma said with a nod. "Oh, Cliff did want a word before you go, though," she added. "Something to do with the charms we seized, he said."

"Right-o. See you later."

She headed down the corridor to poke her head in on Cliff. "Issues with the evidence on the charms case?"

"Possibly." Cliff was alone in his lab today, but he looked around nervously as she entered the room, and waited for her to come all the way inside and shut the door before he continued. "I wondered if you might humour me by taking a look at the animal spirit charms we seized."

Pierce blinked blearily as Cliff spread the collection of wooden charms before her. "What am I looking for?"

"I wouldn't want to prejudice you," he said, pursing his lips. There was a grimness to his tone that stopped her pleading exhaustion, and she studied the things more closely. To her inexpert eye the wooden medallions they'd seized at Miller's arrest looked pretty much the same as the one Cliff had already examined; in fact, she was fairly sure it was included in the mix—she recognised the running hare design.

Or maybe that wasn't the only reason it stood out from its fellows. Now that her eye had been drawn to it, she couldn't help but feel there was something subtly different about the way that the runes were formed, like the mismatched handwriting of a forged signature. "This one's different," she said, pointing it out to Cliff. "I'd say it was made by someone else."

"Yes," he said. "And though I'm afraid I can offer you no concrete proof of this, I *don't* think it's the same charm you originally gave me."

Her gaze snapped up to meet his. "You think it's been replaced with a fake since you've had it in the lab?"

He grimaced. "As I say, I can't offer any definitive proof, but it feels different to me—slightly lighter, perhaps, a little rougher around the edges. I doubt I'd have noticed if you hadn't brought me all these others to compare... and if I didn't have good reason to be paranoid."

If Cliff was right, then whoever had made the substitution had to have had repeated access to the lab to examine and photograph the medallion and then replace it with a convincing fake. Meaning Maitland's people's theft of the shapeshifting pelt hadn't been a one-time thing—he had someone positioned here at the RCU full time, monitoring their activities and keeping an eye out for any artefacts her team encountered. Who knew how many other items they'd seized had gone missing from storage without their knowing?

And that wasn't the worst part. Someone among her small group of coworkers had to be aiding these people. Snow? Dawson? One of her two constables? They were all new to the unit—any one of them could be a plant.

And they weren't the only possibilities. What about Deepan, the sergeant she'd trusted with her life for years? The research team, some of whom she'd known for even longer? She didn't want to believe that any of them could be persuaded to turn mole, or that they could have been replaced by impostors without her spotting it.

But what if she was wrong?

"Keep this to yourself," she told Cliff. "From now on, we can't trust anybody."

He nodded soberly. "So what do we do now?" he asked.

Pierce let out her breath in a heavy sigh. "I wish I bloody knew," she said.

Everything seemed hopeless lately.

HER MOOD WAS grim as she drove home, mind alternating between the implications of Cliff's news and even darker thoughts of the scene back in the warehouse. Despite feeling utterly worn down by the day's events, she couldn't settle, keeping herself occupied in hopes her mind would stay that way too.

Item one, do something about her broken phone. It wasn't

the first to come a cropper in the line of duty, especially in recent years—she couldn't help but miss the bloody great brick of a phone she'd had back in the old days, a pain to lug about but not nearly so fragile. At least she still had all the numbers written down on paper; no doubt the two children she called constables would be hopelessly at sea if ever they lost track of their precious gadgets.

Pierce let out a slow sigh at the thought. She hadn't worked with either of them long, but they both seemed like good kids. She didn't *want* to believe that one of them might be a spy in her department, but she knew she had to stay wary of the possibility. The only people she could trust now were those outside of the police completely.

Even if that was more by misfortune than by choice. She paused as she came to the Gs in her address book. Leo Grey. Should she update him on the latest wrinkle in their investigation? It wasn't as if there was anything he could do... and, yet somehow she thought it might make her feel better to have a conversation with someone where she could put all her cards on the table.

She picked up the landline and dialled Leo's number.

"Hello?" His wife answered the phone on the second ring, catching Pierce slightly unprepared.

"Er, hi, this is Claire Pierce from the RCU. Is Leo there?"

"No, he's not," she said. She sounded faintly worried, which put Pierce on alert. "Is he working on something for you? I've been trying to get hold of him all day, but his phone's switched off." She tutted a little at her own concern. "Oh, I know I shouldn't fuss, and I'm sure it's important... It's just that he was out half the night last night as well, and I don't want him to push himself too hard doing ten times the work you even asked him for, you know? He's really not recovered enough to drive himself like this."

It was probably more a general outpouring of worries to a sympathetic ear than anything aimed at Pierce specifically, but it still hit her like an accusation. "I did ask him to look into a few things for me," she admitted, "but there's no reason for him to be burning the midnight oil over it." Especially when their investigation seemed to have hit a dead end with the Hardison Group site—a site that she was prepared to bet Leo was sitting outside right now, keeping up a lonely, dangerous surveillance.

"Look, I might have an idea where he's taken himself off to," she said. "I need to speak to him anyway, so I'll have a word, tell him to take a break. It's really not that urgent." Not when there was no obvious way to proceed from here.

"Could you?" The gratitude in his wife's voice only made her feel worse. "It's just that it's difficult coming from me, you know? I don't want to feel like I'm nagging, but you know how stubborn he is."

"I do," she said.

What his wife didn't know was that it could already have got him into much bigger trouble than just setting back his recovery from his injuries.

It took Pierce several wrong turns to find her way back to the Hardison site; she was grateful her own car was still being examined for evidence back at the barn so she was driving one no one would find familiar. It still felt reckless to be returning this soon, and she drove past several more turns before parking to return on foot. She saw no other cars along the way; if Leo was here, he'd either brought in a third party to drop him off or hiked further than he probably should with his injured leg. Both options struck her as unnecessarily reckless.

Of course, maybe she was wrong, and he hadn't come here at all.

Or maybe he'd already been caught. Pierce cursed to herself. She'd brought him in on this mess so that she wouldn't have to keep going out on a limb all by herself, with no one knowing where she'd gone or why. It hadn't been part of the plan for Leo to start doing the same thing.

She picked her way cautiously across the fields towards the Hardison building. In the dimming light, she could just about make out the glint of the high metal fence. There was no way Leo would have been able to get past that level of security. But if he'd set up surveillance on the place, then where would he be? She headed towards a small copse of trees beside the access road to the site, the only obvious source of cover around.

Too obvious? As she approached, she thought she saw a moving shadow shift beneath trees, and she hesitated. If it wasn't Leo, but one of Maitland's people...

Then she was already caught. She stepped backwards, reaching for her warrant card, as a dark shape emerged from under the trees.

On four legs rather than two. Shit, shit, shit. Pierce turned to run, but the big dog leapt after her, eerily silent as it bounded past her and herded her back towards the trees. In the face of gaping mastiff jaws that could crush her bones, she raised her hands and backed down, mind ticking away furiously. Malodorant spray—had she grabbed another canister after discharging hers in the scuffle at the park? Shit, she didn't think she had. She had the silver cuffs, which would neutralise the pelt, but she'd never get them on the shifter while it was in dog form.

Yet even as she thought it, the dog's outline was folding and shifting, like some grotesque contortionist act with bones that bent in the wrong places. The canine body rapidly melted into the form of a slim-built man weighed down by the bulky pelt strapped to his back.

A man who staggered and grunted, clutching his left thigh as he tried to climb back to his feet.

"*Leo?*" Pierce blurted in disbelief.

She caught the faint flash of his grin as he reached up to touch the heavy head of the dog pelt on his back. "Found a way I can infiltrate the patrols," he said.

"A shapeshifting pelt? Leo, are you *nuts?*" she said. Leaving aside the obscene amount of money he must have sunk into commissioning the thing—if Firearms paid that well, she'd clearly picked the wrong specialisation—shapeshifting pelts were highly regulated... and dangerous. A pelt wasn't something you threw on like a coat: he must have had the activation rune tattooed on his skin, inextricably linking himself to the pelt's enchantments. Every time he used it, he'd become a little more animal and less human.

Leo didn't seem too bothered by any of those concerns, almost high with uncharacteristic excitement. "It's a legal pelt," he hurried to assure her. "Got it made at the Darville skin shop—guy who works there owes me a favour. All the paperwork's in order, he's just... going to delay registering it a little while."

Pierce sighed, vainly massaging at her headache. "Leo..." she said, and then didn't know where to go from there. The awkward position he was putting her in, given her job enforcing pelt regulations, barely even registered on the scale of problems with this idea. Except it wasn't just an idea, it was already a fait accompli.

"Leo, what the hell were you thinking?" she demanded. "You went out and got yourself a permanent magical binding, based on some half-baked plan to—what—sneak in the gate with a pack of their dogs and hope they don't notice an extra? You've seen what shapeshifting does to people—you're the one out there with the silver bullets bringing them down when they lose too much of their humanity to keep control."

"Not anymore," he said forcefully, with a sting of bitterness that silenced her briefly. He met her eyes, serious now, though she could see the jittery restlessness bubbling beneath. "Claire. You know what we're up against. Police tactics aren't going to cut it; they *control* the police. We're going to have to get creative, and we're going to have to get dangerous. We're not going to beat them without playing their game."

"Yeah," she said with a weary sigh, although she only felt bruised and defeated. He might be right that there was no way to win against these people within the law, but that didn't make her any happier at the prospect of stepping outside it. "The thing is, if we start playing their game, then we've already pretty much given up on winning."

Leo gave a thin smile in response, but she could tell he didn't really agree. Would *he* have, before he'd lost his career to the injuries she'd caused by dragging him into this fight? He'd always been calm and dependable, not someone she'd ever believe would be advocating vigilante justice... but how much could you ever know somebody, really?

Pierce might have an ally in her fight against this conspiracy now—but she couldn't help but feel like she was as alone as ever.

ABOUT THE AUTHOR

E.E. Richardson has been writing books since she was eleven years old, and had her first novel *The Devil's Footsteps* picked up for publication at the age of twenty. Since then she's had seven more young adult horror novels published by Random House and Barrington Stoke. *Spirit Animals* is her third novel for Abaddon Books.

She also has a BSc. in Cybernetics and Virtual Worlds, which hasn't been useful for much but does sound impressive.